The yellowbacks... classics of popular fiction

The yellowjackets or yellowbacks were a great series of bestselling adventure and crime thrillers that had its origins in the mid to late 19th century following on from the 'penny dreadfuls'. They virtually began the mass market revolution of the early 20th century with a clear standard format and imprint/series livery (what would today be called branding). Hodder & Stoughton published the yellow jackets in two main series with series run dates of: 1923-1939 and later 1949-1957.

As the tagline ('where thrillers really began') on the back cover implies, the imprint and series focused on thrillers that were the bestsellers of their time. This current reissue or retro revival if you will, brings back many of these masterpieces, now classics in their own way and extends it further by including key titles from that period that were either great crime or thriller or even general commercial fiction (including sub-genres of noir, horror, gothic, romance, westerns etc) influences of their time. There are some perennial favourites and many rarities either lost or not easily available being revived in the current series. Writers and characters ranged from adventure heroes like Bulldog Drummond, Allan Quatermain, Richard Hannay or the Saint through thriller grandmasters Edgar Wallace and E. Phillips Oppenheim, crime and mystery maestros like Patricia Wentworth, GK Chesterton, Agatha Christie and the Detection club, to western and swashbucklers like Zane Grey, Max Brand, Captain Blood and even romance or general fiction classics like Hermina Black, Denise Robins, Marie Corelli or Stella Morton. These were books that had storytelling at their heart and always entertained.

The yellowbacks had both hardback (with varying design elements) and paperback (which built the series look) versions with the latter still carrying the imprint 'yellowjacket'. The current reissues pay tribute to both and use an amalgam of elements from both editions while retaining the complete yellow (or 'mustard-plaster') livery with the author's name in blue beveled type with a 'simulated emboss' effect and a white outer 'outline', and the book title in black. These reissues retain the distinctive size of the original mass market paperback and follow the three main category variations—the thrillers (crime, westerns, mystery, adventure) had blue lettering for the author's name, while Romance and 'softer general fiction had red; and other categories like humour had green.

For more detail and a full list of titles visit https://www.hachetteindia.com/home/yellowbacks

THE REMINISCENCES OF SOLAR PONS

THE REMINISCENCES OF SOLAR PONS

August William Derleth (February 24, 1909 – July 4, 1971) was an American writer and anthologist. Though best remembered as the first book publisher of the writings of H. P. Lovecraft, and for his own contributions to the Cthulhu Mythos and the cosmic horror genre, as well as his founding of the publisher Arkham House (which did much to bring supernatural fiction into print in hardcover in the US that had only been readily available in the UK), Derleth was a leading American regional writer of his day, as well as prolific in several other genres, including historical fiction, poetry, detective fiction, science fiction, and biography. Derleth wrote more than 150 short stories and more than 100 books during his lifetime.

THE REMINISCENCES OF SOLAR PONS

August Derleth

Hodder and Stoughton Yellow Jacket

hachette INDIA

The Reminiscences of Solar Pons

(Registered Name: Hachette Book Publishing India Pvt. Ltd.)
An Hachette UK Company www.hachetteindia.com

1

The texts in these editions in most cases have been reprinted as is, with minimal editorial changes and by and large no bowdlerizing for political correctness; though in some editions, a few words and phrases considered archaic, or those considered offensive now, along with archaic punctuation may have been modified in places to make the text more accessible to today's readers. The narratives, language, beliefs, social mores and/or cultural depictions, in these volumes are a reflection of their times and must be viewed as such. They may also contain certain cultural, racial and gender prejudices and stereotypes that may be outdated or clearly wrong then and wrong today; but their removal would be tantamount to claiming these prejudices never existed. The Publisher does not endorse or support those depictions or stereotypes; and these books have been made available for a discerning audience that will read it for entertainment value and a chronicle/record of popular fiction of past times.

Cover design by Priya Singh adapted from the original classic yellowjacket by Hodder & Stoughton.

Cover illustration by Ishan Trivedi.

Series note: Some of the books in the series (unless otherwise credited) may have cover or inside illustrations from the original yellowbacks or early editions, and while full restoration has been attempted, some images may be grainy or faded due to the condition of the original material. The end notes or bonus material or blurb details may have been sourced from the public domain or free use publications such as Wikipedia and attribution is hereby made also allowing similar free use reproduction from here. Sources requiring further specific attribution may write in and further detailing and/or corrections shall be made in subsequent printings/editions.

Reprint specifications may be subject to change including but not limited to finishes, paper, colour sections.

ISBN: 978-93-5731-187-8

Hachette Book Publishing India Pvt. Ltd.
4th & 5th Floors, Corporate Centre,
Plot No. 94, Sector 44, Gurugram - 122 003, India

Typeset in Electra LT STD 10/12.5 pt by Manipal Technologies Limited

Printed and bound in India by Manipal Technologies Limited

MIX
Paper from responsible sources
FSC™ C043100

CONTENTS

Foreword

AUGUST DERLETH
THE REMINISCENCES of SOLAR PONS
foreword by ANTHONY BOUCHER

Foreword

A PATTERN OF EXCELLENCE
BY DAVID MARCUM

By the time *The Reminiscences of Solar Pons* was published in 1961, August Derleth was well established as an author of historical novels, and the man who had rescued the works of H.P. Lovecraft from possible obscurity, publishing those stories in editions that were easier to find than the old magazines in which they'd first appeared – and where they likely would have been forgotten otherwise. His work in these fields often led many people to forget, or possibly not know at all, that his Solar Pons stories were beloved within the Sherlockian community. However, even in those circles, far too many people were still unaware of "The Sherlock Holmes of Praed Street". It would be a number of years before the Pons stories became available to a wider audience.

The Reminiscences is a tidy volume of eight adventures, to match the number stories in the Sherlock Holmes collection *His Last Bow*, which was subtitled, *Some Reminiscences of Sherlock Holmes*. Here we have a whole tale devoted to Pons's "The Praed Street Irregulars". "The Black Cardinal" gives a tight picture of European tensions in those years between the World Wars... and one might note some ties to a certain "lost" Pons story that appears in Volume 8 of this new edition of *The Complete Solar Pons*, entitled *The Apocrypha of Solar Pons*. "The Blind Clairaudient" features a few obscure references to several other Pons cases for those who wish to puzzle them out.

And "The Hats of M. Dulac" shows that the Diogenes Club of the 1920's has apparently become a little more social than in the days when Mycroft Holmes spent time there, watching from the bow-window in the Stranger's Room as humanity passed by in Pall Mall below him.

Also included in this volume is an early attempt at a Pons Chronology by the late Robert Pattrick. He passed away long before subsequent volumes of Pons tales could appear, so his effort is woefully incomplete, but it's an important effort nonetheless, and as a part of the original volume, it couldn't be ignored.

These stories continue the pattern of excellence established by Derleth in previous volumes, and are an important part of the Pontine Canon.

For those meeting him for the first time, Pons is very much like Holmes. He solves crimes by using ratiocination and deduction. He plays the violin, smokes pipes, and lounges around his rooms in dressing gowns, as well as occasionally conducting chemical experiments there. His brother, Bancroft Pons, is an important fixture in the British Government, rather like Sherlock Holmes's brother, Mycroft. His landlady is Mrs. Johnson, and his closest contact at Scotland Yard is Inspector Jamison. And his friend and biographer, in the mold of Dr. John H. Watson, is Dr. Lyndon Parker.

While most of Holmes's Canonically-recorded adventures stretch from the 1870's until his retirement to Sussex in 1903, Pons operates in the post-World War I era, with his cases extending from when he and Dr. Parker meet in 1919, after Parker has returned to England following his war service, to 1939, just before the beginning of World War II. Pons had also served in the War, in cryptography, and when the two meet, Parker is disillusioned at the England to which he has returned. However, this is quickly subsumed as the doctor's interest in his new flat-mate and friend grows when he joins Pons on a series of cases that he later records.

For too long, the Solar Pons adventures have been too difficult to obtain. Fortunately, these new editions will change that. Here's how that came about.

In the late 1970's, I had been a Sherlockian for just a few years, having found Mr. Holmes in 1975. Those were the early days of the Sherlockian Golden Age that began with the publication of Nicholas Meyer's *The Seven-Per-Cent Solution* in 1974, and has continued to the present. Meyer reminded people that there were *other* manuscripts by Dr. Watson out there, still waiting to be found – hidden in attics, filed away in libraries, or suppressed by paranoid individuals for a plethora of reasons. These began to be discovered, one by one. Meyer himself subsequently published the amazing *The West End Horror* (1976), along with an explanation as to how the appearance of the first book had led to the second. Other Sherlockian adventures continued to surface – *Hellbirds* by Austin Mitchelson and Nicholas Utechin (1976), *Sherlock Holmes and the Golden Bird* by Frank Thomas (1979), and *Enter the Lion* by Sean Hodel and Michael Wright (1979), to name just a very few. The Great Sherlockian Tapestry, after consisting of mainly just sixty main fibers for so long, was about to get much heavier.

And around that time, someone with great wisdom realized that Solar Pons should be a part of that.

Pinnacle Books began reprinting the Pons adventures in late 1974, just months after the July publication date of *The Seven-Per-Cent Solution*. In the world of book publication, at least in those days when things took forever, Pinnacle certainly didn't jump on the bandwagon at the last minute to get the books immediately into print, after seeing how popular both *The Seven-Per-Cent Solution* and Sherlock Holmes were. Rather, the re-publication of the Pons books must have been planned for quite a while, and it was just their great good luck that their Pons editions appeared right around the same time as Meyer's *The Seven-Per-Cent Solution.* Planning and setup would have required a great deal of effort, as would designing the distinctive "Solar Pons" logo that they would use on both their Pons books, and later on Sherlock Holmes books by Frank Thomas. And most of all, they would have needed time to solicit the wonderful cover paintings of Solar Pons and Dr. Parker.

It was these paintings that drew me into the World of Solar Pons.

Living in a small town in eastern Tennessee, finding things related to Sherlock Holmes in the latter 1970's was difficult. My hometown had both a new and used bookstore, and I regularly scoured them looking for new titles. Strangely, several of my most treasured Sherlockian books from these years were found – not in the bookstores – but on rotating paperback racks at a local drugstore. However, it was at the new bookstore, a few weeks before my fourteenth birthday, that I happened to notice seven books lined up in a row, all featuring a man wearing an Inverness and a deerstalker.

I grabbed them, thinking I'd found a Holmesian motherlode. Instead, I saw that they were about... *Solar Pons?*

I had a limited amount of Sherlockian research material then, and I don't recall if I found anything about Mr. Pons to explain why he dressed like Sherlock Holmes. (I had quite forgotten then, although it came back to me later, that I'd first read a Pons story back in 1973 – before I'd ever truly encountered Sherlock Holmes. That story, "The Grice-Paterson Curse", was contained in an Alfred Hitchcock children's mystery anthology, and I credit how much I enjoyed it then with shaping my brain to be so appreciative when I first read about Holmes a couple of years later, in 1975. That one is still my favorite Pons story to this day.)

Those seven books haunted me, and I somehow managed to hint strongly enough to my parents about it that they ended up being birthday gifts a few weeks later – along with some other cool Holmes books. And so I started reading the Pontine Canon, as it's called – the first of countless times that I've been through it. (It's strange what the brain records. I vividly remember reading and re-reading those books frequently in an Algebra class throughout that year – particularly one story on one certain day, "The Man With the Broken Face". I was lost and behind for a lot of that year in that class, and instead of trying to catch up, I'd pull out a Pons book, which felt much more comfortable. The teacher, who later went on to be beloved and award-winning for some reason that escapes me, knew what I was doing and did nothing to pull me back. Pfui on her! But I did like reading about Pons.)

As time went on, I discovered additional Pinnacle paperbacks, featuring new Pons stories by British horror author Basil Copper. It was great to have more Pons adventures, but his weren't quite the same. Around the time I started college, I discovered that Copper had edited a complete *Omnibus* of the original Pons stories, and it was the first grown-up purchase that I made with my first real paycheck. (Many thanks to Otto Penzler and The Mysterious Bookshop!) I was thrilled to see that the stories had been arranged in chronological order, which appealed to me. (That kind of thing still does.) Little did I realize then that Copper's editing had been so controversial within the Pons community.

For it turned out that Copper had taken it upon himself to make a number of unjustified changes. For instance, he altered a lot of Derleth's spellings in the *Omnibus* edition from American to British, causing some people to become rather upset. I wasn't too vexed by that, however, as I was there for the stories.

Copper continued to write new Pons stories of his own, published in various editions. I snapped those up, too, very happy to have new visits to 7B Praed Street. Over the years, I noted with some curiosity that Copper's books came to take on a certain implied and vague aspect – just a whiff, just a tinge – that Pons was *his* and not Derleth's.

Meanwhile, the Battered Silicon Dispatch Box published several "lost" Pons items, and also a new and massive set of the complete stories, *The Original Text Solar Pons* (2000), restoring Derleth's original intentions. It was in this book that I read Peter Ruber's extensive essay explaining Copper's changes in greater depth, and the reaction to them within the Ponsian community. However, Ruber didn't mention what I found to be Copper's even more egregious sin. But first a little background...

Over the years, there have been various editions of the Pons books – the originals published by Derleth's Mycroft & Moran imprint, the Pinnacle paperbacks, the Copper *Omnibus*, and the Battered Silicon Dispatch Box *Original Text Omnibus*. (There has also been an incomplete set of a few titles from British publisher Robson Books, Ltd.) Only a few thousand of the original Mycroft & Moran books were ever printed, and for decades, Pons was only known to a loyal group of Sherlockian enthusiasts by way of these very limited volumes. The Pinnacle books made Pons available to a whole generation of 1970's Sherlockians – such as me – that would have never had a chance to meet him otherwise if he'd only remained in the hard-to-find original editions.

As time has passed, however, even these Pinnacle books have become rare and quite expensive. For modern readers who have heard of Pons and are interested in learning more about him, or for those of us who are Pons enthusiasts who wish to introduce him to the larger world, it's been quite difficult, as all editions of his adventures are now quite rare and expensive, unless one is stumbled upon by accident. The Mycroft & Moran books can be purchased online, usually for a substantial investment of money, and the Copper and Battered Silicon Dispatch Box *Omnibi* were always expensive and hard to come by, and now it's only worse. Finally, with these new publications, the Solar Pons books will be available for everyone in easily found and affordable editions. With this, it's hoped that a new wave of Pons interest will spread, particularly within the Sherlockian community which will so appreciate him.

In 2014, my friend and Pons Scholar Bob Byrne floated the idea of having an issue of his online journal, *The Solar Pons Gazette*, contain new Pons stories. Having already written some Sherlock Holmes adventures, I was intrigued, and sat down and wrote a Pons tale – possibly almost as fast as Derleth had written his first Pons story in 1928. It was so much fun that I quickly wrote two more. After that, I pestered Bob for a while, saying that he should explore having the stories published in a real book. (I choose real books every time – none of those ephemeral e-blip books that can disappear in a blink for me!) When that didn't happen, I became more ambitious. Bob put me in touch with Tracy Heron of The August Derleth Society, and he in turn told me how to reach Danielle Hackett, August Derleth's granddaughter. I made my case to be allowed to write a new collection of Pons stories, as authorized by the Estate, and amazingly, I received permission. I introduced Danielle (in this modern email way of meeting people) to Derick Belanger of Belanger Books, and then set about writing some more stories, enough to make a whole book. Amazingly, the first new authorized Pons book in decades, *The Papers of Solar Pons*, was published in 2017.

But that started me thinking...

Realizing that this new book had the possibility to reawaken interest in Pons, or spread the word to those who didn't know about him, I wondered if the original volumes could be reprinted. After all, interest in Sherlock Holmes around the world is at an all-time high, getting the word out by way of the internet has never been easier, and shifts in the publishing paradigm mean that the old ways of grinding through the process for several years before a book appears no longer apply.

The Derleth Estate was very happy with the plan. Now came the hard part.

Being fully aware of the controversy surrounding Copper's *Omnibus* edition, it was evident that that new editions had to be from Derleth's original Mycroft & Moran volumes – for after all, he had edited and approved those himself. Thankfully, modern technology allows for these books to be converted to electronic files with only a moderate amount of pain and toil.

I had several friends, upon hearing of this project, who very graciously offered to help me to "re-type" the original books. I can assure you that, if these books had needed to be re-typed from scratch, there would have been no new editions – at least not as provided by me. Instead, I took a copy of each of the original Mycroft & Moran Pons books, of which I am a very happy and proud owner, and scanned them, converting them all into electronic files. So far so good – that only took several hours of standing at a copy machine, flipping the pages of the books one at a time, and hitting the green button. (And sometimes re-doing it if a scanned page had a gremlin or two.)

After that, I used a text conversion software to turn the scans into a Word document. That raw text then had to be converted into another, more easily fixed, Word document. Then came the actual fixing. Early on, it was decided to try and make the new editions look as much like the originals as possible. Therefore, many inconsistent things that niggled me as an editor-type remain in the finished product, because they were that way in the originals. For instance, Derleth's punctuation improved quite a bit from his early books to the latter – but it was very tempting to start fixing his punctuation in the earlier books. If you see something that looks not-quite-right, chances are it was that way in the original books.

There were times that a letter or a note, as quoted in a story, would be indented, while on other occasions it would simply be a part of the paragraph. I wanted to set up all of those letters and notes in a consistent way throughout the various books, but instead I kept them as they had appeared in the original editions, no matter how much the style varied from story to story. Finally, some of the racial stereotyping from those stories would not be written that way today. However, these are historical documents of sorts, and as such, they are presented as written, with the understanding that times have changed, and hopefully we have a greater awareness now than before.

Since the early 1980's, whenever I've re-read the Pons stories – and I've done so many times – it's been by way of the Copper *Omnibus* editions. I enjoyed having them all in one place in two matching handsome and heavy books, and I was very pleased that they were rearranged for reading in chronological order. The fixing of British-versus-American spelling didn't bother me a bit. This time, as part of the process to prepare the converted-to-text files, I was reading the stories as they had originally appeared, in the order that they had been published in the original volumes. I hadn't done it that way for years. The conversion process captures everything, and that means some items do have to be corrected. For instance, when setting up for printing, original books from the old days often *split* words at the end of a line with hyphens, whereas modern computer programs *wrap* the text, allowing for hyphens to be ignored. When converting the text of the original books, the program picked up every one of those end-of-line hyphens and split words, and they all had to be found and removed. Likewise, the text-conversion program ignores words that are italicized in the original, and these each have to be relocated and re-italicized. (However, in some cases, Derleth himself was inconsistent, italicizing a word, such as a book title or the name of a ship, at one point in a story, and not at a later point. That had to be verified too.)

I have long been a chronologicist, organizing all of the thousands of traditional Sherlock Holmes stories that I've collected and read into a massive Holmes Chronology, breaking various adventures (book, story, chapter, and paragraph) down into year, month, day, and even hour to form a *complete* life of Holmes, from birth to death, covering both the Holmes Canon and traditional pastiches. It was inevitable that I would do the same with Pons. For several decades, I've had a satisfying Pons Chronology as well, based on research by various individuals, and largely on Copper's arrangement of the stories within his *Omnibus* – with a few disagreements. By re-reading the original stories in their original form, for the first time in years, I realized that, in addition to changing spelling, Copper had committed – as referred to earlier – a far bigger sin.

I discovered as I re-read the original stories for this project that a number of them weren't matching up with my long-established Pons Chronology, based a great deal upon Copper's arrangement in his *Omnibus*. Some of the stories from the originals would give a specific date that would be a whole decade different from where I had placed the story in my own chronology. A quick check against Copper's *Omnibus* revealed that he had actually changed these dates in his revisions, sometimes shifting from the 1920's to the 1930's, a whole decade, in order to place the story where he thought that it ought to go. Worse, he sometimes eliminated a whole sentence from an original story if it contradicted his placement of that story within his *Omnibus*.

As a chronologist, I was horrified and sickened. This affront wasn't mentioned in Ruber's 2000 essay explaining why Ponsians were irritated with Copper. I can't believe that this wasn't noticed before.

There has always been ample material for the chronologist with the Pons books, even without these changes. Granted, the original versions, as written, open up a lot of problems and contradictions about when various stories occur that Copper smoothed out – apparently without anyone noticing. For this reason, and many others, I'm very glad and proud that the original Solar Pons adventures, as originally published by Derleth, are being presented here in these new volumes for a new generation.

David Marcum
"The Obrisset Snuffbox", PSI
(excerpted from the Belanger edition reissues)

THE SOLAR PONS FANDOM BEGINS
BY DERRICK BELANGER

Solar Pons is the great torch bearer of Sherlock Holmes, but as I noted in my introduction to *The Return of Solar Pons*, the Praed Street detective is his own man, fully fleshed out in these adventures, and as Anthony Boucher aptly notes in his introduction to this book, unlike Sherlock Holmes, he is a flexible detective. What does he mean by flexible? He means a man that can deal with the known as well as the unknown, a detective who can solve a crime dealing with the rational as well as that which deals with the supernatural or irrational.

In *The Reminiscences*, we get both types of adventures, from the rational like "The Adventure of the Mazarine Blue", to the irrational and otherworldly like "The Adventure of the Blind Clairaudient". Pons moves between these two types of cases seamlessly, and unlike Holmes, is open to otherworldly explanations to his cases.

Beyond the excellent stories in this collection, we also have another defining moment for the Sherlock Holmes of Praed Street. We have his first published chronology. Chronologer Robert Patrick does an excellent job putting the stories in a sequential order, with precise dates no less. As Holmes fans know, the great detective's stories were most famously ordered by William Baring-Gould. Mr. Baring-Gould provided a chronology of all the Holmes stories, but some of his story arrangements were controversial, such as having "The Red

Headed League" take place in 1887, even though the story specifically states that The Red Headed League was dissolved in 1890. Mr. Patrick also has some controversy to his sequence, with some critics believing that his meeting date for Pons and Parker was far too late in 1921 and should be moved to 1919.

My point is not to argue over correct dates for the Solar Pons stories. My point is that people saw fit to create a timeline and argue over the dates. That means Pons had hit a certain level of importance. He had his own fan base that would take the time to argue *minutiae* over the character. The fandom was solidified in 1966 when Luther Norris formed The Praed Street Irregulars, a group dedicated to the study and preservation of the Solar Pons stories. Over fifty years later, there are now Solar Pons fan groups throughout the world, groups which ensure that the Sherlock Holmes of Praed Street shall be remembered as long as his predecessor.

Derrick Belanger
May 2018

The Reminiscences of Solar Pons

INTRODUCTION

BY ANTHONY BOUCHER

(From the 1961 Mycroft & Moran Edition)

Small puzzle for Baker Street Irregulars: Why should the fourth volume of Solar Pons stories, after the Adventures, Memoirs, *and* Return, *be logically and inevitably titled* The Reminiscences?

One of the most appealing qualities of Solar Pons is the clear fact that he is not Sherlock Holmes.

Offhand, this statement may seem at least a paradox, if not a heresy, since his greatest following is among those readers who find a Pons story the best possible substitute for a new adventure of Holmes himself.

But a mere effort to make a facsimile of the Master is not enough to give life and readability to a story – as the Agent himself demonstrated in *The Crown Diamond* and its offspring, *The Mazarin Stone*, and as the Agent's son proved even more clearly in *The Exploits*.

Of all the 48 variants on the Holmes name and character listed by Ellery Queen in *The Memoirs of Solar Pons*, hardly any other has the independent vitality of Pons. (The two major exceptions might be Maurice Leblanc's Herlock Sholmes and H. F. Heard's Mr. Mycroft – both intended to be direct portraits of the Master, but each viewed so differently through un-Watsonian eyes as to become a separate and living character.)

As Vincent Starrett wrote in introducing the first Pontian collection, Pons is "a clever impersonator, with a twinkle in his eye, which tells us that he knows he is not Sherlock Holmes, and knows that *we* know it, but that he hopes we will like him anyway for what he symbolizes" – and, I might add, for what he *is* as well.

In a delicate and all but indefinable way, he is not, like Holmes, a man of the Nineteenth Century foreshadowing the Twentieth, but rather a man of the Twentieth Century recalling the Nineteenth. The "twinkle" (which is also perceptible in the eye of Dr. Parker and perhaps even in that of the Sauk City Agent) is faintly self-mocking; the note of gaiety and a sort of ironic playfulness, which marks Holmes upon rare occasions (as in the opening section of *The Valley of Fear*), is more common with Pons, especially when he contemplates his relationship to his "illustrious predecessor."

Pons is even independent enough to have interests of his own, nowhere adumbrated in the Canon of Watson. Although Dr. Parker lists among Pons' "varied interests" his "addiction to good music of all kinds" (obviously the comment of an unmusical man), he is apparently simply an auditor and, unlike Holmes, neither performer nor musicologist. But Pons is (Parker tells us) absorbed equally by "occult lore and scientific treatises on the nature of evidence"; and the official Pons bibliography lists, along with such works as *The Varieties of the Criminal Method* (1911), a monograph dealing with *An Examination of the Cthulhu Cult and Others* (1931). (The reference, for those unfamiliar with other publications handled by Pons' Agent, is to a singularly terrible Mythos of eldritch and arcane horror, created – or revealed – by the late Howard Phillips Lovecraft, which once dominated American fiction of the supernatural in *Weird Tales* and other magazines.)

It is doubtless because of this interest that Solar Pons has on rare occasions found himself involved, as Holmes never was,[1] in cases which contain a definite and undeniable element of "fantasy" – occurrences which pass the bounds of what is (at this moment) believed possible by science. One such adventure you will find in this volume (*The Blind Clairaudient*). Two others (jointly agented by Derleth and Mack Reynolds) appear in *The Science-Fictional Sherlock Holmes* (Denver, 1960).

Few of the detectives whose exploits have been chronicled for us are competent to handle a case which does not have a "rational explanation." Holmes and such later masters as Dr. Fell and the Great Merlini – yes, and even Father Brown, with his devout faith in the supernatural – approach a seemingly paranormal situation with a firm attitude of "Stuff and nonsense! How was this gimmicked?" – an attitude that may invite disaster if no human gimmickry is involved.

A very few detectives, notably Algernon Blackwood's John Silence, Manly Wade Wellman's John Thunston, and Seabury Quinn's Jules de Grandin, have specialized exclusively in the supernatural; but this too has the limitations of inflexibility, and one can imagine de Grandin brandishing a clove of garlic or an aspergillum as protection against Jack the Ripper.

With more suitable ambivalence, the cases of Richard Sale's too-little-known Captain McGrail, like those of my own Dr. Verner (all save one of which, I regret to say, still repose in their box at the Wells Fargo Bank), end inconclusively, or rather with two conclusions, evenly balanced between the rational and the fantastic.

A certain few detectives have on occasion adapted themselves to a case outside the normal pattern. Lord Peter Wimsey once (in *The Bone of Contention*) employed good occult reasoning to dispel the supernatural. The career of C. Daly King's Tarrant (another of the Great Neglected Detectives – there's a title for an anthology!) seemed to draw him more and more into occult involvements. My own Fergus O'Breen, who has coped only with murderers in novels, has met (and I hope competently) with werewolves and time machines in shorter adventures. F. Tennyson Jesse's Solange Fontaine (yet another candidate demanding rescue from oblivion) employs something very like ESP in her deductions, and has occasionally found herself in an unarguably supernatural episode. [2]

In addition to the somewhat specialized *Dream Detective*, Morris Klaw, Sax Rohmer has chronicled the fortunes and misfortunes of Assistant Commissioner (of Scotland Yard) Sir Denis Nayland Smith and of private detective (ex-FBI) Drake Roscoe, each of whom has often faced an adversary whose catholic and unscrupulous arsenal of weapons includes the supernatural and the parascientific – Smith's enemy being, of course, the (apparently literally) immortal Dr. Fu Manchu and Drake's the less well known but no less insidious Astar, by first marriage the Marquise Sumuru.

(It is regrettable that the infamous Doctor has no more worthy antagonist than the often startlingly inept Nayland Smith; he should have been matched with Holmes, or at the very least with Cleek of the Forty Faces – as a subsidiary matter, the prose style of his exploits and those of Cleek would have jibed admirably. Aficionados, however, will recall that a certain unnamed Oriental doctor crossed the path of Solar Pons in *The Camberwell Beauty*, and will be happy to learn that he reappears in this current volume.)

The detective of ideal flexibility is William Hope Hodgson's "ghostfinder," Carnacki (of whom Dennis Wheatley's Niels Orsen is a pallid and regrettable imitation). Carnacki is a specialist, called in only for seemingly supernatural problems; but unlike either Gideon Fell or Jules de Grandin, he aims his efforts at determining whether the specific problem is or is not supernatural in origin. Once having determined its nature, he treats it on its own terms, by "realistic" or by occult methods.

You will discover many individual, non-Holmesian virtues of Solar Pons in this volume, as well as many more felicitous echoes of 221B Baker Street in 7B Praed Street. But high among the independent qualities of Pons must rank the fact that his name can be inscribed on the all-too-short list of the Flexible Detectives.

His Last Bow, *the fourth collection of Sherlock Holmes' shorter adventures (and I trust you have observed that each volume of the Pontian canon contains precisely as many stories as its Holmesian parallel?), bears in its original English edition (John Murray, 1917) the subtitle:* Some Reminiscences of Sherlock Holmes. *(The U. S. edition, mysteriously as always, is subtitled:* A Reminiscence...)

– ANTHONY BOUCHER
Berkeley, California
April 28, 1961

1 – At least not to our knowledge. There is some reason to believe that the extraordinary "unfathomed cases" listed in *Thor Bridge* – Phillimore, Persano and the cutter *Alicia* – may have been supernatural or at least science-fictional in essence.

2 – I have a vivid recollection of a short story by H. C. Bailey, in the 1920's or early 1930's, in which Reggie Fortune confronted genuine witchcraft, but I have never been able to rediscover it. I shall be grateful if any reader can help me.

I

THE ADVENTURE OF THE MAZARINE BLUE

On the tempestuous spring night, my friend Solar Pons had just paused at the fireplace to knock out his pipe of shag, when from the street below, in a lull between the wind's gusts, came the sound of a motor. A gleam of anticipation came into Pons' eyes.

"Surely that is not a visitor at this hour!" I cried. "Why, it is eleven o'clock!"

"Not a visitor, I trust, but perhaps a client. A powerful car, Parker. And, short of sudden emergency in the city, come from some distance."

At this instant the outer door below opened and closed. There was not immediately any step on the stair.

"A stranger to these environs," said Pons dryly. "He is pausing to light his way and determine which floor it is he wants. Ah, he has seen your card, Parker; he is coming up."

In a moment the footsteps came to our ears.

"A man not yet in middle age, carrying a cane under his arm – listen to it occasionally strike the rail or draw along the wall. In some haste, too."

The knock that fell upon the door of 7B interrupted my companion's further deduction.

"Come in, come in," called Pons, all alert now, and still before the fireplace, his hands clasped behind him, his faded blue dressing-gown lax about his rangy figure.

In response to his call, the door was flung open, and a man of about thirty burst into the room. He was tall, thin, clad in what was once a military coat which reached to his knees, and did indeed carry a stick under one arm. He was hatless, but wore a monocle in his right eye. His face was pale, his eyes were somewhat feverish, and his dark moustache seemed almost black above his bloodless lips. His glance ignored me entirely and fixed at once on Pons.

"Mr. Solar Pons," he cried without preamble, "I am prepared to pay you any retainer you name if only you can solve the mystery of our ghastly discovery. We have not called the police since we discovered the body."

"Pray compose yourself, sir," said Pons. "You have obviously come from some little distance and have allowed yourself to become overwrought. Just sit down – Dr. Parker will bring you a stimulant – and tell us your story from the beginning."

"Mr. Pons, I beg you – there is no time to be lost. I have come all the way from Chetley Old Place near Stroud, Gloucestershire. I beg of you to come with me now, at once, and let me tell you my story on the way. My car is below."

"Chetley Old Place," mused Pons. "Then you are Sir Richard Chetley."

"Yes, Mr. Pons. You were of service to my late father when I was in Australia over ten years ago."

"A pause for hot lemonade and brandy will not take much time," said Pons then, as I came up with that stimulant for our client. "And you might just say in brief what it is that has upset you to the extent of your coming away without a hat in such inclement weather and driving over a hundred miles to our quarters."

Sir Richard accepted the glass I proffered him, thanked me curtly, and turned once again to Pons. "Mr. Pons, late this afternoon we had occasion to open the family vault, our burial place for many decades. Twelve of us have been laid away in it – yet, today, there were thirteen coffins. And the thirteenth contained the decomposing remains of someone utterly unknown to me. Who he was, how he came there – we do not know. Will you come, Mr. Pons?"

There was no need for Pons to answer; he was already removing his dressing-gown, and I knew that to take issue with him would be folly.

As we drove through the night toward the Cotswolds, our client told his story without interruption. His aged aunt, the last remaining member of the preceding generation of his father's family, lay seriously ill at Chetley Old Place. Her life was despaired of, and, after dinner, our client had thought of making sure that all would be in readiness in the family burial vault, which he had not entered since the death of his father six years before. Old Sir Malcolm had been the twelfth member of the family to be laid in the vault. Sir Richard had taken with him one Jasper Nason, one of the two servants on the estate, the other being Mrs. Nason; indeed, it was Nason who drove the Rolls-Royce in which we rode.

"Our home, as you know, lies in the Cotswolds, and the vault is perhaps half a mile from the house, well away from the road, built into the side of a small knoll which is part of the foothills," explained Sir Richard. "The lock on the vault door is a very old one, fashioned many years ago, and it yields only to an ancient handwrought key; indeed, the whole lock is handwrought. Nason carried the key, and it was he who opened the door while I held a lantern. The moment we stepped into the vault, we were aware of a very strong stench of decomposing flesh. This was astonishing, since to the best of my knowledge, no one had been in the vault during the six years following my father's death. But, in truth, we thought little of it, since the air flowing through the opened door soon seemed to dissipate it. I went directly to the place where we expected to lay Aunt Agatha, next to my father's coffin. Judge my amazement to find a coffin there, and with every sign of belonging there, save that it bore no name plate, and was plainly a very inexpensive coffin. Nason was as astonished as I was.

"To add to our wonder, we discovered that the coffin was not sealed, but only nailed shut, and forthwith we pried it open. In it lay all that remained of a gentleman who could not have been dead very many months, slain by a savage blow on the head, for it was plain that his skull had been broken in from behind. He was unknown to me, and as unknown to Nason. I thought immediately of calling the police, but then I hesitated; I knew that once the local police had been called, there would be no keeping the mystery from the papers, and the discovery of an unidentified corpse in our family vault could hardly be kept from my aunt, and might prove to be a fatal shock to her. I thought of you at once, Mr. Pons. We closed the vault again, locked it, and set out immediately for London. That was three hours ago."

For a few moments Pons said nothing, and the only sound we heard was that of the motor as we rode into the west. Indeed, Pons seemed asleep, though I knew he was not, for I knew that attitude of intent listening only too well. Without opening his eyes, he spoke at last.

"The coffins in your vault, I take it, are placed in order and are reasonably uniform?" he asked.

"Yes, Mr. Pons. That was why I noticed at once that the thirteenth coffin was not one of ours. It could not have cost more than ten pounds."

"Yes it was placed similarly to the others – as if it belonged there?"

"It was."

"How many places are then left for the family, Sir Richard?"

"Well, sir, there are easily ten, I should say. There is a place for my aunt, for one. There are places for myself and such family as I might have."

"You are not married, however," said Pons.

"No, sir. I am the last of the line."

"Is that not the direct line only? I seem to remember that your father had a brother, as well as two half-brothers, and a cousin, and that you, yourself, once had a cousin."

"So I did, Mr. Pons. That is a painful memory. You should recall it before me, since it was in the matter of my cousin Leonard that you were of service to my father; you sent him to Borstall with his bad companions, Hugo Mays and Alfred Tetlark, all of whom were engaged in a series of burglaries in this vicinity. The two younger fellows were given but four years at Borstall; the old lag, Alfred, was sent to Dartmoor for nine. When Leonard was freed after four years, he and his father left England for Australia and were lost when their ship went down in a storm off the coast of New Zealand. Leonard's father was my father's half-brother, Henry. The other half-brother, Edward, also broke with my father over the prosecution of cousin Leonard, and we have lost sight of him – if, indeed, he is still alive. My father's only brother died before my father by a year, and is buried in our vault next to my mother's coffin, and thus but one coffin removed from my father's. My father's only cousin is dead, too, I believe; he died in America three years ago."

"There was no evidence that the lock had been tampered with?" asked Pons then.

"We did not stop to see, Mr. Pons. Certainly there was no obvious evidence, for we had to unlock the door to get it open, and the lock offered no more resistance than is customary. It is an old lock – by several generations – and it is a wonder that it still serves so well. But, then, the old things were more sturdily built."

"The vault itself is out of sight of the house?"

"Yes, Mr. Pons."

"And, doubtless, in an unfrequented place, so that anyone could obtain access to it without much fear of immediate discovery?"

"I suppose that is so, Mr. Pons."

"Very well. We shall see in good time. If you will forgive me, I will catch a few winks while we are riding to our destination. Pray let us go directly to the vault on our arrival. Wake me there."

So saying, he composed himself for sleep for the two hours of driving before us.

It was still dark as midnight when we reached the Chetley vault.

Our client, red-eyed now from strain and lack of sleep, led the way with a powerful lantern to the door, and would have unlocked it at once had not Pons stayed his hand.

"Let us just examine the lock, Sir Richard."

He whipped out his magnifying glass, motioned for the light, which our client held high upon the heavy door, and bent over the lock. He looked at it carefully for some time; then crossed to the other side of the door, beckoning for the light, and studied the hinges.

"Ah," he murmured almost at once. "The hinges were removed. That then was the way entry was made." He turned and beckoned to Nason, a sallow-faced man in his fifties.

"Unlock the door."

Thus bidden, Nason stepped forward, took the key from his master, and, while Sir Richard directed light upon the ponderous lock, manipulated the heavy key, which was fully ten inches in length. The door swung back, and immediately the charnel odor of the crypt swept over us from the deep blackness inside. The light reflected eerily on the coffins beyond.

Sir Richard took the lead and entered the vault. Inside, a brick ceiling was domed overhead, arched over to reach the floor on both sides. There was room enough for a double row of coffins, and we walked down between them – some obviously very old, since they were of the seventeenth century in origin – six on either side, until we came to the thirteenth, to which the light held. This was clearly a coffin of the cheapest manufacture, and quite out of place among the others in the vault; so much was evident at a glance.

Pons now took the lantern, and methodically went around the coffin, scrutinizing it closely on all sides. Only when he had finished was he willing to open the coffin, seeing which Nason stepped well back. My own inclination was to do likewise, but I had no choice, for even as he was about raising the lid, Pons spoke.

"Your department, I think, Parker."

The stench of decomposition was almost overpowering. Pons betrayed none of his distaste for it save in the twitching of his nostrils and the grimness of his mouth. Our client, at facing his unwelcome tenant once again, went even paler than before. The light of the lantern disclosed all that remained of a portly man well past middle age. Decomposition had progressed to such a point that identification of the remains might indeed be difficult; yet it was possible to say, I concluded after a cursory examination, that the fellow had come to his death by means of some blunt instrument which had smashed in his skull from the rear. He was a heavily bearded man, and in his beard, otherwise black, there were the beginnings of grey hair. His arms had been folded neatly across his breast, and he had been clad in a suit of brown tweed. He was not a tall man, nor yet small; he measured approximately five and a half feet. The past winter having been cool, decomposition would not have progressed to the stage of revealing so much of the skeleton if the body had been in the vault for only six months; in my opinion, the body had been in its present resting-place for at least nine months.

So much I could tell Pons and our client. Having done so, I stepped back and Pons in turn bent to the gruesome examination. He looked in vain for identifying marks on the clothing, and reached with great care into all visible pockets, none of which gave up contents. It was only when Pons felt about under the remains that he brought forth what appeared to me to be a few tiny fragments of colored paper; these he put into one of the small envelopes he carried from time to time for just such a purpose as this. By assiduous search, he discovered a few more such pieces before he was ready to abandon further examination, and covered the remains in the thirteenth coffin once again.

We lost no time leaving the vault, and breathed the air outside once more with gratitude. Standing before the locked door of the vault, our client turned to Pons.

"What must I do now, Mr. Pons?" he asked. "I hesitate to call the police."

"Nevertheless, the police must be notified. However, it can do no harm to wait yet a little while – the corpse is not likely to move. And nothing more will be disclosed by the body in its present state than its state in a day or two hence. Let us repair to some place where we can rest. Perhaps there is an inn at Stroud?"

"Mr. Pons, Chetley Old Place is at your disposal," said our client.

"There is no danger that we may disturb your aunt, Sir Richard?

"I doubt it."

"What, incidentally, is ailing her?"

"Her doctor tells me that she has a combination of diseases common to her advanced age."

"She has been ill for some time, then?"

"Indeed she has. She has been abed for two months."

Pons nodded absently, stood for a moment tugging at the lobe of his left ear, and then started toward the car, remarking that it would be best to get to bed before returning early in the morning to London, where my practice demanded my presence, since I had failed to notify my *locum* that I might be away from the city.

Once in the room to which Sir Richard had shown us, Pons turned to me, his face quickened with the excitement of the chase. "What a pretty puzzle, eh, Parker?" he cried. "What do you make of it?"

"Murder, certainly."

"Most foul, indeed! No more?"

"Well, one could hardly ask for a better place of concealment. Quite likely had it been anyone but Sir Richard, the thirteenth coffin would never have been opened – or perhaps even challenged."

"You saw nothing odd in the choice of the Chetley vault?"

"Any other vault would have done as well."

"Capital! my dear fellow. That is precisely the point. Why this one? I submit that whoever made such fell use of it knew that it was advantageously reached and well out of sight of both house and highway; that, moreover, it was seldom visited by members of the family, and thus peculiar to his need."

"I should imagine that several hundred people knew of its existence," I said, not without some asperity.

"Granted. But even 'several hundred' is a limiting factor. There were no identifying marks on the clothing. Does that not suggest to you that whoever deposited the corpse in that place might have thought identification possible by some member of the family?"

"Perhaps."

"Reluctantly spoken, and without spirit," said Pons, a vexing smile on his thin lips. "A man well past middle age, you said. That suggests nothing to you?"

"My dear fellow, why should it?"

"Why indeed!"

He took from his pocket the envelope he had used in the crypt, looked about for a piece of white paper, and, finding a sheet of writing paper in the drawer of a small desk in our room, he dumped the contents of the envelope thereon. I looked down at a little pile of veined blue fragments, having very much the appearance of brittle onion skin paper. "What in the world is that, Pons?"

"That is what I hope to discover," he answered.

So saying, he drew up a chair and began with infinite patience to try to fit the various fragments together. After watching him at this well-nigh hopeless task for a minute or two, I left his side, with the announcement that I, for one, intended to sleep, and he could do what he liked. Since he was doing so, he made no reply.

When I awoke an hour after dawn, I found Pons already up.

"I suppose you have found the murderer," I said testily.

"Perhaps not quite. We shall see when once we have had a look at a heavy man of some five and a half feet in height, well past middle age, bearded, and very probably a lepidopterist."

"Ah, that blue paper!" I retorted.

"It is not paper."

I went over and looked down at the result of Pons' nocturnal labor. What he had put together on the white paper out of the fragments he had assembled from the coffin looked like all that remained of one wing of some insect. A moth? But no, it was not that.

"Why, it looks like a butterfly!" I cried.

"Indeed, and you are right, Parker," he said. "It is such a discovery as one on which to construct the entire meaning and *modus operandi* of the crime. Have you ever seen its like before?"

I confessed that I had not.

"I thought as much. Unless I am sadly mistaken, these are the remains of a Mazarine Blue, a rare immigrant. Less than a hundred have been found in all the Isles in the past century and ten years, and of these, no less than twenty were captured in the year 1825 alone. That should give you some indication of how rare this butterfly has been since then. A member of the subfamily *Plebeiinae*, I think. But then, I am no expert. I shall need to call on Lord Kerners, who is the recognized authority in London."

"But how came such a rarity in the place where you found it?"

"Ah! That is the question, Parker. None but a lepidopterist is likely to have possessed a Mazarine Blue. And a large number of those which have been taken are undoubtedly in public collections. We are thus limited, for obvious reasons, to a collector within not too great a radius of the immediate Cotswold country where we find ourselves this morning. And is it not a lovely morning!" he added, peering from the window.

Indeed, the view from the window was the epitome of England in all her rural beauty, for the hill slopes, the tidy fields and pastures, the blue beeches and birch trees among the pines, at this hour wreathed in rising mists, with the dew gleaming in the patches of sunlight conveyed instantly both the essence of this green isle and the freshness of the season in the country. Pons, however, did not give even this enchanting view his undivided attention, for, as I moved closer to him, he lowered his voice and spoke rapidly.

"Before we go, Parker, do contrive to have a look at our client's aunt. I am curious especially to know how long she may linger."

"Surely you do not suspect him or her... ?"

"Fie, Parker! You are far ahead of the game. We have not yet made such progress!"

"But you were only a little while ago describing the murderer," I protested. Pons clucked impatiently. "I did not identify him as such. Our first quarry – a lepidopterist. I submit that no true collector would permit a specimen of the Mazarine Blue to escape him, no matter what the circumstance."

"Perhaps he did not see the butterfly."

"That is always a possibility. Or seeing, did not care."

"Then he was not the collector."

"Ah, Parker, it warms me to observe such definite proof of my good influence. The faculty of observation is basic before the science of deduction can be employed. But I am persuaded to believe you, too, now have all the facts, and should be able to apply your experience to the solution of this gruesome little problem. Let us just look up our host."

Sir Richard was up and waiting for us. He looked haggard. I inquired solicitously about his aunt at the breakfast table, and found it unnecessary to suggest that I look in on her, for he himself asked whether I would care to do so.

We were soon thereafter on our way to London in our client's car, though he did not accompany us. Pons, as usual, sat in deep thought. How he could close his eyes to the scenic beauty of that fair land I could never hope to understand; but so he did, slumped into one corner of the tonneau, and while I took delight in the ever-changing view, he sat in brooding silence, unaware of all else but the problem in hand. Presently, however, he opened one eye half way and shot a glance at me.

"The aunt, Parker. How did you find her?"

"She has at least a week. But if you are thinking that anything about her condition is unnatural, put it out of your mind. She is dying of the debilities of old age – of just what Sir Richard said, a complex of senile diseases."

Pons waved one hand impatiently. "Sir Richard, at any rate, is safe from harm for at least a week – if indeed harm impends. I am persuaded that it does."

"You gave him no warning," I protested indignantly.

"There is plenty of time for that."

He relapsed into silence again.

"I must say," I said presently, "I, am extremely confused by the various and apparently unconnected directions in which you have shown an interest. What has the old lady's condition to do with Sir Richard's safety? Why is the Mazarine Blue of such signal importance? And what have we to do with a collector of butterflies when it is manifest that no collector would ever have allowed a Mazarine Blue to escape him? – in your own words."

"Ah, Parker, surely you jest! The answers are so obvious that not even you could be unaware of them!"

If he had wished to silence me, he could not have chosen a better weapon.

We reached our quarters at 7B Praed Street just before noon, and, though I was then ravenously hungry, for all that we had had breakfast at Chetley Old Place, Pons did not wish even to look at food. He lost no time in making an appointment to see Lord Kerners, and then turned upon his files, which were shortly scattered about his chair, as he sought the information he expected to find among them.

"Ah, here we are," he said at last. "'Conviction of Leonard Jones'. Here is the whole sorry mess. Sir Malcolm was adamant about punishment, and the young man seemed incorrigible. There was, in any case, an appreciable prejudice on Leonard's part – he felt resentment against his wealthier relatives. Four years in Borstall, thereafter three years knocking about London – I seem to recall meeting him once in Soho and then at last his tragic end."

"There is no doubt about his end, then? Down off the coast of New Zealand in a storm, I think Sir Richard said."

"Ah, Parker – you have been chronicling too many of these little adventures. I fear there is no question about Leonard's death. The ship went down within sight of shore. Some hands were saved, but neither Leonard nor his father was among them. The sea was searched for some time, and anyone reaching the beach would certainly have been noticed."

"Mistaken identity, then," I suggested.

"To what end," Pons shook his head. "No, no, that is entirely too fanciful, though I agree that the probability would be bound to occur, since Leonard, at least, knew very well about the burial vault. So did his father and his uncle."

"There is an uncle who still survives."

"He has been out of touch with the family for ten years," replied Pons. "Besides, if his motive were vengeance, surely he is starting late to accomplish it, since Sir Richard's father has been dead these past six years."

"The fact remains that something dastardly is afoot," I insisted.

"We are in perfect agreement as to that," answered Pons dryly.

Soon after, Pons left for his appointment with Lord Kerners, and I went on professional calls I could put off no longer. It was not until that evening that we met again, when I entered our rooms to find Pons just turning from the telephone, explaining that he had put through a trunk call to Dartmoor to make some enquiries.

"You saw Lord Kerners?" I pressed him.

"I did. There is no doubt about it. The fragments are of a Mazarine Blue. There is sufficient evidence to indicate that the entire butterfly was very probably pressed beneath the corpse. Having had my own guess verified, I made inquiry about the number of Mazarine Blues known to be in private collections, particularly in the Cotswolds and the vicinity of Stroud. Would it surprise you to learn that one Edward Jones is a lepidopterist?"

"Nothing you turn up can surprise me. But 'Edward Jones' is a common name. Can it be Sir Richard's surviving relative?"

"We shall see. He lives at Evesham on the Avon, which is not too far from the ancestral estate of Chetley Old Place. That is surely within easy transportation of Stroud, and it must have occurred to you that the transportation of a body, even by night, becomes increasingly hazardous with every mile. I submit that a journey from London could hardly be accomplished without attracting someone's attention. But a journey from anywhere within a radius of Stroud that includes Evesham is far more likely to be accomplished without a hitch. A visit to Evesham is indicated."

Without waiting for my reply, Pons drew a railway guide to him. "Let me see – we can take a train for Evesham out of Paddington by way of Oxford at eight-ten tomorrow morning We shall reach Evesham just after eleven."

"You are coming back to my theory," I said, not without a note of triumph.

Pons favored me with an enigmatic smile. "I shall be most interested to learn how a collector could lose a Mazarine Blue with equanimity," he said.

We reached Evesham before noon of the following day.

No one who knew Pons was likely to have recognized him, for he was clad as an outdoorsman, a hunter of butterflies, no less, complete with net. By presenting himself as a fellow collector, he expected to be received with considerably less suspicion by Edward Jones at the address Lord Kerners had given him. The place we sought was a modest but secluded dwelling in the north end of the town, not far from the Abbey Manor House; it was surrounded by iron palings, from the gate of which a flagstone walk led to a tree-embowered terrace. The day being warm, the door of the house, visible from the gate, stood partly ajar. So much we saw in a brief reconnoitering journey, for Pons was not yet ready to go in.

"Before we set foot in that idyllic scene, let us just go around to the police station and make ourselves known," he said.

"In case you should have to produce your revolver?" I asked. "I saw you take it."

"Ah, Parker, you are indeed growing more observing. Soon I shall have no secrets left, and my poor powers will be exposed for what they are."

At the police station, Pons introduced himself to Sergeant Moore, who was at this hour in charge. He was a heavy, florid-faced man, who, once he was convinced of Pons' identity, was eager to be as cooperative as possible.

"I should first like to know whether any local tradesman has reported the theft of a coffin within the past year," asked Pons.

Sergeant Moore scratched his head. "Not as I know of, Mr. Pons. And I think I'd know that if it'd been reported."

"Let us say, then, the sale in peculiar circumstances – not necessarily only within the last year," pressed Pons.

Sergeant Moore's face broke into a grin. "Why, you must mean Mr. Jones!" he cried. "He bought himself a coffin four, five years ago, and he's been sleepin' in it ever since. Oh, but he's a queer one, all right!"

Pons smiled. His next request was somewhat more sobering. Could the Sergeant detail a man to follow us, to respond to Pons' signal?

The Sergeant could and did, and when we left the police station, we were followed by Constable Peter Maugham, who, following Pons' instructions, remained as unobtrusive as possible, staying a street or so behind us.

This time Pons went forthrightly up the flagstone walk to the door of Edward Jones' house and gave the bell-pull a prolonged ring. Then we stood until footsteps approached from inside and a bearded face was thrust out at us from the dusk of the house.

"What can I do for you, Gentlemen?"

"Have I the honor of speaking to Mr. Edward Jones?" asked Pons.

The old gentleman nodded benignly. "You do, sir."

"The well-known lepidopterist, whose collection of butterflies is so widely respected?" continued Pons.

There was a brief, suspicious moment of silence. The old fellow's bull-like neck turned as he moved his head a little so that his narrowed eyes measured Pons from head to toe. "My collection," he said. "I *am* sorry, sir, to have put you to any trouble. I sold my collection, good three years ago – perhaps even more."

"Come, sir, you jest. No true collector could bring himself to part with his life's work!"

"Nevertheless, sir, I sold my collection." Then, after a moment of hesitation, Jones added, "Do not let me keep you from your hunting, sir. Good-day, Gentlemen."

He closed the door softly but firmly in our faces.

"A rude old man," I said, as we walked toward the street. Pons' eyes danced. He walked almost too rapidly for me to keep up, and, as soon as we were out of sight of the house, he waited for Constable Maugham to catch up.

"Dr. Parker and I are doubling around to the back of the house. Will you return to the front, Maugham, and arrest Mr. Jones if he attempts to leave?"

"Arrest him, Mr. Pons?" Constable Maugham was incredulous. "But on what charge?"

"The charge is murder. Have no fear. I will substantiate it. Come, we have no time to lose."

"Pons, this is madness," I protested as I hastened after him, where he made his way around to the rear of Jones' property.

We reached there just in time. As we came up, the burly old man we had last seen at the front door was opening the gate at the rear of his property. He was red-faced and obviously in grievous haste, for he had scarcely paused to snatch more than enough of his belongings to fill a small hand-bag. Before he caught sight of us, Pons had his revolver in his hand.

"Not so fast, Alfred," said Pons. "I thought you had recognized me."

Our quarry stood where he was, cursing. "Next time, Pons," he muttered furiously and ominously.

"There won't be another time, Alfred. It's murder this time. The murder of Edward Jones, committed nine months ago. Parker, just summon Constable Maugham."

"There was really no other alternative," said Pons as we sat in our compartment on the return trip to London, "though I suppose the crux of the matter was the delay in the matter of vengeance. This in itself posed no great problem and actually served to cast still further doubt on the highly theoretical question of the possible escape of Leonard Jones and his father in that shipwreck off New Zealand's coast. Had they been engaged in this, they might have been expected to move far sooner. I was left then with Leonard's companions in that robbery of a decade ago. Hugo Mays had been released at the same time as Leonard, and had gone his separate way. Alfred served his full time, and was released last year. Nine years, you will recall, Parker. The coincidence did not escape me – last year was the ninth year, and it was immediately after his release that Alfred set in motion the events which culminated in the murder of Edward Jones.

"No doubt Leonard had remarked on his resemblance to his uncle Edward. Doubtless, too, Leonard had set forth with admirable clarity his feelings about the Chetleys, so that Alfred was fully armed with all the information he needed when he left Dartmoor. Besides, Alfred surely knew of the death of Leonard and his father; he may also have known that Edward Jones was the only surviving relative after Sir Richard and his

Aunt Agatha – and she was dying. Edward Jones offered him a suitable victim – an elderly man, bush-bearded like himself, living alone in a secluded house. Perhaps he even posed as a fellow collector to obtain entrance. And then to find that his intended victim was one of those eccentrics who are given to sleeping in coffins – was that not temptation with a vengeance? I submit that Alfred killed Jones on his very first visit and took his place; I submit that the old man was showing him his collection of butterflies at the time of his murder, which accounts for the presence of the rare Mazarine Blue.

"Alfred's goal was perhaps worth the gamble in his eyes. His victim's living was modest, but enough. But the game might have been extended to win a genuine prize – Chetley Old Place and the entire estate. Once Aunt Agatha had departed this life, a convenient accident to Sir Richard would have left the spurious Edward Jones the only heir. Could this have been Leonard's hope, fallen on Alfred's fertile brain?

"I fancy this is Alfred's last journey. The police will turn Spilsbury on poor Edward Jones' remains, and that with such evidence as we have gathered will complete the case and send Alfred to the noose."

II

THE ADVENTURE OF THE HATS OF M. DULAC

His eyes twinkling, Solar Pons lowered the paper as I came into our quarters at 7B Praed Street one morning, and said, "Ah, Parker, this little matter of the honorable members' hats will certainly offer a new topic of conversation to supersede the unfortunate scandal at the Diogenes Club."

"Scandal seldom touches the Club," I said, I fear, somewhat pompously, since the subject of the Diogenes Club was one close to me, the Diogenes having been my earliest affection.

"I refer to the violence done to Colonel Mowbray, who was so outrageously searched within its hallowed precincts," continued Pons, as if to torment me. "Now, I fancy, the honorable members will talk of nothing else but the bedevilment they are suffering in the matter of their hats. The morning papers say that no less than seventeen hats have been stolen from the Club."

"Or mislaid," I said.

Pons shook his head. "Not all seventeen. You require too much of chance."

"Besides, as I recall it, they haven't all been taken from the Club."

"Quite true. But so far, only members of the Diogenes seem to have suffered the loss of their hats."

"A coincidence."

"Tush! It is nonsense to speak of coincidence of such magnitude."

"Someone's knavery, then, expressing itself in malice against our members," I said.

"It wears the face of desperation, Parker," replied Pons. "It intrigues me. It tickles my fancy. I am almost tempted to propose to the House Committee of the Diogenes that I be retained to look into it."

"Oh, come, Pons – it is too trivial a matter for your special talents," I protested.

"Nothing is too trivial which promises to alleviate for a time the monotony of existence," retorted Pons. "However, at the moment – through the good offices of my brother, Bancroft – we seem to have some sort of problem in the offing."

He reached under the newspaper on the table and tossed a sheet of notepaper over to me. It was expensive paper, of a high rag content – obviously the property of a man of taste and refinement, and perhaps of wealth. I opened it and read:

"Sir: Your esteemed brother has been kind enough to suggest that I call on you about a little matter which troubles me. Perhaps at one o'clock today?

"Hercule Dulac."

Below, in Bancroft Pons' unmistakable scrawl, was written: "Solar, more in your line than mine. Bancroft."

"What do you make of it, Parker?" challenged Pons.

"'A little matter,' he writes," I said without hesitation. "It does not seem to be a capital crime, does it? He is a man of good connections, or else he would hardly have had your brother's ear. Since he has some access to the Foreign Office, and thus to Bancroft, perhaps it is not too much to guess that he is in the diplomatic service. Of France, perhaps?"

Pons smiled. "Splendid, Parker! I am delighted to observe how much of my methods rubs off on you. French, certainly.

His name tells us that. The paper is unofficial. The French are punctilious in matters of this kind. Thus M. Dulac's problem is likely to be unofficial. Had it been otherwise, Bancroft would have taken it up. I do not recognize our client's name. He is likely to be a minor official, perhaps in the consular service. He writes with a heavy hand, which suggests that he is not physically slight. And what troubles him would seem to be more in the nature of a puzzle to him than something serious, for the casual air of his note suggests as much.

"But come, sit down and take a little lunch. He will call at a considerate hour, which is not far hence. I trust you found your patient improved and are in good appetite. Mrs. Johnson is even now on the way up the stairs with a delicious steak and kidney pie."

We had hardly finished lunch – indeed, Mrs. Johnson had just left our rooms with the dishes – when the outer bell rang, and our landlady's voice could be heard on the stairs directing our visitor to our door.

"A big man," said Pons, cocking his head to mark the ascending steps.

"Heavy," I said. "Elementary."

"Ah, forgive me, Parker. These little deductions come as naturally to me as food and drink. I forget how they must on occasion tire you."

Our client's knock fell upon the door. I hastened to open it.

Hercule Dulac stood on the threshold. He was not as tall as he was broad-shouldered and well-muscled, offering the appearance of a man who was much given to athletics. His features, however, were finely cut and delicate, and he wore a moustache to cover a short upper lip. His lower lip was slightly out-thrust. His pale blue eyes swept past me and fixed at once upon Pons. He bowed.

"Mr. Pons?"

"Come in, M. Dulac," Pons called out.

Our client crossed the threshold as Pons introduced me.

"Dr. Parker is my old and valued friend, sir," said Pons, waving M. Dulac to a chair. "Pray be seated," he added. "I am curious to learn of the matter that troubles you."

Once seated, M. Dulac put his walking stick across his knees and laid his hat upon it. Observing Pons' expectant air, he began to speak at once.

"I hope you won't think my problem too trivial for your good offices, Mr. Pons, but I assure you it has caused me no little annoyance. It concerns, sir, my three hats."

Pons flashed a glance toward me; his eyes danced.

"The cost of the hats is of no consequence," continued M. Dulac. "It is the internal irritation I suffer and the not inconsiderable mystification. Two hats have been stolen from my house and one was knocked from my head and carried off by a ruffian in the street near my house. Mr. Pons, to the best of my knowledge, I have incurred no enemies since I came to London, and I am at a loss to explain this singular matter."

"When did these thefts take place?" asked Pons.

"My house in St. John's Wood was entered four nights ago. Two nights past, my hat was knocked off in the street."

"You caught sight of your assailant?"

"A big man, Mr. Pons, but very nimble. I took after him, but he outdistanced me without trouble. His face was covered with a silk handkerchief."

"You are in the consular service, M. Dulac?" Pons asked then.

"I am, sir. I am the secretary to M. Fliege, the French consul in London."

"Are you by any chance a member of the Diogenes Club?"

"No sir. I have exchange cards, of course, which are honored at several London clubs, but the Diogenes is not one of them."

I coughed.

Pons sat with his eyes closed, undisturbed by my thrust. He pulled his ear lobe between the thumb and index finger of his right hand, a familiar gesture which told me that some train of thought had begun behind those keen eyes.

"M. Dulac," he said presently, "I am no lover of coincidence, however much it occurs in life. You are not a member of the Diogenes. You have been a guest there?"

"On one occasion."

"Ah!"

"It is not, however, a Club to which I would have any desire to belong," M. Dulac went on in a disapproving voice. "On the evening I dined there, I had the misfortune to witness a scandalous matter – the search of one of the members by the police. Moreover, on that same evening I found that someone had gone off with my hat, and I had to content myself with the somewhat more used hat left in its place."

"I assure you, sir," I could not refrain from breaking in, "such incidents as you describe are by no means everyday occurrences at the Diogenes, which is one of the oldest and most respected clubs in the city."

"Pray overlook Dr. Parker's outburst," said Pons, with a wry smile and mocking eyes. "He speaks as a member."

"Colonel Mowbray," I went on, "is even now consulting his solicitors in regard to an action against the police for that disgraceful episode."

"I mean no disrespect to your institutions, Doctor," M. Dulac hastened to say.

Pons brushed this aside. "Actually, then, M. Dulac, you have lost four hats – not three."

"I haven't recovered the hat lost at the Diogenes Club, no. Mr. Pons – but that, I assume, was a simple mistake, for the hat I had to take was quite similar, only somewhat older. The other three, however, were unquestionably stolen."

"The hat you took from the Diogenes in place of your own," pressed Pons. "What has become of it?"

"I still have it, sir. I waited for someone to return my hat, since it had my name and address sewn into the band, like all my hats. Thus far, no one has done so. I can only conclude that the error has not been noticed. The hat I took from the Diogenes Club is in a box at my home."

"None of your stolen hats has been recovered?"

"Two of them, quite badly torn, were found floating in the Thames, Mr. Pons. A clear case of vandalism, the reason for which completely escapes me. I had thought I had some familiarity with the British character, but the key to this puzzle eludes me."

"What kind of hat was it that you left at the Club?"

"A bowler."

"And the hats which were stolen?"

"Also bowlers."

"Dear me – someone has an affinity for our common bowler! Were not the honorable members' stolen hats also bowlers, Parker?" asked Pons.

"I believe they were."

"Perhaps, more than likely, he has a horror of bowlers, since he destroyed two of M. Dulac's," said Pons. So saying, he came to his feet. "M. Dulac, I will look into this matter for you. If you are at home, I will call on you within the hour."

"Sir, I will be there." M. Dulac, too, got to his feet. "The number is 71 St. John's Wood Road, Mr. Pons."

Our client bade us a ceremonious good-afternoon and took his departure.

Pons waited until he heard the outer door close. Then he asked, "Did not M. Dulac's little problem strike you as curious."

"I confess that the most curious aspect of it is your evident willingness to take up a matter so slight."

"Nothing is slight, my dear Parker. Everything is relative. This matter is sufficiently important to M. Dulac to take him to my brother, and bring him from Bancroft to me."

"He could purchase a lifetime of wearing apparel for what it might cost him to catch the thief who has stolen his three hats," I said.

"Four," said Pons.

"I beg to differ," I insisted. "One was taken by mistake."

"Perhaps," agreed Pons with uncommon amiability. "But let us just examine our client's story for a moment. It suggests nothing to you?"

"Certainly the parallel with what has been happening to the members' hats at the Diogenes Club begs to be acknowledged," I said. "It would appear that the hat-thief is expanding his activities from club members to guests."

"The sequence of events certainly does suggest as much," agreed Pons. "The news accounts have it that all the hats removed from the Diogenes Club were common black bowlers, not particularly costly. So were M. Dulac's hats. I submit that this is not common thievery, for a thief would already have acquired all the bowlers he could use. Doubtless the psychoanalytic gentry might conceive of the bowler as a symbol, but I daresay the problem is more elementary than that."

"Oh, come, Pons, there is surely no great mystery to be made of this affair," I cried. "You are always the first to chide me when I look away from the obvious."

"Ah, a distinct touch, Parker," said Pons. "You are right. There is no mystery on the surface of this puzzle. A gentleman at the Diogenes Club took someone else's hat and left his own. Before he could return for it, his hat had been taken. For some reason which we must fathom, he cannot openly inquire for his hat – that would seem to be the crux of the matter. He therefore resorts to stealing hats, which he subsequently discards as soon as he finds they are not the missing hat he seeks. He then learns, perhaps after a more complete examination of the hat he took from the Club, that it is the property of M. Dulac, and, reasoning that our client might very well have taken his hat in place of the missing one, he turns his somewhat unwelcome attention to M. Dulac."

"Do you seriously believe that anyone would go to such lengths for a common bowler?" I cried.

"This gentlemen evidently *wants* his hat very much," said Pons. "Come along, we'll take a look at it."

Since St. John's Wood Road was not far from our Praed Street quarters, we soon had the missing bowler in our possession. It seemed to me a very ordinary sort of hat, no longer new, but well kept. Our client viewed it with considerable distaste which he took no pains to conceal.

"It fits me, Mr. Pons, but poorly," he said.

"Lacking any distinguishing mark, it might be hard to distinguish in haste," observed Pons. "So that anyone, coming up behind you, might mistake one of your own for it – and knock it off."

"Yes, that is true, Mr. Pons."

"With your permission, I'll just take this bowler along," proposed Pons. "For the time being, you may not be able to hope for immunity from further thefts – though I daresay anyone invading your house will be interested only in bowlers."

"I am happy to be rid of it, Mr. Pons," our client assured us. "But surely a simple application made at the Diogenes Club might have avoided such a roundabout way and such a distinctly criminal manner."

"Quite true," murmured Pons, peering into the hat, lifting its lining, and fingering it. "The average Englishman would have done so. Fortunately, we are as a nation given to the proper way in which to conduct ourselves – thus it is left to nonconformists like the owner of this bowler to keep up interest in the human animal."

We bade M. Dulac good-day.

On our way back to No. 7B, Pons put the missing bowler into my hands. "Examine it, Parker," he said.

I turned the hat about. It was of good quality, but there was nothing about it to indicate the identity of its owner. It manifestly belonged to a man whose head was a size or two larger than average, but who yet required that some padding be put inside the lining up from the brim.

"A man of middle age," said Pons.

"Ah, yes – I see an iron-grey hair or two," I conceded. "Some dandruff, too."

Pons clucked. "A man who uses cologne."

I sniffed the hat. "Common lilac."

"No, Parker. Expensive lilac. The hat is the costliest bowler of its kind on the British market. Its appearance may deceive you at first glance – costly products often look very ordinary at casual scrutiny. Its owner is obviously a man about town, much given to soft living, a man who appreciates what we tritely refer to as the finer things of life. And thus, in the eyes of such a man, the costliest."

"There is nothing about this hat to warrant its being the object of such an unethical search," I said. "That is surely out of keeping with your description of its owner."

"Ah, that is a *non sequitur*," Pons chided. "A man's morals and ethics are not determined by his tastes. It is sounder to believe that it is the other way 'round."

"There is one thing," I said. "I refuse to believe that a man of wealth would permit himself to wear a padded hat. He would obtain a perfect fit."

"Capital, Parker!" cried Pons. "I see plainly that when the time comes for me to retire, you ought to be able to step into my shoes. The hat is not of the slightest interest. Nor, I submit, is it the true object of the search which has annoyed so many more people than our client. It is the padding – not the hat."

As he spoke, he inserted thumb and forefinger into the lining of the hat and drew forth a long, folded and crumpled envelope. He unfolded it and held it up for me to see. Across its face had been typewritten: "Last Will and Testament of Herbert Comparr, Baron Darnavon." Below, in a corner of the envelope, in ink, was a date but two months before.

"Lord Darnavon died in a fall down his beach steps three weeks ago or thereabouts," said Pons. "You may recall the incident, Parker."

"I do. It happened at his place near Highcliffe."

"The steps gave way; the old man went down. He broke his neck, as I remember the account."

"Yes, he was seventy-eight. He had no business on a beach ladder at that age. But was not his will offered?"

"I believe it was. He left his estate to his granddaughter, Mrs. Alan Upway, in Australia. She is presumably on her way here, though her husband was with Darnavon when the old man died."

"There was surely no reason to challenge the will?"

"None. It was with a highly reputable firm of solicitors and had been executed only last year."

"Then this will is the more recent," I said. "Pons, we should lose no time returning it to the executors of Darnavon's estates."

"Gently, Parker," said Pons. "The appearance of this will gives rise to some interesting questions. I propose to examine them."

Back in our quarters, Pons proceeded without ceremony to put on a pot of hot water so that he could steam open the envelope found in the lost bowler. I took a dim view of his plan and said as much.

"What you are about, Pons, is precisely as illegal as making off with someone's hat," I said.

"Surely it is a matter of degree," said Pons. "We ought to determine whether the executors of the estate are in fact the proper owners of this document."

"Are they not the best judges of that?"

"Who am I to say so without knowing what is in the document?"

I said no more, but watched as he carefully steamed open the envelope and extracted the document within. He read it with obvious eagerness, his keen grey eyes flashing from line to line.

"Mrs. Upway has been reduced to half the estate in this will," he said presently, looking up, "and Darnavon's London nephew, Arthur Comparr, is to receive the other half."

"If those are his only two living heirs," I said, "that would seem a more equitable distribution of the old man's assets. They were considerable, I believe."

"Ample. Darnavon was wealthy. The Crown, of course, will receive a major share, in any case. The granddaughter, however, is in the direct line, and the nephew is not."

"Was there not some bitterness when she left to marry an Australian? I seem to recall something of that kind."

"Some furore in the newspapers, in any event."

I leaned forward. "Pons, doesn't it strike you as more than a coincidence, then, that her husband should have been visiting Darnavon at the time of the old man's death?"

"It is odd that you should say so," replied Pons, his eyes narrowed.

"It would have been to his interest to spirit this will away," I went on, "for by it his wife loses half the estate."

"A logical speculation, Parker, but we have no present connection between young Mr. Alan Upway and the bowler found in the possession of our client."

"I believe such a connection can be disclosed."

"We shall see. In the meantime, what do you make of Darnavon's signature?" He held the final page of the will up to the light before me.

I examined it closely. "It is obviously the signature of an old and probably no longer well man," I said. "It is shaky, unsure – that would be typical of a man of Darnavon's age."

"The witnesses' signatures, in any case, are firm enough," observed Pons. He lowered the will, and sat for a moment with his eyes closed in that attitude of deep thought so usual for him, his face mask-like, with not a muscle moving. He sat thus for fully five minutes before he spoke again to say, "I rather think, on the strength of this little discovery, we ought to pay a visit to Highcliffe."

"Ah, you're planning after all to restore the will to its rightful owners," I cried.

"That, I fancy, is the art of deduction from a medical background," said Pons cryptically.

Next morning found us on a train from Waterloo to Southampton, where Pons engaged a cab to take us to Highcliffe, a small seaside resort, just out of which, along the coast, was the late Lord Darnavon's estate. Pons was annoyingly silent about the reason for his journey, preferring to speak, when he did speak, about the features of the region through which we made our way – the ancient oaks, beeches, and yews of the New Forest, rising among the heathland and farmlands – the Burne-Jones windows in the church at Lyndhurst – the milieu of the original of Alice in Wonderland – the home of the Montagus at Beaulieu – and, above all, the singular sombreness of the Thomas Hardy country which lay near, subjects in which, for all Pons' quiet enthusiasm, I was not at the moment primarily interested. Pons said nothing at all to satisfy my curiosity.

It was afternoon by the time we presented ourselves at the seaside home of the late Baron Darnavon and were shown into the presence of Alan Upway, a dark-eyed, reserved and somewhat suspicious young man, who plainly regarded our visit as an intrusion. He still wore on his arm a mourning band, which I thought somewhat ostentatious and unusual for a grandson-in-law. Yet his attitude toward us could not be described as offensive.

"I am somewhat familiar with your name – and occupation, Mr. Pons," he said. "What can I do for you?"

"Mr. Upway, we have a fancy to walk upon the private beach belonging to the estate," replied Pons. "I thought it only proper that we obtain your permission before venturing to do so."

Upway was astonished – and, I thought, relieved. His face told us as much. He was also puzzled, but no more than I. "By all means, sir," he answered, when his surprise had worn off. "The readiest access is by means of the ladder to the beach house. My wife's grandfather always used it instead of having steps cut into the steep declivity to the beach. If you care to come with me... ?"

Following our host, we made our way down through the gracious gardens and lawns of the Darnavon estate to the hedge which grew thickly at the edge of the cliff upon which the house rose. The hedge was of yew and was interrupted only by a stout gate, opening upon a plain ladder of wood, which led down for some twenty steps to a beach house built snugly against the cliff on the sand below.

"Here it is, Mr. Pons," said Upway. "You'll forgive me for not coming along, but the place has an unpleasant memory for me. It was here that Lord Darnavon died."

"The ladder, I take it, has been repaired since then?"

"An entirely new ladder was put in. If my wife now elects to take up her residence here, we shall, of course, do away with it altogether, and have steps cut into the wall."

"That is eminently sensible," agreed Pons.

He thanked Upway and led the way down the ladder. I followed.

I looked back once, and received a most disagreeable impression of Upway's touseled head, grim mouth, and narrowed, searching eyes looking down at us. But he whisked out of sight even as I gazed upward, and I found it necessary to watch my footing rather than look back again.

Pons waited impatiently at the foot of the ladder. "A pronounced risk for an old man," he said reflectively.

"A risk even for one younger," I added.

"You speak for yourself, Parker. I found it easy enough. But then, you've grown a little portly – evidence that your success in your practice has gone to your waist, which is always better than to your head."

"What are we doing here?" I demanded. "This is madness. You never so much as mentioned Darnavon's will!"

"I had no intention of doing so. Now, Parker, do me the favor of walking out toward the sea a little and calling to me if you should see young Upway anywhere about above, peering at us."

I walked out past the beach-house toward the sea, which was not far away, for the beach among the rocks was narrow. The Channel rolled gently, making a pleasant water music along the shore, and sea birds flew crying past. Looking back, I saw Pons on his knees at the foot of the ladder, scrabbling about in the sand like a child. He was, unless my eyes deceived me, actually sifting the sand through his fingers, carrying it up in his palm, studying it. But my task was to watch the hedge above for sight of Upway.

I sought our host in vain. Having drawn back before my eyes when I was on the ladder, he did not again show himself. The long line of thickly grown yew revealed no sign of a watcher.

I glanced once again at Pons. He had now taken some envelopes from his pocket and was putting into them sand from that in his palm. What could he have found? It seemed to me that we had come a long way from the matter of M. Dulac's hats.

Pons rose to his feet and beckoned to me. Waiting but to see that I was coming, he began to mount the ladder.

I came along at his heels. He offered not a word of explanation of his puzzling conduct.

We reached the top of the ladder and passed through the hedge. Standing with the gate once again closed behind us, Pons looked about. Our host was not to be seen. But across the garden, near to what I took to be a potting shed, an old man was at work cutting back rose bushes.

Pons' long strides carried him quickly to the gardener's side. "You, sir," said Pons. "I'd like a word with you."

The old fellow looked up from under grizzled brows, keen dark eyes flashing from one to the other of us. Then, surprisingly, he smiled. "I be pleased to talk wi' Mr. Solar Pons any time of day," he said. "I reads the papers, I do. Ye've come to make inquiry, I'm bound!"

I was delighted to observe that Pons was too startled to speak.

The gardener's cackled laughter was subdued; his face darkened suddenly. He nodded toward the house and said, "'*E* told me to burn the ladder. I did burn some after the new one was put in – but not all. No, sir. You come along wi' old Fred Hoskins, Mr. Pons."

He turned toward the potting shed, continuing to talk. "Ever since *'e* come from down under, the old man had nothing but accidents. There was that potted plant almost fell on him below-stairs. And the upset of the book shelves in the library. Then the ladder – that took him. I saved a piece right 'ere, Mr. Pons."

We had entered the potting shed, where the old man went directly to a row of potted plants. He reached behind them and removed a rung and a small section of ladder frame. He handed these pieces to Pons.

"Broke clean off at the frame on the one side, Mr. Pons. Many time I told the old man it was bound to go some day, but 'e was tight wi' his money. Still, none thought it was that rotten. His Lordship wasn't a heavy man – only medium."

"Thank you, Mr. Hoskins," said Pons, having found his voice at last. I was by this time almost bursting with laughter I dared not release.

"All I wants, sir – all anybody wants, sir – is justice, plain justice," said the gardener fervently.

When we stepped out of the potting shed, Hoskins seemed to shrink together. He fell silent. I gazed past him. There, standing at the back of the house, was Upway, staring fixedly in our direction.

Fortunately, Pons had concealed the portion of the ladder the gardener had given him under his coat. He seemed not a whit abashed by our host's intent scrutiny, though we had, after all, strayed from the beach. Indeed, Pons passed Hoskins and went directly to Upway.

"I hope, Mr. Upway, you won't think it an imposition," he said, "but I wonder if you would be so good as to answer a question or two about Lord Darnavon's death."

Upway frowned fleetingly and hesitated a little before answering cautiously, "What I had to say about it is on record, Mr. Pons. But I have no objection to answering your questions, if I can."

"Thank you. You were the only member of the family present at the time of His Lordship's death?"

"Yes, Mr. Pons." Upway moistened his lips a little and added, "I had been here a week. I had come down from London. I was in London from down under on business, and I couldn't very well return home without paying a visit to my wife's grandfather. I had written him from Melbourne, of course; so he expected me."

"You were alone with him for a week, then? Apart from the servants?"

"Yes – though there was one afternoon when he sent me away. My wife's cousin was due to spend the afternoon with him. Lord Darnavon expected a bit of thickness because he planned to take Arthur to task for his gambling and sporting."

"I see. What precisely did Lord Darnavon say about him, if you can recall?"

"Well, let me think." Upway paused for a moment to cast his thoughts back. "It was something like this," he said calculatingly. "'That fellow spends money like water. Not as if he had it. I talk to him and fume at him and he sulks and mutters and promises he'll reform. Pah! My brother's only child, too! I'll give it to him once and for all.' Something of that nature, Mr. Pons."

"And did he succeed?"

Upway permitted himself a fleeting smile. "I should think not! A day or so after he'd gone, Lord Darnavon missed something of value and had to take the trouble to lodge a complaint with the police, suspecting that his nephew had taken it.

"What was it, Mr. Upway?"

He shrugged. "Oh, something he could sell for ready money, I fancy."

"Thank you, sir."

"Is that all, Mr. Pons?" His voice was markedly cool.

I broke in. "I wonder, sir, whether you've ever been in the Diogenes Club in London?"

Upway studied me for a moment before he answered, "I was a dinner guest at the Club two days after I landed from Australia."

Pons took me firmly by the arm and bade Upway good-day.

For most of the journey to London, Pons sat in silence, wearing that annoyingly supercilious smile which suggested that he held some knowledge I did not share. I had resolved not to speak, but his attitude so irritated me that, as we neared London, I could contain myself no longer.

"Sometimes I fail to understand you, Pons," I burst forth. "This whole matter is as plain as a pikestaff; yet you've walked away from the culprit as if he would always be at your command."

"That the matter is plain as a pikestaff, I grant," replied Pons, his eyes twinkling. "But I'm not sure we have the same matter in mind."

"The crime!" I cried.

"So far," retorted Pons dryly, "we have evidence only of the theft of three hats belonging to M. Henri Dulac – and, if we can believe the papers, to others belonging to members of the Diogenes Club."

"What about the stolen will?"

"I submit, Parker, that we know nothing of a stolen will."

"Oh, come, Pons" I cried. "You're playing upon words. Are you simply going to sit by and let Upway escape?"

Pons smiled dreamily. "I should think it highly unlikely that he would leave the prize within his grasp, even if he had reason to do so. But, no matter. I shall summon the culprit to our quarters when I'm ready to receive him."

After this, he would say no more.

Back at 7B late that night, Pons pushed aside the supper Mrs. Johnson insisted upon bringing up to us – though I did justice to it – and went to work in his chemical laboratory in the alcove off the living-room. He dumped the contents of the envelopes he had filled at Lord Darnavon's beach to the table before him. I saw plainly that his envelopes contained only sand, pebbles, and bits of wood. He added to all this, the fragment of the fatal ladder. Then he drew over his microscope, and I retreated to the evening papers. From time to time I heard him murmur, but he might not have known that I existed, and he was still deeply immersed in the problem he had set for himself when I went to bed.

Pons was at the breakfast table when I got up in the morning. He did not appear to have slept at all. He wore a quiet look of satisfaction and greeted me almost gaily.

"Well, Parker, I have turned up one or two little things which somewhat alter the aspect of the matter of M. Dulac's hats," he said.

"Indeed," I replied. "I venture to say your discoveries will come as no great surprise to me."

"Perhaps not. But guesses are never as good as solid facts. What do you make of this?"

He reached down beside his chair and brought up a sheet of cardboard upon which he had affixed several articles. They were, in order: the very end of one of the rungs of a ladder – several tiny shavings, which seemed to be fresh; very small grains of wood, likewise fresh. In his other hand Pons held the portion of the ladder frame he had obtained in Lord Darnavon's potting shed, that containing the broken end of the rung.

"If you examine these articles closely," said Pons, "you will observe that the ladder was deliberately weakened by very small, worm-like borings, made at the juncture of frame and rung in such a way as to cause the rung to give way under weight."

"But there is nothing about either the rung or the ladder to show that such borings were recent," I objected, after having examined both.

"Quite so. The shavings, however, are a different matter. They are manifestly fresh, and readily lost in the sand. Moreover, there is nothing on their surface to show that they did not come from the new ladder. However, a chemical analysis and a comparison of grain indicates beyond cavil that these fresh shavings came from this ladder and rung. I have subjected the borings to analysis, and I find that a stain simulating aged wood was used to conceal their freshness."

"Very clever," I agreed. "Now let me carry on. Lord Darnavon was aided to his death by this simulated accident. His last will was then stolen so that his previous will would become valid. Why on earth have you hesitated to send word to Scotland Yard and have them make the arrest?"

"Ah, Parker, you continually amaze me," said Pons good-naturedly, as he rose and crossed to the mantel to fill his pipe with shag from the toe of his slipper stuck into the coal scuttle. "There is such a little thing as evidence sufficient to convict. The fact that the ladder was tampered with affords us no clue to the identity of the man who weakened it."

"But who stood to benefit by this dastardly murder of a defenceless old man?" I asked hotly.

"His granddaughter, plainly."

"And her husband, who was fortuitously at the scene," I cried. "Need you know more?"

"I think so. We shall see, however. I have sent for the culprit. I dispatched a note early this morning by hand of one of the Praed Street Irregulars. I fancy he will not be long in coming. And, by the way," he added, "I shall take it as a favor if you delayed making your rounds a bit and stood by." He crossed to his desk, from the drawer of which he took his revolver. "Just to be on the safe side, I think you had better keep this in your pocket on the ready."

I stared at him, I fear, mouth agape.

It was not yet ten o'clock when the outer bell rang.

"That may be our man," said Pons. He sat listening to Mrs. Johnson's familiar steps, and then the heavy tread which followed her up the stairs to our quarters.

"It is much too heavy a man for Upway," I said.

"I fear it is," agreed Pons.

Mrs. Johnson threw open the door, and stood aside.

There on the threshold, his hat in his hand, and a broad smile on his ruddy, cheerful face, stood Colonel Arthur Mowbray, my fellow member of the Diogenes Club.

"Mowbray!" I exclaimed, coming to my feet. "You know Solar Pons?"

"I have not had that pleasure," said Mowbray, bowing.

"Ah, Colonel Mowbray – you had my note about your hat?" asked Pons.

"I did, sir. I came directly to recover it."

"Pray come in," urged Pons. "Sit down. Just over there, if you please."

I closed the door behind Mowbray as he went over to sit with his back to the windows.

The Colonel waited expectantly, saying, "Just a common bowler, you might say, but a man grows accustomed to a hat that has – well, as one might put it – grown accustomed to his head." He laughed heartily.

"Here it is, sir," said Pons, and handed him the bowler he had taken from M. Dulac's home.

"Thank you, Mr. Pons. But how you ever recovered it is beyond me, it is indeed." He stopped talking abruptly, and the expression on his face changed with the suddenness of a summer sky beset by storm.

"I observe you are searching the lining, Colonel," said Pons airily. "I removed the padding."

Mowbray jumped up, allowing the bowler to drop unheeded to the floor and roll to the wall. His fists were clenched; his face worked with rage. He took a step forward.

Pons was unperturbed. "I read it, Colonel," he added coolly.

For a moment I thought that Colonel Mowbray was about to attack Pons. Nervously, I grasped the weapon in my pocket.

"Pray restrain yourself, Colonel," said Pons. "Dr. Parker is armed. I thought that will a lamentably crude attempt at forgery. Not quite your line, is it, Colonel? Gambling, I think, is more to your taste. How much are you in for, Mowbray, to drive you to such desperation?" He gestured over his shoulder toward the alcove. "You may observe a portion of the ladder which collapsed under your late uncle. I have analyzed the borings, the shavings, even the stain you used to simulate age. A clever touch. A pity you resorted to murder. I need hardly say, sir, that Scotland Yard is alert, and these pieces of evidence, together with certain other facts I can impart, will be in the hands of officers at the Yard before the day is out."

"You infernal meddler, sir!" cried Mowbray, his great hands working convulsively. He restrained his rage with difficulty and only because I had drawn Pons' revolver and held it trained upon him.

Pons walked across the room and threw open the door. "Good-day, Colonel Mowbray."

Mowbray flung himself violently from the room.

Pons closed the door and turned to me. "I fear, Parker, it was a nasty jolt to learn that one of the honorable members of the Diogenes Club could be guilty of murder. But, alas! The distinction of membership hardly precludes the possibility. 'Mowbray,' as I thought you knew, was an assumed name – to go with the 'Colonel'. Your fellow-member is Arthur Comparr, Lord Darnavon's sporting nephew. It was he who was responsible for the accidents at Darnavon's place, including the one which terminated fatally, as Mowbray had hoped one of his traps – set on the day of his visit – might be. And it was Mowbray who was forced to steal hats to find the bowler he deliberately abandoned at the Diogenes when confronted by the police who were acting on Lord Darnavon's earlier complaint. He could not afford to have the padding in that hat discovered in his possession."

"But the will, Pons!" I cried. "Surely..."

"Ah, yes, the will," Pons broke in. "You made a simple but understandable error, Parker. Had it been Upway who wanted that will out of sight, he would surely have burned it with dispatch upon Darnavon's death. You assumed the will had been stolen and was meant for destruction. On the contrary, it was meant to be discovered later, after Colonel Mowbray had had time to conceal it somewhere at Darnavon's place."

"What was it you told Scotland Yard, Pons?"

"Nothing yet. The evidence is thin – too thin to hope for conviction. Lacking further developments, I will call Inspector Jamison tomorrow. However, Mowbray is a gambler. He may rush forth headlong without pausing to assess the nature of such evidence as I may have – and he is not quite sure of what I can prove. I am taking a chance on Mowbray's gambling instincts."

Pons won his gamble. The morning papers carried the intelligence that Arthur Comparr, generally known as Colonel Mowbray, had shot himself in his quarters during the night.

"Justice," observed Pons, "was what Mr. Hoskins asked. This, I fancy, will do."

III

THE ADVENTURE OF THE MOSAIC CYLINDERS

"No, Parker," Solar Pons broke in suddenly, "while circumstances cannot lie, they are only too prone to misinterpretation."

"In this case," I began, lowering the *News of the World*, and paused. "But how the devil did you know what I was thinking?"

"That expression of smug satisfaction on your face could only have taken rise from a profound belief that the police are on the right track in their suspicion of Mr. Cecil Bowne's ward in Bowne's murder, an account of which you are manifestly reading."

"How elementary!" I cried. "Angus Birrell was the only one on the scene. The night of the murder was the servants' night off, which Birrell would know, certainly. Moreover, Birrell was Bowne's sole heir."

"Is that not a little too pat?" asked Pons with that annoyingly supercilious air he could so easily assume.

"And his story about running downstairs when he heard Bowne struck down is thin, very thin," I went on.

"I've read the newspaper accounts. Nothing is so blinding as the obvious! I submit that if Birrell had wanted to murder his benefactor, he could hardly have done so in a manner calculated to cast more suspicion upon himself."

"He's described as a hot-tempered brute of a man," I began again.

"Dear me! How we do embroider what we read! I do not recall that anyone called him a 'brute'."

"Very well. I retract it."

Pons smiled. "If there has been any evidence of disagreement between the men – or any immediate altercation – it has escaped me," he went on. "And the newspapers have an annoying habit of painting persons and places in accordance with their private prejudices. But it is idle to speculate about the matter when we shall shortly hear from Mr. Birrell himself."

"You're going to Birdlip?" I asked, astonished.

"At the moment, no." Pons drew a crumpled paper from the pocket of his purple dressing gown and dropped it into the coal-scuttle as he crossed to the mantel for the abominable shag he used to fill his pipe. "I've had a wire from Detective-Sergeant Howard Burnham of Birdlip. He and Birrell are on their way to Number Seven. I expect them at any moment."

Pons had just begun to fill the room with the pungent odor of his pipe when the outer bell rang.

"Ah, I fancy that will be our visitors," said Pons.

In a few moments, Mrs. Johnson knocked at the door to our quarters and, at Pons' invitation, showed our callers in. Detective-Sergeant Burnham was a rotund man of fifty or a little more, clean-shaven, with cherubic cheeks and merry eyes and a generally florid complexion. Angus Birrell, however, was a dark-haired, dark-browed young man to whom a frown seemed to come naturally. He had almost black eyes, which smouldered with ill-concealed anger, it seemed to me, and a mouth that could only be described as petulant. He was athletically built, broad of shoulder, with powerful arms.

Detective-Sergeant Burnham performed the introductions, adding, "Mr. Birrell here insisted on coming, Mr. Pons, and I'll admit I was glad to take the opportunity, as you might say, sir.

I don't know what to make of it – murder's not what you'd call common at Birdlip."

"Is murder ever common, Sergeant? Pray be seated, Gentlemen." Pons turned to our client. "Harrovian, I see," he said, eyeing the colors woven into Birrell's cravat.

"Yes, Mr. Pons."

"Self-employed, Mr. Birrell?"

"You put it very considerately."

"Engaged in writing – and with a pen rather than a typewriter. I recommend the latter; it is no source of callouses."

Our client smiled, a trifle wanly. "I never found a machine conducive to creative work."

"We've read the papers, of course, Mr. Birrell, but let us for the moment assume that we haven't. May we hear your story?"

"Certainly, Mr. Pons. I suppose the best place to begin is at dinner last evening, when Mr. Bowne told me he had just had a letter asking him to an urgent appointment last night. He didn't say why or where he was going; that wasn't his custom. Directly after dinner, I went to my quarters. I had a book I wished to read, and I wanted to listen to a program on the B.B.C. It was the servants' night off, and I heard them go soon after I left the table."

"One moment," interposed Pons. "At the moment that Mr. Bowne mentioned having to go out, was anyone else in the room?"

"No, Mr. Pons."

"Thank you. Pray continue."

"Well, Mr. Bowne was upstairs and down, getting ready to go. He stopped once at the threshold to ask what I was reading. I said, 'Eliot.' 'I'm afraid he's beyond me,' he said. 'When I was a student we didn't read stuff like that.' He laughed. He said I shouldn't be surprised if he came home quite late. Then he went downstairs for the last time. He went into his study, which is just below my quarters. Then he left the house by the French windows, which open out of the study. He was on the way to the garage for his car.

"He couldn't have got far from the house when I stepped over to open a window. At that very moment I heard a dull sound – like a fall – then a groan. I thought of Mr. Bowne at once and called out to him. He didn't answer, though I was convinced he couldn't have reached the garage in so short a time. I ran down immediately and out of the house the way he had gone.

"Mr. Pons, I found him lying on the walk next to a little grove of yew. I thought I heard someone running – then the noise of a motor starting, but I can't be sure because, of course, I didn't think of murder. There was no reason why I should. We live quiet lives. We surely had no enemies. I thought Mr. Bowne had had an attack of some kind. It was the most natural thing for me just to pick him up and carry him back into the house. It wasn't until I got into the study that I noticed he had been struck violently on the side of his head. My clothes were bloodied where his head rested.

"I was horrified. I laid him on a lounge in the study. I ran to the telephone at once and called Dr. Fielding of Birdlip. Then I returned to Mr. Bowne. He was still breathing. As I unbuttoned his topcoat and loosened his collar, he opened his eyes. I don't think he saw me clearly. He tried to speak. I listened very closely, but what he said didn't seem to make very much sense."

"But you *did* hear what he said, Mr. Birrell."

"Yes, Mr. Pons. He said this: 'Go... read... box... sovereign... moor tell you... ask moor... read... linnet start from... nest... don't think badly of me, Angus.' That was all, Mr. Pons. He died in my arms."

Pons had copied down Bowne's last words as Birrell repeated them. "Curious, curious," he muttered, his eyes dancing.

"What do you think Mr. Bowne meant by his dying adjuration to you, Mr. Birrell?"

"Mr. Pons, I haven't the vaguest idea. Mr. Bowne took me as a boy when my father, an old friend of his, died. He has been more than a father to me, and as you know – since it has already been widely bruited about," our client added bitterly, "I am his sole heir. I'm aware of what many people are thinking. Even my profession is against me, since writers are forever in need of money."

"Have you been published, Mr. Birrell?" asked Pons.

"Yes. In Mr. Wyndham Lewis's *Blast*, Mr. Lindsay's *London Aphrodite*, and in the *American Little Review*."

"Ah, an *avant-gardist*," said Pons.

"Mr. Bowne was sympathetic, Mr. Pons."

Pons nodded thoughtfully and changed the subject. "I've observed that the newspapers refer to your late benefactor as 'retired'. No mention is made of the position from which he retired. Can you tell me?"

"When I was a boy, Mr. Pons, he was off for indefinite lengths of time. Irregularly. I always thought he was in some kind of business which required him to travel. Since that time, he has spent his time in his gardens and about his grounds, which were modestly extensive."

"'Since then', you say, Mr. Birrell. How long is it, approximately, since Mr. Bowne retired?"

"Fifteen years or so."

"He would then have been forty, since he was fifty-five when he was slain last night, according to the press reports."

"I was then ten," said our client.

"Mr. Bowne was evidently a man of independent means."

"I'm not familiar with his affairs. To the best of my knowledge, he received payments of some kind by post."

"By the month or the quarter?"

"Neither. They were not at all regular. Sometimes they came twice a quarter, sometimes not for four to six months."

"Did Mr. Bowne at any time offer you an explanation of such remittances as he received?"

"No, sir," said our client somewhat stiffly. "There was no reason why he should do so."

"Quite so. How did he customarily spend his evenings?"

"He frequented a pub in Birdlip on some evenings. He played whist with a group of neighbors one evening a week. The rest of his time he spent reading. He was a great reader, Mr. Pons, and even if he had little sympathy for experimental prose and verse, he had sound tastes, very sound. Hardy, Fielding, Dickens, Galsworthy, Keats, Shakespeare – all of them. And he was always very much interested in history, archaeology, anthropology, and such subjects. He had quite a library and never lacked a book to read."

"We could do with more people of such tastes," observed Pons. "You aren't aware of any enemies he might have had?"

"No, Mr. Pons. How could he have made them? I've asked myself that a hundred times since last night. He was rather oftener a loser at whist than a winner. He was an indifferent darts player at the pub. He never gambled more than a bob at a time. He was a conservative, solitary-minded country gentleman. That he should have been struck down so wantonly fills me with the greatest confusion. It is monstrous. It is a base crime without a motive."

"Say rather without an obvious motive," replied Pons. "Time and events may provide one. Could anything have been taken from his pockets in the interval between your call from the window and your arrival beside him?"

"If so, I wouldn't know what it was. His wallet was intact; as far as I know, nothing had been taken from it. He wasn't in the habit of carrying more than ten pounds at the very most; he had eight on him. But there would hardly have been time to rifle his pockets, Mr. Pons. Believe me, I lost no time reaching him."

At this point, Detective-Sergeant Burnham cleared his throat and caught our client's eye.

"Oh, yes, there's one thing should be mentioned," Birrell said then. "The thing in his pocket. Mr. Bowne wore a top-coat..."

"It did seem on examination that the pockets of the top-coat had been looked into," said the Detective-Sergeant in a flat, reportorial voice. "That it did. One flap up and part of the lining pulled out."

"But there was this thing in the pocket of his jacket," Birrell continued. "Detective-Sergeant Burnham has it."

The Detective-Sergeant reached into his pocket and produced a strange little cylindrical container. It appeared to be made of wood, with mosaic decorations on top and bottom. The letters of the alphabet, quite jumbled, decorated the sides in twenty-four columns and seven circular rows. He handed it to Pons, whose eyes lit up with pleasure at sight of it. "Mr. Bowne's?" asked Pons.

"I've never seen it before," answered our client. "I couldn't testify that it belonged to him."

"Evidence suggests that it did," said Burnham phlegmatically. "It was carried from the house; it could hardly have been put into his pocket outside. His topcoat was buttoned; it hadn't been unbuttoned except by Mr. Birrell here after Mr. Bowne was carried into the house."

Pons turned it about in his fingers. He held it to one ear and shook it. It bore every evidence of being a solid block of wood cut into cylindrical shape and ornamented by some carver's intricate art.

"It's old," offered Detective-Sergeant Burnham. "You can see it's worn."

Pons nodded. He glanced again at our client. "Yet you've never seen this object in Mr. Bowne's possession or in the house?"

"No, sir." Birrell flushed a little. "I'm not in the habit of looking about where it's none of my business. I never was. Mr. Bowne brought me up to mind my own affairs."

"Commendable," murmured Pons. "What, precisely, was the general relationship between your benefactor and yourself."

"Each of us went his own way. I suppose you could say we were good friends and good companions."

"You discussed each other's daily occupations?"

"Not to any very great extent, Mr. Pons. We talked about the weather and the gardens. He was always interested whenever I placed something with a magazine. And very often when he received one of his remittances we celebrated by going out to dinner."

"Let us return for a moment to the message your benefactor received which, he told you, summoned him to an urgent appointment last night. Who customarily took in the post?"

"I did. I always have work on submission to the magazines, and I naturally wait word on it."

"And yesterday?"

"I took in the post, Mr. Pons, as usual."

"Was there anything in it which might have been the message Mr. Bowne said he had received?"

"I've thought about that, sir. I don't think there was. Mr. Bowne had only two letters. One was a tradesman's bill. The other was a notice of expiration from a magazine to which he subscribed."

"So that a message such as he described must have been delivered by hand?"

"It would seem so."

"Yet Mr. Bowne was preparing to use his car to go to the appointment. Would he have done so for a meeting in Birdlip?"

"No, Mr. Pons. He liked to walk too well."

"The meeting then was at some place beyond Birdlip."

"I took it that it was – from his plan to use the car and from his saying he might be late."

"The question is," put in Detective-Sergeant Burnham, "will you lend us a hand, Mr. Pons?"

"I'll be happy to do so, Sergeant. I have had three whole days without a single problem to tax me, and I am near to suffocating of boredom. One thing – I would like to retain this little cylinder until tomorrow."

"Certainly, sir."

"Then you may expect us at the Royal George in Birdlip by noon tomorrow. Failing any word from you, Sergeant, I will wait upon Mr. Birrell at the scene of the tragedy directly after luncheon."

After our visitors had taken their leave, Pons said dryly, "The circumstances seem to have taken on a different complexion."

"On the contrary," I said heatedly, "only if you accept Birrell's story at face value."

"Detective-Sergeant Burnham, who has evidently known Birrell for some time, put enough credence in his account to come to London with him. The Sergeant seems sound enough."

"If I have not mistaken the trend of your inquiries, Pons, the message Bowne received was intended to lure him to his death. Yet Birrell, by his own admission, was the only other person to know of Bowne's appointment."

"Not quite," said Pons softly, "there was also the person who wrote it. I think we may safely conjecture that the author of the message was not the man whose name was signed to it."

I would have protested further, but Pons held up a restraining hand.

"In matters of this kind, Parker, one must begin either by accepting the available evidence or rejecting it. Plainly, you reject it. Let us start by accepting it. Our client is clearly not a fool. Fools are not commonly published in the magazines in which his work has appeared. He is a man of intelligence, a trifle bitter at the world and somewhat frustrated because his ambition to make a name for himself as a writer is not being fulfilled soon enough to please him – a fate common to thousands of men and women who take up pen in the mistaken delusion that writing is an easy way to earn a living. I submit that he is far too intelligent to commit so bungling a crime. Had he wished to eliminate his benefactor, I rather think he would have worked out an ingenious scheme. Something in the line of a death trap to be sprung when he was miles away – perhaps in London – surely that would be truer to his nature."

"Perhaps I'm prejudiced against him," I conceded.

"Patently. His very manner offends you. Moreover, you have scant patience with scribblers of modern ephemera, and the newspaper accounts have helped make up your mind. This little matter promises unexpected ramifications to come. At the outset, there are several points about it which intrigue me. Mr. Bowne's dying message, for one..."

"Which we have solely on the word of the principal suspect," I put in.

Pons ignored me. "... The intruder on the scene at whose presence our client only hinted – mark it well; he has not *claimed* someone was there, but only that he *thought* someone had been running, a poor defense if such it was intended to be – and, finally, this little box. What do you make of it?"

So saying, he tossed it to me. I examined it carefully. It was light to hold. Because of the mosaic decoration, I could not determine of what wood it was wrought, but I thought it was of yew. It was smooth to the touch, testifying to its age.

"Hold it to your ear and shake it," instructed Pons.

I did so. "It whispers!" I cried.

"Does it not!" exclaimed Pons. "There is manifestly something in it – I should make it paper or some such substance."

"Then it is hollow!"

"An elementary deduction, Parker. If I am not mistaken, it holds the key to the mystery."

"How can you say so without more than such a casual glance?" I protested.

"Why, that, too, is elementary, if we accept our client's account. Mr. Bowne had an appointment. He carried no briefcase, book, paper – nothing of that sort – nor any large sum of money. But he *did* carry this most unusual box. It is not too much to suppose that his appointment concerned this box in some fashion of which we have yet to learn."

"What is the thing?"

"Why, it's a sovereign box." He took it from my fingers, and began to turn the lettered rings, which I saw now were not wrought of a solid piece of wood.

"Ah, it comes apart then," I said.

"Must it not if it contains something?"

Pons sat for some time working at the mosaic cylinder. He turned one ring after another, repeatedly. He turned several together, clockwise and counter-clockwise. By watching him closely, I concluded that he was attempting to arrange some of the letters on the box to spell words – or at least one word – from top to bottom. It seemed to me an utterly futile task and I said as much.

"Why, there must be close to two hundred combinations which are possible. Do you mean to try them all?"

"If need be. However, I fear you underrate the task. Since there are twenty-four letters in each ring, and seven rings, the possible combinations would, of course, be the seventh power of twenty-four."

"That would be in the millions!" I cried.

"To be exact," continued Pons, unruffled, "4,586,471,424."

"It would take you a lifetime to make them all!"

"I submit, however, that the combinations forming words are somewhat more limited – only a preponderance of seven-letter words in such languages as are written in Roman letters. We shall begin, therefore, with relatively common words. This cylinder is intricately and carefully wrought by a craftsman whose hand has long been stilled. Let me concentrate."

Half an hour passed. I had long since returned to my perusal of the evening papers when Pons cried out.

"*England*! The word is *England*!" cried Pons triumphantly.

I came to my feet and strode to his side even as the mosaic cylinder came apart in his hands. He had clearly found the combination which unlocked the cylinder by spelling the word *England* downwards. A vertical slot was thus brought into line in the yew-wood rings which formed the inner lining of the box, and this allowed ivory teeth which held it together to be withdrawn. The sovereign box lay in two parts before Pons – the outer shell, consisting of inner and outer rings and top, and the bottom, attached to a hollow cone down one side of which projected the ivory teeth.

Pons upended the hollow cone. A little curl of paper fluttered out. Pons snatched it up in his lean fingers and in a trice had it spread out before him.

What was written on the paper in somewhat faded ink was this:

The linnet starts from its nest
And goes high up into the west

Nothing more.

I stared at Pons in astonishment. "What on earth does it mean?"

His eyes danced with delight. "Patience, Parker, patience. We shall just see. But does this not touch a chord or two in your memory?"

"Surely this is riddle enough more," I cried.

Pons smiled. "Pray indulge me. Let us consult Mr. Bowne's dying words." He drew over the pad upon which he had written what our client had reported Bowne had said. "Ah, yes – here we are – 'box... sovereign' – well, Parker, this is a sovereign box; I am confident that we can safely overlook the involuntary inversion in Mr. Bowne's labored speech. And here we have 'linnet start from... nest'." He rubbed his hands together in a gratified manner. "We seem to have made a start, Parker."

"But what is the significance of these lines?" I pressed him.

"It would appear to be a rhymed couplet."

"Aha! I see. And our client is a poet."

"I don't recall that he admitted to writing poetry, though your deduction isn't out of place, in view of his liking for Eliot. I suspect, however, that the point is irrelevant; I fear Mr. Birrell would have little regard for this couplet as poetry."

"Is it in code, then?"

"If so, a most ingenious one. Only a comparatively brief message could be hidden in these two lines. Yet I am convinced it is a message of some kind. It is plainly this which he was expected to bring to his appointment and which carried Bowne to his death instead. It follows, therefore, that someone else knew of the existence of this cylinder; if a name was signed to the letter Bowne received, than two other people at least knew of it, since the signature would certainly have been that of a man Bowne would expect to know about it."

"That presupposes the involvement of two people our client at least does not suspect."

"I fancy Mr. Birrell has lived a long while in a world of his own creation," said Pons cryptically. "Now, let me see what can be done to solve the riddle of this couplet."

So saying, he pushed the mosaic cylinder aside and bent to the paper.

Though his light burned late that night, Pons gave no indication next morning that he had solved the puzzle of the paper; indeed, I saw by his knit brows and clouded eyes that he had not, and when I asked him, as we boarded a train at Paddington for Cheltenham at seven-thirty, he said only, "It is not a formal code."

With that I had to be content, for he offered no further comment, either immediately or during the three and a half hour ride through the lovely spring countryside on our way to the Cotswolds. He sat in our compartment shrouded in silence, while his hawk-like face was host to a variety of lively emotions – from time to time a suggestive smile touched his thin lips, sometimes his eyes laughed; at other times he sat with his eyes closed, the fingers of one hand fondling the lobe of an ear. He was obviously in no mood to brook interruption, and I held my own counsel throughout the journey to Malvern Road Station in Cheltenham.

There at last Pons seemed to come to life. He began to talk animatedly of the picturesque stone cottages with their mullioned windows and stone-slabbed roofs we were destined to see in the Cotswolds, and he expressed his pleasure at seeing again Leckhampton Hill, which was on our course to Birdlip two miles out of Cheltenham. But of the problem in hand, he uttered not a word, much to my disappointment.

We took a cab at the station in Cheltenham and set out for Birdlip, which was only a short drive from the city. Except for exclamations of delight at some particularly attractive stone frontage or vista, Pons rode in silence. On our right rose the rampart of the great escarpment, a ridge of impressively beautiful hills, made all the more so by the soft green of the beech woods which began to show on their near slopes at Birdlip.

The Royal George at Birdlip was a small hotel of but eight beds. Pons took a room on the top floor, from which the windows afforded us a magnificent view of the Cotswold country. At Birdlip and south from there, the escarpment was less imposing, and perhaps because of this, more beautiful, with beech woods and the hills rising skyward on the one side of Birdlip, and on the other the descending wolds, which lay like a dream with clusters of dwellings, groves, streams and lovely vales.

"We are in the midst of antiquities here, Parker," observed Pons.

"As old as that mosaic cylinder?" I asked, not without a touch of sarcasm.

"Far older. At the very site of this hotel there was a posting station during the Roman occupation, and Roman remains abound throughout the region. Even older – the Dobuni who ruled on Cotswold before the Romans and artifacts, sparingly found, to be sure – like the pieces once belonging to their queen now to be seen at Gloucester Museum."

"It may come as a surprise to you," I replied with some asperity, "but I have a slight acquaintance with British history. Considerably more than I have of the problem in hand."

Pons smiled wintrily. "You overrate my poor powers if you suggest I know much more of this intriguing problem than you, Parker. I have certain suspicions, true, but knowledge, no. Come, let us take a little lunch and be on our way."

After lunch, Pons enquired at the desk whether any message had been left for him. None had. Thereupon, with ostentation unusual for him, he asked to be directed to the home of the late Cecil Bowne. He seemed to take unwonted pleasure at the attention he stirred by mention of his name, and his manifest intention of pressing an enquiry into the murder. "You did yourself proud," I could not help saying when we were on our way on foot through the village.

"Ah, Parker, one can never tell upon what shores the ripples of village gossip may touch," he observed. "These are dark waters."

The object of our search lay on the south edge of Birdlip. It was a country house, evidently remodeled and made rather more modern, for all the untouched outbuildings were of the native stone and obviously very old. There were several of these, in a semicircle, well apart one from another, between the house and the edge of the village. Immediately beside the lane as we came to it was the garage; beyond it stood a dark grove of yew trees, and beyond this grove the other outbuildings, curved around the house at a respectable distance from it. The house itself stood away at a slight angle from the yew grove, and the French windows through which our client's benefactor had walked to his death were plain to see, for the area from the windows to the grove was roped off, evidently by the police, and very probably for Pons's examination.

Pons entered the grounds and made directly for the grove along the limestone walk from the garage. A small pool of dried blood marked the spot where Bowne had been struck down. It could be seen on a stone in the walk just opposite a thick-boled yew, which indicated where Bowne's murderer might have stood – if Birrell's testimony could be accepted without question.

Characteristically, Pons ignored the walk entirely and gave all his attention to the edge of the grove. First he came to his knees at the base of the old yew next to the site of the attack on Bowne; then he took out his magnifying glass and scrutinized the trunk of the tree, from the bark of which he removed some infinitesimal threads or hairs and put them into a small envelope. He came around the tree just as our client emerged from the house to greet us.

"I'm happy to see you," said Birrell.

"And I to find that the good Sergeant hasn't yet put you in irons, Mr. Birrell," said Pons.

"Will you come in, gentlemen?" Birrell turned to lead the way back to the house. "I should tell you, Mr. Pons – I've not been idle this morning. I got hold of Mr. Harris, Mr. Bowne's solicitor, and the two of us went to his bank to make some proper enquiries there. I trust I interpreted the direction of your questions last evening correctly, sir?"

"Ah. You asked about the source of Mr. Bowne's income?"

"Exactly. Mr. Pons, apart from the few dividends on investments, really of little consequence, that he received, for the past fifteen years my benefactor's principal source of income has been his old schoolmaster, the late Cornelius Muir."

"Muir," murmured Pons thoughtfully. "Muir." He stood for a moment at the French windows. "Did he not once publish a monograph on Britain's Roman antiquities?"

"That's the man, Mr. Pons. Mr. Bowne was a student of his at a small private college in Bristol when Muir taught there. History and archeology were his subjects, I believe. Then Muir turned to collecting and retired from the teaching profession. Evidently Mr. Bowne was of some continuing service to him. Only," he added, speaking with hesitation, "I'm hanged if I know when it could have been, for I can't recall that he ever visited Muir. At least, he didn't do so to my knowledge. Yet the remittances came with fair regularity in their uncertain pattern over a decade and a half."

"Were they in equal amounts?" asked Pons.

"That's a rather perplexing aspect, sir – they varied greatly. Naturally, I thought at once – and so did Mr. Harris – that Muir might possibly have made some investments in his name for his former student. The great variation among payments leaves considerable doubt as to this."

"What were the limits of that variation?"

"From two to one hundred and seventeen pounds," answered Birrell. "I don't know much of financial matters, investments and the like, but it seems to me highly unlikely that there exists any stock or bond issue which would pay off such varied amounts in such short and irregular periods of time. I'm under the impression that dividends are seldom paid oftener than annually or semi-annually – rarely quarterly – but these payments were made without any plan at all except their very marked irregularity. That seems to have been the rule from the beginning."

"Interesting," said Pons crisply, his eyes twinkling.

"But come in, please."

Our client stood aside while Pons and I entered the study of the house, a somewhat cramped room all available wall space of which was occupied by deep shelves packed with books. A glance at the titles confirmed our client's statement that his late benefactor's literary tastes were very sound; almost nothing of a lighter nature, except a single novel by Compton Mackenzie, met my eye. A lounge against one panelled wall, slightly recessed under shelving, was evidently the spot where Cecil Bowne had died the previous night, for a white cloth poorly concealed a bloodstain.

Pons stood just inside the French windows, saying nothing. His keen eyes darted here and there. I saw him glance toward the ceiling, then toward the threshold opening on to the hall and the stairs beyond, and deduced that he was computing the time it would have taken our client to rush from his room to the side of his stricken benefactor.

Presently Pons spoke. "I don't recall your mentioning anything about a weapon last night, Mr. Birrell. Was one found?"

"No, sir."

"The inference being that the murderer made off with it?"

"I think so. Dr. Fielding gave it as his opinion that the weapon used was either a poker or an iron bar, and he will so testify at the inquest two days hence."

"If, as circumstances suggest, the mosaic cylinder or sovereign box found in Mr. Bowne's pocket was kept on the premises, where would your late benefactor have been likely to keep it?"

Our client strode across to the wall above the lounge and removed a section of books from a shelf at shoulder height, revealing a wall safe behind.

"Here, sir."

"You have the combination?" asked Pons.

"No. But it will surely be found among his papers in his box at the bank."

"If Mr. Bowne had a deposit box, what was he likely to keep here?"

"I don't know, Mr. Pons. I've never looked into it, even when it stood open on such occasions as I happened to come into the room when he was at it. Papers, perhaps. Or such things as the sovereign box."

"Let us return to the remittances your benefactor received for so long a time," said Pons then. "When was the last of them received?"

"Five weeks ago almost to the day, Mr. Pons. A week before Muir died of a heart attack, quite suddenly."

"In what amount?"

"Twenty pounds."

"There have been no payments since then?"

"None."

"Nor any communication from Muir's estate?"

"None, Mr. Pons. Muir was a widower; there were no children. His nearest relative is, I believe, a cousin in Canada. I really don't know the circumstances relating to the disposal of his estate, but I suppose these matters are in the hands of his solicitors. Enquiry could be made at Gloucester, where he lived."

Pons nodded absently. From the pocket of his jacket he took out a slip of paper which he handed to our client.

"Have you ever read these lines before, Mr. Birrell?"

Our client glanced at the couplet discovered in the mosaic cylinder. His face was expressionless, save for a faint air of disapproval which came into it presently. "Never, Mr. Pons. This is meant to be a rhymed couplet, but as poetry, it's bad, very bad. The metre is abominable." He did not ask how Pons had come by it, but his eyes betrayed a lively curiosity which Pons had no intention of satisfying at the moment.

"They mean no more to you?"

"No." His brows came down darkly. "Should they?"

"If they should, you would know it, Mr. Birrell."

Our client glanced at the couplet again, then, baffled, handed it back to Pons, who reached into his pocket once more, took out the mosaic cylinder, and opened it. He restored the couplet to its hiding place and closed the sovereign box again.

Birrell watched in fascination. I could not be positive, but it seemed to me his astonishment was too genuine to have been feigned.

"Mr. Pons, what does it mean?"

"At this moment, I myself am not sure, though I'm beginning to draw certain inferences from it," answered Pons.

Our client made no attempt to press Pons further. "Is there anything you would care to examine here, sir?"

"I should like to take a look at your benefactor's recent correspondence," said Pons. "We should determine, if possible, with whom his appointment was made on the night of his death."

"Oh, that. I can spare you the trouble," said our client, striding over toward a desk in one corner of the study. "I think this is what you're looking for."

He handed Pons a small fold of paper, evidently torn from a common tablet. I looked over his shoulder as he read the message typewritten on it –

"Bowne: We'd better get together before it's too late. How about Tuesday evening next, 8:30 or 9:00, my place? You can get around easier than I can these days. Reed."

Pons shot a glance of enquiry toward Birrell.

"I believe that would be Austin Reed at Tewkesbury. Mr. Bowne had a very spare correspondence. Apart from Muir and the customary business affairs about taxes and investments, he wrote to only three people, and these only occasionally – to Reed, a cousin of his named Carroll in Edinburgh, and a Mr. Sidney Hawes of Bishop's Cleeve."

"If you have their precise addresses, I'll take them down."

"Certainly, Mr. Pons."

Our client, not without some obvious bafflement, copied down the addresses Pons wanted from what appeared to be the late Bowne's address-book.

"Muir's, too, if you don't mind," said Pons.

"But he's dead!"

"Just the same – I may have need for it."

As he handed the list of addresses to Pons, our client shook his head and said, "I must confess, Mr. Pons, your methods leave me more puzzled than ever."

"At this juncture, Mr. Birrell, an investigation must proceed blindly. I think we have finished here, at least for the time being. Once we've returned this interesting little cylinder to Detective-Sergeant Burnham, I shall consider what line of enquiry to follow... By the way, Mr. Bowne's murderer was a slender man, very agile, about five feet, three inches in height, wearing on the night of the murder what I take to be brown tweed."

Pons thereupon thanked our client, and we took our leave.

Birrell stood with astonishment on his features, but I could see also that he was disappointed and plainly felt that he was being locked out of Pons' investigation. His dark looks followed us from the house to the lane.

Through tea, which Pons had sent up to our quarters at the Royal George, he sat absorbed before his notes, his eyes narrowed and thoughtful. But from time to time a thin smile played about his austere face, and his eyes danced. At last he leaned back.

"In the light of such discoveries as we have made, Parker, what do you make of it?"

"Precious few discoveries we've made," I retorted. "And what the devil did you mean by telling Birrell his benefactor's murderer was a short, slender man?"

"Oh, come, Parker – that is surely as elementary a deduction as I could possibly have made. Even you could have made it. If a man leans against a tree and his shoulders, judging by the brown tweed threads left on the rough bark, come to roughly four feet, three inches, and there is scarcely an imprint to mark where he waited, it's hardly a feat to conclude that he was slight of build and short of stature. That little matter, however, is relatively inconsequential. Let us consider Bowne's dying statement again. Does it not now take on new light?"

"I see very little light, Pons."

"Come, come, it isn't as bad as that. Look at his first words – 'Go... read... box sovereign'..."

"Ah, that clearly means our client was intended to read the couplet in the mosaic cylinder," I said.

"An excellent example of the misinterpretation of circumstances," observed Pons dryly. "It could hardly have meant that, when Bowne might have shown his ward the message at any time in the course of several years. No, I fancy it meant, 'Go to see Austin Reed.' Now then – 'moor tell you... ask moor.' I submit that what Bowne said was 'Muir,' in the confused state of his mind forgetting that Muir had died. Then he repeated 'read', which, following so close upon 'ask Muir' must certainly refer to asking 'Reed'. The quotation from the couplet is obvious, of course. What do you make of his dying adjuration, Parker? 'Do not think badly of me, Angus.' Is that not a curious final statement?"

"It suggests that Bowne had been guilty of some wrong."

"Toward Angus?"

"Possibly."

"I submit that Bowne's adjuration referred to what Angus Birrell was destined to learn if and when he followed his benefactor's dying instructions. Our client himself has said he hadn't the vaguest idea of what Bowne could have meant, and stressed the fact that Bowne had been very good to him. Moreover, Birrell is his sole heir." Pons shook his head. "I think we may definitely conclude that Bowne's reference was toward what was to come, not to anything which had already affected their relationship."

I conceded that this made sense.

"Now let us turn for a moment to this note so casually making an appointment which Bowne evidently never thought of not keeping. What do you deduce from it?" Pons tossed it to me as he spoke.

I read it carefully once more. "For one thing," I said cautiously, "it is entirely typewritten, including the signature. Anyone could have written and sent it."

"Certainly Reed did not," agreed Pons. "Go on."

"Reed had reason for haste. There is a note of urgence in the letter."

"Capital, capital, Parker! I am happy to see this development in your ability to rationalize. Go on."

"So that if Bowne unhesitatingly responded to it, he, too, must have recognized that urgence. It must then have been a common urgence."

Pons' eyes danced with delight. "You do me proud, Parker! Quite so. Pray continue."

"Reed writes that Bowne can get around easier than Reed can. So Reed must have been ill or unable to travel far, and Bowne must have known this not to have questioned the source of his letter."

"He corresponded with him."

"Well, that seems to be the sum total of what's to be made of this," I said, handling the note back to him.

He folded it and restored it to his pocket. "Except for one thing. The urgent matter which inspired both the note and Bowne's willingness to accept it was almost certainly the death of Cornelius Muir. Something subsequent to that may have heightened the urgence of the matter. 'We'd better get together before it's too late.' Too late for what – if not the solution of the riddle of the mosaic cylinder? I submit, Parker, that Reed also owns a portion of the 'poem' begun with the couplet in Bowne's cylinder. By the same token, we had better lose no time in getting to Reed. I fancy we can hire a car and driver to take us up the Severn valley. I shall be happy to see Tewkesbury again; it is surely one of the most attractive towns in all England."

A lithe, short-statured young man answered our knock at Austin Reed's door. He held the door ajar only a little way and looked out at us suspiciously, his hard blue eyes clearly hostile.

"Mr. Austin Reed?" asked Pons.

"Can't see him. He's abed. Very ill."

Pons took from his pocket the note sent to Bowne, wrote across the back of it, "Must speak to you about this. Solar Pons," and handed it to the reluctant young man guarding the threshold.

"Take this to Mr. Reed at once," he commanded.

"I'll do it, but it won't do any good," said the young man, in a somewhat more courteous manner, now that he had caught sight of Pons' signature. "I'm sorry to seem so ungracious – but we've been upset by the burglary and all. I'll take it to him. Just step inside and wait. I'm Harold Reed, his son."

He opened the door to us and walked away.

We stepped into the hallway and looked around. The house seemed to be reasonably well appointed; it was not a wealthy man's home, but it was certainly not a poor man's dwelling. But we had little time to examine our surroundings, for young Reed's quickened footsteps sounded very soon.

"Come in, gentlemen," he said. "Come in. Your note excited Father."

He showed us into a bedroom, where a gaunt man of sixty-odd years lay in what seemed to me a terminal illness. He was grizzled for lack of shaving, and his condition was fully as grave as his son had hinted. Bony fingers trembled on the note Pons had sent in, and as Pons bent to retrieve it, the sick man spoke.

"Not mine. Not mine," he said.

"Father means he didn't write this message, sir," said young Reed.

The sick man turned feebly toward his son. "Box... Harry. Get me... box."

A little impatiently, the younger man replied, "Dad – it's gone. Don't you remember? It was stolen." He turned to Pons and explained. "He's talking about a little curio he had here. He set great store by it, though I never could see that it had any value. Father always said that little box assured our future."

Pons took Bowne's mosaic cylinder from his pocket. "Like this, Mr. Reed?"

Young Reed's eyes widened. "Yes, sir. That's it! Where did you find it?"

"No, Mr. Reed. This is not it, but only one similar to it. It was found on the night before last in the pocket of a murdered man. It had belonged to him."

"Alike as two peas," said the younger Reed, staring at the sovereign box as if unable to take his eyes from it. Indeed, his fingers trembled with excitement or eagerness as he held out his hand as if to take it for a moment before he withdrew it.

"Your father's was stolen," pressed Pons. "When?"

"A week ago, sir. Someone entered the house one night. Father had been in hospital in Gloucester for a while, and I was there part of the time – living in Gloucester, to be near him – and when we got back here the day after I went down to bring him home, we saw someone had broken in by the back door."

"When was this?" interrupted Pons.

"Ten days ago. We couldn't find that anything had been taken – but when Father asked for his curio, it was gone. Since it was here when I left for Gloucester, it must have been stolen while I was gone. I asked the nurse about it, but she hadn't touched it – hadn't even seen it, according to her, and that's probably true because Father kept it behind some books on the top shelf of his little library."

The elder Reed began to speak suddenly, brokenly, with gasping effort. "Hawes first... blinded... Bowe next.... Then me... Blinded – all blinded... Sworn to secrecy... Never told... None of us.... He bound us.... We pledged him.... Counted on us.... Trusted him.... Hard work... careful... by night... Harry – Harry – the box... The box!"

"Dad, it's gone," said his son patiently.

"Lost. All lost," murmured the older man.

"Semi-delirious," I could not keep from pointing out. "What he says is probably dredged up from the past but has some meaning for him."

"And for us," said Pons sharply, motioning me to silence.

The old man lay with eyes closed now, breathing heavily from the exertion of speaking at such length. The fingers of his right hand twitched in a grasping motion, as if he dreamed of attempting to seize hold of some object.

"The box – Harry," he muttered again. "All lost... All gone... Her diadem... Cross... red and the green.... Great queen!... I promise – on my honor as English gentleman – to speak no word... to speak no word. So are we... bound... we four..." And again he half raised up in bed and cried out, "Harry – Harry... the box!"

Then he fell back, utterly exhausted.

"Pons, we dare not stir him farther," I protested.

Pons nodded absently. His eyes strayed from the old man in the bed and fell upon a typewriter in an alcove nearby.

"I wonder, Mr. Reed," he said to the younger man, "whether you would be so kind as to insert this false message into your machine and type to my dictation."

"Certainly, Mr. Pons."

Pons handed him the message Bowne had received, watched him insert it into the typewriter, and then dictated, "Not written by Austin Reed – Now just sign it, Mr. Reed."

The younger Reed did as he was asked, whereupon Pons bade him good-day, and we withdrew.

Outside once more, I said. "Well, that was surely a fruitless visit. Except for the matter of a second cylinder, we heard nothing but the disconnected ravings of delirium. Did you expect to turn up another sovereign box?"

"Say rather I was not surprised to learn of the existence of a second. As for not learning anything – alas! Parker, you disappoint me grievously. We have just learned all."

"Pons! You cannot mean it!"

"I was never more in earnest. Those disconnected ravings, as you called them, unlocked the secret of the mosaic cylinders. And even a cursory glance at what Reed typed at my dictation tells us that message and dictation were written on the same machine." He looked at his watch. "It is late in the day, but

I think we had better go on to Bishop's Cleeve and look up Sidney Hawes."

We reached our destination at dusk, but though we found the house of Sidney Hawes without trouble, it was dark save for a small night light. Nevertheless, Pons' knock brought a response from within, and the turning up of a stronger light.

"Who is it?" came in an uncertain voice.

"A friend of Sidney Hawes," answered Pons.

"Come in, then. The door's not locked."

Pons opened the door and we walked in to find ourselves confronting a young man in an easy chair. It was manifest at once why he had not answered Pons' knock in person. He wore a heavy bandage on his head, and another on one arm. His legs were covered with a robe, despite the relative warmth of the evening, and it was not unlikely that he had difficulty getting about.

"Accident," said the young man cheerfully. "I expect you've not heard. I'm Tom Hawkins, his nephew."

Pons introduced himself and me. It amused me to see that Pons' name apparently meant nothing to Hawkins, a fact which was bound to touch Pons' vanity.

"Glad to know you, gentlemen. I'm sorry not to be a better host – but there's a decanter on the sideboard if you'd care to help yourselves. My uncle's man's out and I find it a little hard to get around the way I'd like."

"And Mr. Hawes?" asked Pons.

"My uncle – God rest his soul! – died in the accident, Mr. Pons. And him only fifty-six, too! I was driving the car – it was that, most likely, saved me from being thrown about when we went out of control and left the road."

"How long ago, Mr. Hawkins?"

"Three weeks, sir."

His cheerfulness had given way to a more proper gravity now; he bit his lip and sighed. "My uncle was a fine man, sir, in every respect."

"Badly injured?"

"Oh, no, sir. It wasn't that alone. It was just as much his heart. His heart had been bad, and I expect the shock of the accident and the scare and all did for him. He'd had a bad fall on the stairs just a day or two before, too. I don't know how the accident came about, and that's a fact. Something with the brake, they told me at the mechanic's. I can't understand it. The car was all right only the day before. Then that day my uncle decided suddenlike to go down to Birdlip and call on an old friend there. We set out, and got almost to Cheltenham when the brake gave out and away we went down the slope and off the road."

"You've not changed the name at the gate," I said. "We thought Mr. Hawes was to be found here."

"Oh, it's not my right to do that, sir. I'm staying here only until my cousin – his son – can get home from Calcutta. It's his place now, and I expect I'll move on as soon as he comes."

"Well, I won't say I'm not disappointed, because I am," said Pons in an almost ingratiating manner. "But perhaps you can help me, Mr. Hawkins."

"Any friend of my uncle's has a claim on me, sir."

"Did your uncle mention the name of the man in Birdlip he meant to call upon?"

"Bowne, I think he said."

"And did your uncle ever own a curious little sovereign box decorated with letters of the alphabet and some mosaic scrollwork?" asked Pons bluntly.

Hawkins stared at him, astonished, for a full moment without reply. Then he said, "If my uncle had ever owned such a box, I'm sure he'd have told me about it. I've lived with him ten years, ever since his first heart attack – my cousin Horace couldn't come home, you see, and I was free to come – and there were precious few secrets he kept from me. My uncle kept his sovereigns where they still are, sir – in the bank at

Cheltenham. I don't think it likely that such a box as you describe is in this house."

"Perhaps he kept it, too, in a deposit box," suggested Pons.

"I have access to his bank box, sir." He shook his head. "But what is this sovereign box?"

"A curio, Mr. Hawkins. An interesting curio which may have some bearing on a little problem I am at present investigating."

A light broke suddenly upon Hawkins' thin face. He sat up a little straighter, so that his robe fell away a little from his spare frame. "But, of course – it's Mr. Solar Pons, the London detective!" he cried. "Well, sir – I am honored! But what could you have wanted with my uncle?"

"I had hoped to ask him questions which unfortunately you cannot answer," replied Pons. "Apparently there were a few little secrets Mr. Hawes kept from you. Perhaps his son, once he reaches England, may have the answer to those questions. Thank you, sir, for your kindness to two travellers. We'll be on our way back to Birdlip."

"I'm sorry I can't see you to the door, gentlemen. But as you've been able to make your way in, you'll find your way out. Good night!"

Pons walked out in profound silence and got into the car for the journey back to Birdlip. It was not until we were well on our way that he broke the thoughtful meditation in which he had been plunged.

"I dislike coincidences, Parker, however, much I know them to occur – much more frequently than we recognize. I submit that this chain of events is more than coincidence."

"Which chain of events?"

"That begun with the death of Cornelius Muir, followed by the fatal accident which eliminated Sidney Hawes, the curious illness of Austin Reed, together with the burglarious entry of the Reed home, and the murder of Cecil Bowne. These events suggest nothing to you?"

"Should they?"

"We have four men who were associated in some venture," Pons replied thoughtfully. "They were sworn to silence. Unfortunately – and fatefully – one of those men broke his pledge and precipitated the events which followed upon Muir's death."

"Ah," I said, "this is a familiar pattern. They robbed a train or a bank and have been systematically dividing the loot."

Pons laughed heartily. "I thank Providence for such little touches of humor as you manage to inject into the problems which come our way, Parker, I do indeed."

"It has all the aspects of lost treasure," I cried hotly.

"Lost – or found," said Pons, sobering. "It does indeed."

He said no more, and we rode on in deep silence through the aromatic, night-bound countryside, Pons with his eyes closed against any distraction which might take his thoughts from the perplexing riddle of the mosaic cylinders. Nor did he venture a hint of what he had been thinking when we reached the Royal George, save only to remind me that in the morning we would go to Gloucester "to inquire into the role the late Cornelius Muir played in this little drama."

With this, he turned in and fell asleep at once.

Pons was up and about some time before I woke next morning. I had just finished breakfast when he came into the hotel, ready for the journey to Gloucester, which was but ten miles away. He wore one of those self-satisfied smiles I invariably found peculiarly annoying. He tossed a folded envelope at me. His name had been scrawled across its face.

"This was left for me during the night, Parker," he said.

The envelope was addressed to "Mr. Solar Pons" in broad pencilled script, and had the look of having been written in haste. No address appeared under Pons' name, suggesting that the note had been delivered by hand. The message inside was succinct and pointed.

"Don't meddle in what doesn't concern you. Go home, Mr. Nosey Pons." It was signed: "A Friend."

"I fancy our quarry has the wind up," observed Pons. "That classic signature is all too revealing. I have invariably found that only one who means you ill signs such communications 'A Friend'. I daresay we are uncomfortably close to the heart of this little matter."

"This doesn't have the sound of an ignorant fellow."

"Only an irritated and fearful one. He is literate enough. Bear in mind that all the principal actors in this little entertainment have college backgrounds. Mr. Muir, ex-professor, and three students at his college. Does not that suggest anything to you?"

"I'm afraid not."

"Dear me, morning is not your best time, Parker. But come, let us be off," he said, starting away. "I have had opportunity, early as the hour is, to ascertain the name and address of the solicitor in charge of Muir's estate pending the arrival of the cousin from Canada, who would appear to be Muir's heir. Our business is first of all with Mr. Tooker this morning."

Mr. Norman Tooker proved to be a frosty gentleman of some seventy years, who maintained an office on Eastgate Street. He was expecting us.

"Ah, Mr. Pons," he said with dignified formality as we were announced and shown in, "and Dr. Parker. I've been waiting for you ever since the police advised me to expect you. What can I do for you?"

"I took the liberty of asking the police, with whom I am cooperating in an enquiry, to give you notice of my coming. I'm afraid I may have to ask you to answer some questions which may seem to you somewhat unethical," said Pons.

"Ah, involving a client," said Tooker, visibly drawing into himself.

"The late Cornelius Muir."

Mr. Tooker brightened a little. Manifestly, a dead client was not quite in the same category, ethically, as a living one. "A fine man. I knew him well. He was more than just a client. An old friend, I might say. Surely you can't expect me to believe that he had a part in any crime?"

"We are looking into the death of one of Mr. Muir's former students, and we have reason to believe there may be a connection, however remote, between the death of Mr. Muir and that of Mr. Bowne."

"Ah, the Birdlip assault case," murmured Tooker. "I make a habit of reading news of crime, Mr. Pons; I'm not uninformed. Besides..." And here he hesitated, looking strangely at Pons.

"Do go on, Mr. Tooker."

"I was about to say that in discharging the wishes of my late client, I was on the verge of posting Bowne an envelope left for him by Mr. Muir."

Pons' eyes danced. "May I see it?"

Tooker selected one of three envelopes from a rack on his desk and handed it to Pons. "As you see, I addressed my communication to his estate. The envelope I referred to is inside."

Tooker had not yet gummed down the flap of his envelope.

Apart from the customary notification to the addressee, covering the contents, there was but the envelope to which Tooker had referred. It was addressed, I saw at a glance, in a hand that bore no resemblance to Tooker's signature appended to the covering letter – presumably, therefore, in the script of the late Cornelius Muir.

Pons held the sealed envelope between the thumb and forefinger of one hand. "Do you know what this contains, Mr. Tooker?"

"No, sir. I don't. This was left with, Mr. Muir's instructions to forward unopened to the addressee."

"Let us just examine it."

Pons carried the envelope over to the window and held it up to the light. A smile touched his lips.

"Be good enough to take this down, Parker," he said, and read, slowly, "'Thence by a mile, and turns to face / To where the setting sun last lays its golden grace.'"

"Mr. Pons, this is highly irregular," protested Tooker.

"I daresay it is. Murder, however, is even more so. Do you understand these lines, Mr. Tooker?"

"No, sir. I don't."

"Your late client was also evidently a poet."

"I believe more than one professor has fancied himself a creative writer, Mr. Pons. A poet, eh?"

"The lines are a couplet. They are written in what I take to be Muir's hand."

"I'm afraid it means nothing to me."

"It was evidently intended to mean something to Mr. Bowne, and," added Pons, pointing to two other envelopes which Tooker had prepared, of similar size and appearance, "also to Mr. Sidney Hawes and Mr. Austin Reed."

Tooker snatched up the envelopes in question, took out the inner envelopes, and hurried over to the window with them. He held them up against the pane, one in each hand.

"They are the same lines, are they not, Mr. Tooker?" asked Pons.

"They are indeed. Mr. Pons, I've heard of your ratiocinative powers..."

"Tut, tut, Mr. Tooker. This was not ratiocination at all, but simple conclusion following inevitably from the premise that these three gentlemen and Muir were associated in some venture of common interest. But let us pursue this further," he went on, as Tooker returned to his desk. "Are you familiar with your late client's accounts?"

"Of course, Mr. Pons."

"Some five weeks before his death, he paid Mr. Bowne by cheque the sum of twenty pounds. Ah, I see by your face that this strikes a chord in memory. Tell me, did he not also pay identical sums to Mr. Hawes and Mr. Reed at the same time?"

"He did."

"I submit, Mr. Tooker, that for the past fifteen years your late client made identical payments at irregular intervals to all three of these men, payments ranging all the way from two to a hundred and seventeen pounds."

"Mr. Pons, I would have to check the figures, but I believe you are substantially correct."

"Why were these payments made?"

"I can't tell you that, Mr. Pons. I don't know."

"Perhaps you can tell us how Mr. Muir came by his income?"

"Mr. Muir was quite wealthy. He left a considerable estate, of which the death duties alone will take many thousands of pounds."

"Did he live on interest and dividends, Mr. Tooker?"

"He was a well-known collector of antique and ancient artifacts. His house is cluttered with them even today, Mr. Pons, though he has been systematically selling his collection for a dozen years. There are cheques here from Sotheby's, from the Parke-Bernet Gallery of New York, and from other sources.

"When was Mr. Muir's last sale made?"

"Let me see." Tooker opened a fat folder on his desk, put on his pince-nez, and scrutinized a sheet of paper, his lips working, his brow furrowed. "Here it is," he said presently. "Six weeks and three days ago. A jeweled Dobuni artifact to Sotheby's, who paid him a hundred and ten pounds."

Pons nodded with ill-concealed satisfaction. "Do you think it might be possible to get into Muir's house?" he asked then.

"I'll take you there myself," said Tooker, and rang for his car.

The late Cornelius Muir's house stood in spacious, well-landscaped grounds on the bank of the Severn north of Gloucester. Its modest and relatively unpretentious exterior in no way prepared us for the crowded rooms inside. From the entranceway as far as one could see, and from room to room, the house was crowded with antiques and artifacts, the sight of which wrung a cry of delight from Pons. They were of all kinds – Roman, Celtic, Druidic, Dobuni, of Viking and Norman origin – indeed, it was patent at but a glance that Muir's home was little more than a private museum which must have represented an extensive investment.

"Has an inventory been made, Mr. Tooker?" asked Pons, when he had looked about.

"Not yet. People from the Gloucester Museum have been retained to do it, however." He asked anxiously, "Will you want a copy?"

"No, but I suggest that the police may. Frankly, Mr. Tooker, I didn't come here to view these splendid relics of bygone ages. I have a fancy to see more of Mr. Muir's verses, if possible."

Mr. Tooker looked dubious. "I don't know if I can help, Mr. Pons. This field of his labors was unknown to me until today. – Unless, perhaps – his notebook?"

He crossed to a bookshelf in the study, where we were then standing, and took from it a looseleaf notebook which he brought back to Pons.

"He kept a good many notes and figures here, Mr. Pons – nothing vital in the same sense that his cheque-book was vital – " here he permitted himself a wintry smile "but of matters close to him."

Pons was already leafing through the book, saying nothing.

"It dates back quite a number of years," offered Tooker.

"Sixteen," said Pons dryly, having observed a date on the page bearing the signature of the notebook's owner. "He had some culinary interests, I see by these recipes. Here are some references, too, to a textbook he hoped to write, and a partial outline. Some addresses. Ah, here we are. Here at last is one complete poem. I'll just detach this sheet, if I may," said Pons, suiting his actions to his words, "and post it back to you when I've done with it."

Tooker's expression suggested that he was convinced by this time that my companion was little short of being a madman. Though he held his own counsel, his keen eyes gave him away. He shot a glance at me, he gazed hard at Pons, who now held Muir's notebook out to him, and then barely nodded to sanction Pons' removal of the sheet, which Pons had already unceremoniously folded and stuck into his pocket.

"And now, what next, Mr. Pons?" asked the solicitor, when he had restored the notebook to its niche. He spoke in a tone of voice which plainly indicated that he would not have been surprised at any wild request Pons might make, and I confess I shared something of his feelings, for Pons seemed bent upon anything but pursuit of a murderer.

"Nothing further, Mr. Tooker. You've been most forbearing and helpful."

"The ways of detectives are quite beyond a mere solicitor," said Tooker, not without an edge of sarcasm in his voice. "I hope I've helped you along the road to the identity of Mr. Bowne's murderer."

"Ah, I didn't come for that. I've been quite certain of his identity for some little while. No, I came in search of the final piece of this little puzzle, and I fancy I have it here." He touched his pocket.

We left a sadly baffled solicitor behind us, and, I fear, Pons rode back to Birdlip with an almost equally baffled companion at his side, for Pons offered not one word of explanation. Once back at the Royal George at a late luncheon, I could restrain myself no longer. "What did you mean, Pons, when you told Tooker you knew who Bowne's murderer was?"

"Perhaps I should have said that I am reasonably sure of his identity," replied Pons mildly. "The only pending problem would seem to be that of establishing sufficient legal evidence to convict him. But perhaps we'll be able to trap him. We shall see."

"You cannot mean it!" I cried.

Pons took from his pocket the sheet he had abstracted from Muir's notebook. "It should be as plain to you as it is to me, once you've read that, Parker, and considered it in the light of the known events of the matter," he said.

I read Muir's poem in silence –

The linnet starts from its nest
and goes high up into the west
against the thunder and the crag,
amid the haunts of fox and stag
to where the lightning-wounded beech
points toward the channel's reach,
thence by a mile, and turns to face
to where the setting sun last lays its golden grace.

"You will remember that I postulated the lines discovered in Bowne's mosaic cylinder were but part of a larger unit," said Pons. "Here at last we have that complete unit."

"I'm inclined to agree with our client that the whole is as bad, as poetry, as the part."

"It was hardly meant to be a poem except to those readers who were not intended to read it. It is a suitably constructed riddle."

"Have you solved it?" I asked bluntly.

"Not yet. But I fancy it is not insoluble. I submit, however, that, since Bowne's cylinder contained the first couplet, those owned by Hawes and Reed contained the next two, one in each. Muir alone held the last, without which the preceding three were useless. Does it not impress you as significant that Muir had left instructions for the final couplet to be mailed to his three students after his death?"

"He wanted each of them to have the means to solve the riddle," I said. "That is surely as plain as a pikestaff."

"Not each alone," said Pons, "but as a trio in place of the old quartet. None of the three could solve the riddle without the others. I put it to you, Parker, that the whole thing is now as clear as spring water."

"It is not to me."

"Think on it," said Pons.

"If you're so sure of the identity of the murderer, why not arrest him?" I demanded.

"I prefer to wait until he comes to me," he said enigmatically.

I stared at him, bereft of speech.

"In the meantime," he continued jauntily, "what do you say to a little tour of the Cotswolds? This afternoon, perhaps. Or tomorrow?"

I shook my head. "I can't stay away from my practise so long, Pons," I protested. "I must return to London."

"I'm sorry to hear it," said Pons. "Rejoin me when you can. I know how you like to be in on the conclusion of these little adventures you delight to chronicle." He stroked his lean nose reflectively with one forefinger and gazed calculatingly at the ceiling. "Shall we say not later than three days hence?"

On the morning of the third day after, I arrived at the Royal George to find not only Pons, but also Detective-Sergeant Burnham and our client waiting on my arrival.

"Ah, Parker, you're just in time for an excursion into the hills," cried Pons.

"After three hours on the Great Western, I'm in no mood for a hike," I answered.

"Come, come – the game's afoot. You wouldn't miss it if you were down with pneumonia." He drew a copy of the

Cheltenham daily from his pocket and handed it to me. "You may not have seen this in the fastnesses of London."

The paper was dated two days before – the day after I had taken leave of Pons to return to London – and was folded to a box on the front page, where Cornelius Muir's poem was reproduced in boldface under a brief paragraph headed, "Archaeologist Was Secret Poet."

"I recognize your hand in this, Pons," I said.

"With the connivance of the police," replied Pons, with a bow toward Detective-Sergeant Burnham.

"Yes, Mr. Pons said it was necessary," explained the Sergeant, "so we had it put in all the papers – Cheltenham, Gloucester, Tewkesbury, Winchcombe, Cirencester, Stroud – the lot of 'em. I'm not much for poetry myself, but even I can see that Mr. Muir was a bird-lover. Lot of those folks here-about."

"Let us be on our way," said Pons, glancing at his watch. "We have a short distance to go before we leave the car."

Birrell drove. We went in a northeasterly direction from Birdlip, deep into the hills. I soon lost track of our whereabouts, since I was not familiar with the region east of Cheltenham, but we drove for only a short distance before our client eased his car into an arbored lane where it would be unseen from the road. From this spot, Pons led the way into the hills on foot. The May morning was wonderfully sweet with the perfume of spring flowers and the pungence of foliage, particularly strong after a light rainfall during the night, and the wold through which we walked was surely the most idyllic of that countryside.

We were ascending a rather barren slope when Pons paused suddenly and swept his arm dramatically upward. Before us lay a mounded hilltop, crowned by a rough circle of scrubby bushes.

"That, gentlemen,'" said Pons, "is known locally as the Linnet's Nest."

"I see," said our client keenly, "and I suppose, Mr. Pons, we go west from that point – 'high up'?"

"We do, indeed. Yonder dark promontory is called Thunder Crag." We resumed walking as Pons spoke. "I had some difficulty finding 'the lightning-wounded beech,' primarily because, in the interval of a decade and a half, nothing but the jagged stump of it was left. The channel of the 'channel's reach' is, of course, Bristol Channel, toward which evidence indicates that the beech once leaned."

Detective-Sergeant Burnham expressed his bewilderment. "I'm not sure I know what you two are talking about," he said.

"Sergeant, the couplet found in the sovereign box, which I showed you, was the beginning of a set of directions for reaching a certain place in the escarpment. Since this couplet was also the first couplet of the 'poem' written by the late Cornelius Muir, it is reasonable to assume that the poem constitutes the complete directions. Acting on that assumption, I found successively the places mentioned in the four couplets, and, at last, the goal which Muir sought to conceal from all but the three men who knew what to expect when they reached it.

Detective-Sergeant Burnham looked but little less bewildered; however, he did not press Pons further.

We had now passed the Linnet's Nest, and were advancing upon Thunder Crag, which had a forbidding aspect even in sunlight, and must certainly have worn a menacing appearance in heavy weather. Beyond it lay a little beech woods, then again open slopes, and there, standing alone on a little knoll, an ancient beech stump beside which, when he reached it, Pons came to a stop and pointed

"Bristol Channel lies in that direction. From this place by a mile we shall see a high promontory facing westward – a place 'where the setting sun last lays its golden grace'. We have a mile to go."

We came at last to the west-facing cliff which was Pons' goal. We had walked, I judged, close to five miles from the car, though we might have driven closer to the Linnet's Nest had not Pons deemed it inadvisable. The actual cliff face was not high up from where we stood near its base; it rose from the escarpment in an area that was singularly barren save for a growth of scrubby trees immediately at its base.

"These trees, I submit, were purposely planted," said Pons.

"In this desolate place?" cried Birrell. "Why?"

"Why – if not to conceal from any prying eye what lies behind them?"

"Earth and oolite, Mr. Pons?" asked Detective-Sergeant Burnham. "They have no value hereabout, sir."

"But what lies behind has value, Sergeant."

So saying, Pons descended to the base of the cliff, which lay at the bottom of a slight declivity, doubtless formed by erosion over many years. He parted the trees carefully and disclosed a spill of oolite and earth which had evidently been drawn back and away from the base.

"My work, gentlemen," he said curtly.

Before us was a break in the wall of stone; it had the appearance of having been brought about by erosion a long time ago. It might have seemed the entrance to a cave, were it not that the hard wall of stone that was the cliff could be plainly seen a little way in. Yet it was to this wall that Pons went without hesitation, beckoning us to follow.

As we pressed close, the apparently solid wall of stone opened inward. A cavern yawned beyond.

"Your lantern, Sergeant," said Pons, stepping to one side.

Detective-Sergeant Burnham flashed a light into the cavern, revealing scattered bones, and what appeared to be burial chambers in the walls of the cavern.

"A barrow!" exclaimed our client.

"This is more than an ordinary barrow," said Pons. "If you are thinking of such well-known barrows as Notgrove or Belas Knap or Uley Long Barrow – no, this is decidedly different. This was a burial place used exclusively by rulers of the Dobuni – quite apart from the customary artifacts to be expected here, there are jeweled pieces which have a value transcending what they would bring as antiquities. There were, I surmise, a great many more pieces. There are bronzes, pottery, flint weapons, and the usual crude primitive pieces, suggesting that this burial place was usurped for the Dobuni rulers from an earlier race. Moreover, there is nothing to show that the Romans ever found this place, for there are no Roman signs. It must indeed have seemed a treasure trove when Cornelius Muir stumbled upon it!

"But we have little time in which to explore it. We need not do so now. Unless I am very much mistaken, publication of Muir's 'poem' will certainly not have been missed by our quarry, who has been looking for it so actively, and he in turn will lose no time finding this place."

"Particularly," I could not help adding, "since Mr. Nosey Pons is also looking about."

Pons chuckled. "We shall wait for him here. It is now well into the afternoon, and I fancy he will wait only long enough to mark the sunlight's fall upon the stone above. We'd better leave the door a trifle ajar to prevent the air from going stale. Let us just make ourselves comfortable and bear in mind that silence is the rule."

We waited for an uncomfortable two hours before the sound of a rattling stone from outside gave warning of someone approaching. Even so, it took a while longer for our quarry to discover the door behind the grove of trees. But at last his scraping footsteps came nearer – then there was a tapping on the door, as with a hammer. Then the door swung open. A short, slender man stood there, silhouetted against the fading daylight behind him.

"Mr. Thomas Hawkins, I believe," said Pons, as Detective-Sergeant Burnham's lantern shot its light into our quarry's face.

Hawkins' response was a furious curse. Then he dodged back, crashed through the trees, and ran fleetly around the face of the cliff.

"After him!" shouted Detective-Sergeant Burnham.

We tumbled out of the cave, broke through the trees, and gave chase, our client in the lead.

Our pursuit, however, was not destined to last long. Hawkins was running in unfamiliar territory, and though he was nimble and artful, he came at last to the edge of a steep-walled coombe. Skirting it, with Birrell not far behind him, Hawkins' foot turned on a loose stone. With a wild cry of despair, Hawkins plunged over the edge.

When we reached the place where he had vanished, we looked over and saw him lying motionless below. And when at last we made our way to the spot, it was evident that his neck had been broken.

"I'm not yet quite clear about the details of the puzzle, Pons," I said, as we sat in our compartment riding through the night toward London a few hours later. "One or two little things escape me."

"Small wonder," said Pons handsomely. "The matter, though essentially elementary, had puzzling ramifications. We came to it by the side door, so to speak. But it can be reconstructed quite simply.

"Muir stumbled upon this rich treasure some fifteen years ago. Needing help, he enlisted the aid of three of his former students, whom he knew well enough to know that he could trust them even to the extent of aiding him in a basically illegal act – though, as you know, raiding the ancient barrows was a popular pastime of the nineteenth century. He blindfolded them – you'll recall Reed's delirious mutterings – and took them to the place, which was evidently so filled with treasure that he could not remove it without assistance.

"The agreement among them was obviously to permit Muir to sell off the pieces as portions of his collection, which no one was likely to question, and to divide the proceeds, less duties, four ways. The figure Mr. Tooker quoted us in regard to his last sale, suggests as much, since it amounts approximately to four times the last payment Bowne received, less duties.

"At the same time, Muir agreed to reveal the location of the place to them all together when he died – he intended to will it to them, even though much of the treasure had been removed to his home. To do so, he devised the ingenious method of composing a series of couplets telling them where the barrow was, and enclosing one couplet in each cylinder he gave to his partners, with the provision that the final couplet be posted to each of them at his death, thus making it necessary for all three to meet in order to solve the riddle.

"What he failed to count on was that one of the three might divulge enough of the secret to endanger the success of the plan – and even their very lives. It was obviously Hawes who told his nephew. It was Hawes who died first following Muir's death. He died in a contrived accident. Hawkins admitted to knowing that his heart had been bad; he may have made earlier attempts to frighten him, of which we know nothing. Hawkins had no other motive but to disarm us when he made an attempt to throw us off in regard to the cylinder, and it was most certainly he who subsequently managed to slip a warning to us at the Royal George. It was a calculated touch to type the message to Bowne on Reed's typewriter when he broke into Reed's home.

"He came within one couplet and the last of learning the secret – he had his uncle's, he had stolen Reed's, and he murdered Bowne to steal his cylinder, knowing he would have it on his person when he left to keep the appointment Hawkins had made in Reed's name.

"An entertaining problem, Parker. Would there were more like it!"

IV

THE ADVENTURE OF THE PRAED STREET IRREGULARS

Solar Pons raised his head suddenly from the chess problem he had been contemplating. His feral face was alert.

"Surely that was the scrape of a cycle against the kerb!" he said.

"This April wind makes enough noise to drown out everything else," I answered.

But even as I spoke, the outer door opened and banged shut, and a clatter of footsteps pounded up the stairs.

"That's one of the boys," said Pons, referring to his Praed Street Irregulars – that little band of street urchins whom he called upon to assist him from time to time. "Alfred – he steps more heavily than Pinky or Roger."

The door to our quarters burst open. Alfred Peake stood there, a wildness in his eyes.

"Mr. Pons!" he cried. "The boy's gone. He's been took."

"Come in, Alfred. Pray compose yourself. What boy is this?"

"Our orphing, Mr. Pons. He's ours. We adopted him. Now he's been took."

Pons pushed back his chess game, got to his feet, and went over to close the door behind Alfred. He put an arm around Alfred's thin shoulders and drew the ordinarily bright-eyed lad persuasively forward. Alfred Peake, the leader of Pons' little group of Irregulars, was now fourteen; he had grown a scant foot in height since my first meeting with him in the delightful matter of Mr. Sidney Harris's purloined periapt.

"Now, then, Alfred," said Pons, once Alfred was seated – even if only on the edge of a chair – and Pons was leaning against the mantel, his keen eyes searching Alfred's troubled face, "let us begin at the beginning."

"There was this accident, Mr. Pons."

"Where and when?"

"In Commercial Road. Six days ago. His uncle and aunt got killed. Angel – that ain't his name, Mr. Pons, but he looks like one – he came rolling out, he seen us, and he asked us to help him. So we did. Pinky and Sid and me took him before the bobbies got there, and we put him into Fox & Sons' warehouse. We kept him there, brought him food and drink. Fair cried – he was so glad to be with us! Then tonight, when we got there – a bit late, we were – he was gone. Looked like he fought, too – things all tore up. All we found was a little spill of shag." He drew a fold of newspaper from his pocket. "Here it is, Mr. Pons."

Pons took it, opened it carefully, and lifted a pinch of the shag to his nostrils. "A common shag," he observed. "In ordinary use among laborers everywhere in London." He laid it carefully aside. "Go on, Alfred. That would have been last Tuesday. At what time of the day?"

"Evening."

"I see. And the accident?"

"They got out of a cab, Mr. Pons, to cross the street. There was a car waiting there."

"With a driver?"

"No sir. It had a license plate we never saw before, Mr. Pons."

"Not British?"

"No, sir."

"Go on."

"Well, Mr. Pons, they'd just fair got out into the street when a car came down at 'em. Hit 'em both. Angel saw it coming. He threw himself backward, rolled under a car at the kerb, and right up to where we were standing. 'Quick!' he says. 'Help me get away.' So we took him right off."

"And the car that struck his uncle and aunt?"

"Got clean away. It never stopped, Mr. Pons."

Pons' eyes glittered with interest. "How old would you say the boy is, Alfred?"

"It's hard to tell, sir. Maybe eight."

"Now, Alfred, you'll remember my little lectures on keeping your eyes and ears open. What can you tell me about this boy?"

"Mr. Pons, he wore good clothes. I mean, a lot better than my Dad or Mum could buy. He don't talk much, but he talks funny."

"Do you mean he doesn't speak English well?"

"Oh, Mr. Pons, he talks better English I guess than Pinky or Sid or me. But it sounds queer when he says the words."

"I see. An accent. Go on."

"And he won't say anything about himself."

"His name?"

"Mr. Pons, Pinky come out and said, 'He looks like an angel.' And then we asked him his name and he says, 'Angel'. Mr. Pons, he's been took. He didn't run off. There was a rough scuffle – things knocked over – his bed all tore apart..."

"Bed?"

Alfred looked sheepish. "We brought him some sheets and blankets and there were a lot of sacks to use under 'em. They were all scattered around. Mr. Pons, help us find him!"

"How many of the boys have seen Angel?" asked Pons.

"Oh, they all saw him."

"Good. Then call the boys together and put them to work. Find out first whether anyone saw the boy brought out from

Fox & Son's warehouse. Learn if you can what conveyances were seen in the vicinity during the day. Discover whether any suspicious characters have been seen in the neighborhood within the day before his abduction."

Alfred grinned. "Mr. Pons, ever since that accident, the place has been fair crawling with bobbies and Scotland Yard men – I can tell them when they look like Inspector Jamison."

Pons gazed at Alfred for a long, speculative moment, his eyes narrowed. Plainly, that agile brain had seized upon something which escaped my notice.

"So that the boy cannot have been taken far – under police surveillance. Spread out and search through Stepney. There are enough crannies in Stepney to conceal a small army. A boy would scarcely be a problem. Be off with you, set the boys to work, and come back here before midnight."

"Thank you, sir. I knew we could count on you."

Alfred left our quarters with alacrity, rattling down the stairs as noisily as he had come up.

Pons bent at once to the newspapers stacked beside his chair, searching out, I guessed, last Wednesday's papers. He went through one after another, in intent silence, until at last an exclamation of satisfaction escaped him.

"Here it is, Parker," he said, and read: "'Fatal Accident in Stepney. A middle-aged couple were struck and killed by a speeding car in Commercial Road East late yesterday. The driver of the death car escaped. The identity of the couple could not be learned. They appeared to be foreigners. A calling card picked up at the scene bore the name, Alexander Obrenović. A police enquiry is under way.' "

"That tells us very little."

"Perhaps subsequent reports will say more. Here, Parker," – he seized several of the week's papers and handed them to me – "go through these, while I search the others."

We set to work with diligence, but at the end of half an hour neither of us could discover another mention of the accident in Stepney.

"Most singular," murmured Pons.

"I'm not surprised," I said. "The press of international events crowds out purely local news."

"Are we then becoming so callous that the snuffing out of two lives is of no more concern than a few casual lines in a single newspaper? I fancy not. No, Parker – there is far more to this than meets the eye."

"Oh, come, Pons! Accidents like this take place every day."

"I am not persuaded that it was an accident," retorted Pons. "Most of the evidence in hand is to the contrary."

I stared at him, I fear, in some astonishment, but I waited in vain for any enlightenment.

"I submit this is a matter for my reclusive brother," he went on. "I daresay I can send him a wire that will bring him here before midnight."

"Pons, you're joking."

"I assure you – if ever I was so, I am serious at this moment. There is no time to be lost."

So saying, he scrawled a message on a slip of paper, pushed it into his pocket, and came to his feet. Reaching for his deerstalker and his long grey coat, he said, "I'll take it to Edgware Road myself."

During Pons' absence, I read over several times the brief account in the *Daily Express* which had evidently conveyed to my companion some intelligence I could not discover, and I hunted, again in vain, for further reference to the accident.

When Pons returned and had doffed his outer clothing, he turned again to the little mound of tobacco Alfred Peake had brought him, busying himself briefly with magnifying glass and microscope, which told him little more than he had known before, if his expression could be taken for index to his findings.

"A shag as strong as my own, but of greatly inferior quality," he said. "Quite possibly carried by a seaman or dockworker – which is the most significant fact to be learned from it."

"I don't follow you in that," I said.

"What is important is that the boy's abductors were not foreigners, like himself. The tobacco was evidently spilled in the scuffle, or else Alfred would not have brought it here. We are thus reasonably enabled to deduce that his abductors were fellow Englishmen whose instructions were to take him alive and unharmed."

"You are going well beyond the boundaries of ratiocination," I cried.

"Softly, Parker. I submit, in view of the circumstances as we are able to reconstruct them, that the elderly couple were not the prime target of the automobile that killed them, but that it was the death of the boy that was desired. It follows, then, that the abductors of the boy were not the same people who ran down his relatives, for if their goal had been the boy's death, he might as well have been slain at the warehouse!"

"But that is monstrous, Pons!" I cried. "Who would want to kill a little boy?"

"I can think of several people who might like to do so," said Pons enigmatically. He looked at his watch. "My little message will be delivered by this time. It is half past ten. It will take Bancroft less than an hour to get here."

"Pons, perhaps I am especially obtuse this evening, but I fail to understand your conclusions."

"Pray do not apologize. I am accustomed to it," said Pons. "Yet Alfred plainly told us that this was no ordinary accident when he said that the place swarmed with police and Scotland Yard men. Why – if not in search of the boy? The curious absence of any further mention of the accident in the papers suggests interference. I submit that only the strongest representation on the part of the government could have imposed silence upon the London newspapers. Finally, the name on the calling card. It means nothing to you?"

"Except that it is foreign, nothing."

"I am always happy to discover the burgeoning of deductive powers in you, Parker," said Pons dryly. "Obrenović was the family name of the Serbian rulers in the nineteenth century; perhaps its most illustrious representative was Prince Michael III, who was assassinated in 1868."

"As usual, it is simple when you explain it," I admitted.

"Is it not? It should then, also, be obvious to you that the boy is now being held neither by those who have designs on his life nor by those who wish to save him, but by a third party interested solely in selling him to the highest bidder."

"Because he isn't dead?"

"Because, on the one hand, he was not slain on the premises," said Pons. "And on the other, he would not have struggled if friends had come to take him. His abductors were Englishmen hired by someone who correctly interpreted the events which took place on Commercial Road East six days ago."

So saying, he lapsed into silence.

Scarcely half an hour had passed when the door to our quarters opened noiselessly and disclosed the impressive figure of Bancroft Pons, his customary sleepy eyes glittering with anticipation, his proud, sensuous lips pressed grimly together. He walked catlike into the room, but Pons was aware of him without turning.

"So the Foreign Office was sufficiently interested to send you under escort," he said. "You could have reached here so soon in no other manner."

"Pray spare me these exercises, Solar," said Bancroft Pons. "I was shocked by your wire – deeply shocked. '*Which heir has disappeared?*' How can you possibly know of this matter? We kept the most rigid security."

"Only by the intervention of Providence, my dear fellow," said Pons. "But you have not answered my question."

"Let us say only the heir to one of the Balkan thrones. His disappearance here in London on the eve of the Balkan Conferences is painfully embarrassing to His Majesty's Government."

"To say nothing of the danger the boy now faces," said Pons.

Bancroft Pons sniffed. "I dislike this fencing, Solar. Do you know where he is?"

"Alas, no. Until this evening he was hidden in Fox & Company's warehouse in Stepney. This evening, however, he was abducted, but not by agents associated with the assassins who ran down his uncle and aunt..."

"Cousins," said Bancroft Pons. "The boy was attending a private school, south of London. We have known for some time that anarchistic elements interesting in fomenting trouble in the Balkans may have had designs on the boy. His cousins, who were in England to watch over him, removed the boy at the first sign of danger, and arranged to embark at the East India Docks in the hope of taking him to safety on the Continent. It was a convenient fiction for the boy to think of his cousins as uncle and aunt. But you will have surmised as much. Who had the prince?"

"My boys. You have heard me refer to the Praed Street Irregulars."

"What! You anticipated the crime on Commercial Road East?"

"You flatter me. I knew nothing of it until tonight, when Alfred Peake came to announce that the boy had been taken."

"Taken?"

"He was not slain, which was the goal of his enemies. He struggled with his abductors, which he would not have done if they were friends. So he was seized by some agent independent of the throne and also of his would-be assassins. This was found on the scene."

Pons handed his brother the packet of shag.

Bancroft examined it, held it to his nostrils. "Baggett's," he said.

"Very probably."

"An acrid smell lingers here."

"Gunpowder?"

"I think not. It reminds me of opium."

Pons bounded to his feet and took the shag from Bancroft to hold it again to his own nostrils. He smelled the paper as well.

"No, it is in the tobacco," said Bancroft. "That abominable habit you have of smoking the vile stuff has blunted your olfactory nerve. But enough of this – I grant that a foreigner would not be likely to use Baggett's, but the matter is in any case academic. Who could have the boy? Not Baron Kroll?"

"The Baron is out of the country," said Pons. "Besides, Kroll's interest would have been political; the influence of his government could have been strengthened if the prince were in Germany. No, it is not Kroll."

"Your familiarity in these circles transcends mine," said Bancroft. "Who then?"

"An adventurer not above bargaining with both sides to obtain the highest price for the boy's life," said Pons.

"Name him."

"Very probably Israel Sarpedon. I thought him in Cairo, but evidently he has returned. He is a man utterly devoid of scruples, absolutely without human emotions save only of greed, a man who would sell his mother's life as readily as he would a package of clothing."

"Where can he be found?"

"He has an establishment in Soho, but the boy will certainly not be there."

"How can you be sure of this, Solar?"

"I cannot," replied Pons. "It is only the strongest probability that Sarpedon has the boy. It is the kind of venture which most appeals to him. If he has him, the boy will be in the hands of Sarpedon's agents, waiting upon his instructions. He will hardly have been taken far from the scene of his abduction, since the police are nosing about the vicinity of the accident. Moreover, expedience demands that the boy be kept concealed under guard until the hue and cry have died down. Then Sarpedon will make his move."

"He will offer the boy to the highest bidder," said Bancroft with suppressed fury.

"Precisely."

"We can take him."

"Futile," said Pons.

"He and his place can be watched."

"Equally futile. He will never personally show his hand, but will only issue orders through subordinates. There is nothing to be gained by putting the wind up Sarpedon. Do not alarm him, but let us just spread the word that I am looking for him. Your people will know where to drop this information, Bancroft."

"Other than that?"

"Wait on word from me. There are certain matters in which the Foreign Office is without peer – but this is not one of them."

"You have forty-eight hours," said Bancroft, and bade us good-night.

"Such ultimata," observed Pons as he sprang to his feet, "come with remarkable ease to anyone associated with His Majesty's Government."

He vanished into his chamber, from which came the sounds of rummaging about, together with the strains of London street songs hummed somewhat brokenly. Then a suspicious silence followed; this lengthened into a quarter of an hour.

When at last Pons reappeared, he was transformed. If I had not seen him enter his chamber, I would certainly not have recognized the stooped, illkempt beggar who shuffled into the room asking in a whining voice for a half-penny.

"Good God! Pons – surely you're not going out in that garb!"

"I would scarcely have taken the trouble to assume it purely for your entertainment, Parker," he said crisply. "I'm bound for Stepney and Limehouse. Admirable as the boys are, they may be a little beyond their depth in this matter, considering the brief time we have in which to act. There is a certain Chinese doctor in Limehouse who has a small army of men and women in his employ – his activities, I should add, are even more nefarious than those of Israel Sarpedon – and in this he may be useful to me, as I may some day be to him."

"It surprises me that you have never mentioned Sarpedon to me in all these years," I said.

"He is quite possibly the second most dangerous man in London," said Pons imperturbably.

"Then Baron Kroll is the most dangerous."

Pons smiled. "Yes – but I should add that the Chinese gentleman on whom I am calling tonight takes precedence. He is very probably the most dangerous man in England, if not in Europe. As for Sarpedon," he went on, blunting my astonishment, "I have never had occasion to mention him. For the past eight years he has been in the Middle East, employing his unique talents to the best advantage of his exchequer. He came close to crossing my path once before your time, but we have never actually met. I look forward to that pleasure."

Once more the outer door opened and closed; again there was a rattling on the stairs; and for the second time that night, Alfred Peake burst into our quarters, only to recoil at sight of Pons, his mouth agape. He shot a hasty, alarmed glance at me.

"Where's Mr. Pons, sir?" he asked.

"Alfred, my lad," said Pons. "Have I aged so much since your last visit?"

"Lord love us, Mr. Pons!" cried Alfred, his eyes wide with amazement. "Is it really you?" Then admiration filled his face. "Fooled me, you did, Mr. Pons."

"And the boys?"

"They're out, sir – them who could get out. We'll all be out in the morning."

"Tell me, Alfred," pressed Pons, "do you know a boy of the same age, and the same general size and appearance as Angel?"

Alfred thought deeply. "P'raps David Benjamin would do," he said presently. "He's small for his age."

"Capital!" said Pons crisply. "I'm coming with you, Alfred. Good night, Parker."

Alfred ducked back out of the room, Pons at his heels, leaving me smarting a little at Pons' failure to invite me to accompany him, even though I knew that I could never have carried off a disguise as skillfully as he, and might very well only have been in his way.

I was awakened next morning before dawn by Pons' tapping my cheek.

"Ssst!" he whispered. "We are about to have a visitor."

I slipped out of bed and followed Pons quietly into the living-room, where he stood waiting in the dark.

There was a rustling at the door.

Pons stepped forward and threw it open, revealing a tall, saturnine man of middle age in the act of lighting a cheroot. He favored Pons with a wintry smile as he slipped into the room with the languid grace of a tiger.

"Mr. Solar Pons, I believe. I understand you were looking for me."

"Mr. Israel Sarpedon," said Pons. "A light, Parker."

"Though what prevented you from coming to my place in Soho puzzles me," Sarpedon continued, planting himself insolently at one end of the mantel, to face Pons at the other, as I lit the lamp.

"Because you don't have in Soho what I want."

"That is?"

"Come, Mr. Sarpedon, let us not fence. I want the boy."

"I don't traffic in children, Mr. Pons."

"Not just any children, Mr. Sarpedon. This one, I think you know, has a certain monetary value over and above that of just any child."

"And supposing I had this boy to whom you refer, do you think you could possibly come up with an offer greater than any other I might obtain?"

"Certainly," said Pons.

"Indeed!"

"Your freedom for his safe delivery. Otherwise, you may find yourself uncomfortably detained for a considerable time. His Majesty's Government looks with singular displeasure on being embarrassed."

"Bluff, Mr. Pons, pure bluff! I could hardly be less disturbed." Calmly, he tossed his cheroot into the fireplace and favored Pons with a long, calculating stare, with eyes that were as cold as ice. "Tell me, Mr. Pons," he continued, "does it never occur to you that this meddling of yours is likely some time to lead to consequences of the gravest kind?"

"So is one's most trivial act – like getting out of bed in the morning, or indulging one's curiosity on Praed Street or in Soho – or even, perhaps, in Stepney."

"Let me suggest, Mr. Pons, that interference in affairs which do not concern you may some day be fatal."

"You add zest to my humble existence," said Pons.

"There is something unhealthy about meddlers and meddling," said Sarpedon.

"More so than with those anti-social people who make meddling necessary?" asked Pons.

Sarpedon sniffed disdainfully and strode over to the door. "Good morning, Mr. Solar Pons. You have been warned."

With this, he went out.

I shot a glance at Pons. He seemed unruffled; indeed, he showed a certain satisfaction. "A dangerous man," I said. "Did you expect him, Pons?"

"I was confident that if word reached him that I was looking for him, his vanity couldn't resist the challenge."

"A daring fellow."

"Not at all. He knows he is on sure ground. When he charged me with bluffing, he knew very well what he was talking about."

"Oh, come Pons!"

"The sinuosities of international diplomacy are sometimes beyond mere mortals like us, but the conclusions to which diplomats come are often only too clearly foreseen. That is why it is essential that the utmost haste be resorted to if Sarpedon is to be thwarted."

He had stepped over to the window as he spoke, and stood peering down intently into the dawn-filled street. "Ah, he came in his own car. And Alfred has managed to hop on to the back. Capital! Now we shall have to wait to see whether he drives home or whether he stops at the nearest callbox. I fancy it will be the latter; if so, Alfred may be fortunate enough to discover the number he calls. He'll want to make sure I'm not on to the place where he is keeping the boy."

He turned away from the windows, rubbing his hands together, his eyes merry. "He may not yet have made his contacts. If not, we have time. If he has, events will move rapidly to culminate to his satisfaction. We shall do our best to prevent it. Now we can only wait."

But waiting sorely tried Solar Pons. When the game was afoot, he was dreadfully restless, and nothing engaged his attention for very long. He spent a little while over a problem in chemistry, and he sawed away at his violin, producing sounds which seemed to me uncommonly execrable – though he called it music, and he spurned the breakfast which Mrs. Johnson brought up and implored him to eat.

When at last the telephone rang, he leaped upon it. But hope faded to annoyance as he listened.

"That was Alfred," he said, turning away from the instrument. "Sarpedon called a number in Limehouse, but Alfred failed to get it properly. At least, we can infer that the boy is being held in private quarters somewhere – unless Sarpedon has an outpost at a telephone, which I should think not likely. The fewer men engaged in a venture of this kind the better. He cannot have more than two; there may be only one guarding the boy." He shook his head. "Time speeds past, Parker. We may be too late."

And with this he resumed his restless pacing of our quarters.

I was just passing the telephone close upon the hour of noon when it rang a second time. Even so, Pons reached it before I could take it up. But I was close enough to him to hear the strange, spine-tingling sibilance of the voice that greeted Pons and spoke but a single sentence to him, though I could not hear the words. The effect on Pons, however, was magical; suppressed excitement replaced his tenseness, and he was obviously eager to be off.

"The Doctor has not failed me," he said, putting down the telephone. "The boy is in a house in Salmon Lane. Let me just call Alfred and alert the boys. Then you and I will change our appearance a trifle and go to Limehouse – by the back way, since Sarpedon will almost certainly have No. 7 watched – unless you would prefer to spend a more secure sedentary hour or two at home."

"You know better, Pons," I said indignantly. "If I were to stay here, who would be there to look after you?"

It was just past noon when Pons and I, dressed like common touts, set out by cab for the vicinity of the house in Salmon Lane. Pons rode in silence, chafing visibly at every delay caused by impediments on Oxford Street and High Holborn. In Cheapside we were detained five minutes by a snarl in traffic, while Pons fairly danced in impotent rage. But at last we turned into White Horse Road and left the cab not far down Salmon Lane to walk along the street, which seemed uncommonly crowded with urchins of all ages.

I saw, too, that there were unusually many foreigners present in the street – Orientals of some kind, some Chinese manifestly, but others who seemed to be Burmese or Malay in origin. I plucked nervously at Pons' sleeve, but he shook me off impatiently.

But I had no time to speak, for suddenly the entire street erupted into activity. Cries of "Fire!" and "Stop, Thief!" went up. Boys, Orientals, and the regular habitues of the street began to run and mill about. A column of smoke ballooned up from the doorway of a house just half a street away. Within seconds, Pons and I were rudely jostled and pushed against an adjacent railing, while the crowd of shouting and screaming boys and Orientals pressed all around us.

And did I dream that – just before police whistles began to blow – a tall, stooped Chinese, an ageless old man wearing a skull cap and smoked glasses, drifted past and whispered in a sibilant voice, "Return to Praed Street, Mr. Pons!"? It could hardly have been an hallucination, for Pons gripped my arm hard and at once turned about, starting back the way we had come.

We were hemmed in, however – first by the men and boys running past, then by a crowd of curious people coming into the street from buildings on both sides, finally by a phalanx of policemen – but eventually we made our way back down White Horse Road to Commercial Road, and there, after trying in vain to hail a cab, Pons finally crossed to the Stepney station of the Midland Railway, where we boarded a train for a somewhat roundabout journey back to our quarters, which we reached at last in late afternoon.

Alfred Peake had preceded us. He jumped up as we entered, a little uncertain, but quite sure that he recognized us despite our altered appearance – which had not deceived Pons' Chinese friend.

"He's sleeping, Mr. Pons," he said.

"Capital, Alfred, capital!" cried Pons. "All went well?"

"The moment the smoke bomb went off and they came running out, we went in the back. We had everything ready. David switched clothes with Angel and stayed there. Angel came with us. No danger to David, is there, Mr. Pons?"

"I fancy not."

"All them Chinese – or whatever they were – helped. You got friends, Mr. Pons. They kept those men from coming back – and a lot more."

Pons smiled wryly. "Now then, Alfred – you shall have your reward." He took a handful of guineas from the drawer where he carelessly kept coins, and gave them to Alfred. "Distribute them among the Irregulars, with my gratitude, my lad. Without you, I shouldn't have had the pleasure of this little excursion."

When Alfred had gone, Pons said, "Let us get into more presentable clothing, Parker. I daresay it won't be long before we hear from my estimable brother." He cocked his head to one side. "Is that not Mrs. Johnson's step on the stair?"

"No one could mistake her tread," I said.

Mrs. Johnson knocked gently.

"Come in, come in, Mrs. Johnson," cried Pons.

Our devoted but long-suffering landlady opened the door just enough to stick her head in. "Begging your pardon, Mr. Pons, but a gentleman who said he was your brother telephoned and said you was to do nothing about that matter of the boy until he got here at six o'clock. And will you be wanting supper?"

Pons shot me a triumphant glance. "Thank you, Mrs. Johnson. Yes, supper when you're ready to serve it. And a cup of hot cocoa."

At six, promptly, Bancroft Pons walked into our quarters.

His face was clouded.

"I fear I bring you bad tidings, Solar," he said.

"Mr. Sarpedon has got through to the Balkan embassy concerned about the crown prince?"

Bancroft grimaced. "You anticipate me. The embassy wishes us to do nothing."

"Confident that they have bidden more for the boy's life than his would-be assassins. A pity."

"Is it not? But we are helpless in the face of diplomatic pressure."

"All the more a pity since it puts us in so delicate a position," Pons went on.

Bancroft Pons' eyes narrowed. "Continue," he said dryly.

"What are we to do with the boy? Or are you suggesting that the embassy is willing to pay *us*?" Pons' eyes danced mischievously.

"Solar! You cannot mean – ! But, of course, you *do* mean it!" Pons came to his feet, strode to the bedroom door, opened it, and stood aside. "Gently, Bancroft – he sleeps. Let me introduce you to the crown prince."

Bancroft looked in and withdrew. Pons closed the door again.

"How on earth did you manage it, Solar?"

"I fear I had to employ agents of whom you would not approve. Necessity, you know – and the urgence of the moment. Can we take Sarpedon?"

Bancroft Pons shook his head. "No scandal. The embassy would hope to avoid it."

Pons sighed. "I feared as much. Another time, then. He will not forget."

Bancroft settled himself into Pons' favorite chair. 'I'll just wait until he wakes, and restore him to his uneasy throne myself."

"That may be hours, Bancroft," protested Pons, "and I don't know that I can survive the strain."

"I'll wait," repeated Bancroft. "If we are both silent from time to time, and you can keep away from that infernal violin, we should be able to stand it. Perhaps far easier than that poor lad will find it to face his future!"

Bancroft Pons' words were prophetic. The crown prince, safely returned to his parents, lived only to go into exile – but not before Pons had received a handsome gift from the royal family.

V

THE ADVENTURE OF THE CLOVERDALE KENNELS

The curious puzzle of the Cloverdale Kennels came to the attention of my friend, Solar Pons, late one night in the same summer which saw the deflation of the grandiose pretensions of Arthur Shaplow, the diverting case of the reluctant scholar, Ivor Allanmain, the riddle of the Sussex Archers, and the singular affair of the Lost Dutchman. Indeed, I had just finished filing my notes on two of these cases, and was preparing to retire, content to leave Pons bent like a lean and hungry bird of prey over his retorts, deep in a chemical problem, when the outer bell rang.

Pons glanced at the clock on the mantel. "Mrs. Johnson will surely have retired by this hour," he said. "Run down and see who it is, Parker, like a good fellow."

Our caller proved to be a messenger boy with a wire for Pons. I asked him to wait for an answer.

Pons eagerly tore open the envelope. His keen eyes scanned the message before he handed it to me.

"CAN YOU COME HASLEMERE AT ONCE WOULD APPRECIATE YOUR ASSISTANCE IN MYSTERIOUS DEATH EDWARD HARTON – Hetherman."

"Hetherman," I said, looking up. "Do I know him?"

"You may recall that extraordinary occasion when Inspector Jamison asked me to talk on the science of ratiocination to a group of down country police officers meeting in London, Parker. Detective Sergeant Hetherman was in the contingent from Surrey and came up to speak to me after the meeting. He cannot be more than thirty now, but struck me even then as a bright and promising young man."

There was no need to ask whether Pons intended to run down to Haslemere, for he had already taken up the Railway Guide and had begun to turn its pages.

"Harton's death must have taken place within the past few hours," he said thoughtfully. "There was nothing about it in the evening papers, and the most recent news summary on the B.B.C. made no mention of it." He paused, his eyes arrested. "Ah, here we are. We've just missed the last train from Waterloo by a quarter of an hour. The next is at 5:25 in the morning. If your practise can spare you, we will be on it." His glance challenged me. "What do you say, Parker?"

"You know my answer," I replied.

Pons rapidly scrawled a message to Detective Sergeant Hetherman, and I delivered it to the waiting messenger below. It lacked but a few minutes of seven o'clock next morning when the train drew into the station at Haslemere, which was in the south reaches of Surrey, less than fifty miles from London. Sergeant Hetherman stood waiting for us in the chill, misty dawn. He was a slender chap, as tall as Pons, with close-cropped hair and warm blue eyes. He shook my hand, at our introduction, with genuine heartiness.

"I have a car waiting, Mr. Pons," he said. "This is a country matter, and we must drive out of Haslemere. Have you had breakfast?"

"I prefer to dispense with food when I confront one of those little problems which give me so much pleasure," answered Pons, as we walked toward the car. "I could not help observing,

Sergeant, that you carefully avoided calling Harton's death 'murder'. Is there doubt?"

"Well, sir, there is – but not much in my own mind. There seems to be a rather general acceptance among the neighbors that Harton took his own life. If he did so, his method was singularly roundabout, and there's no motive for suicide that I've been able to uncover."

"Perhaps we had better have an account of the matter," suggested Pons, as we seated ourselves in Sergeant Hetherman's car.

"Very well, Mr. Pons. Harton was an employee of Mr. George Pelham, a businessman in Haslemere. Pelham's hobby is sporting dogs. Harton was manager and trainer of the Cloverdale Kennels, owned by Pelham. These kennels are approximately four miles out of Haslemere, and Harton didn't stay in town; he had rooms with Mr. and Mrs. Martin Coster, whose home is about three fields and a copse or two away from the kennels. Harton had been in the vicinity for six years or so. He was well known and well liked, to hear people talk."

"It always seems possible to prefer the outsider to the native," said Pons. "It is a sad reflection upon human nature that it is so. Where was Harton from?"

"London. Pelham had brought him down."

"A racing man?"

"No record of it, Mr. Pons."

"You certainly made inquiries, of course."

"Certainly, Mr. Pons."

"He came recommended?"

"Very well, sir. Pelham is a man who'd make certain of that – a real martinet and a bit stuffy."

"Very well. Go on, please."

"The kennels are one longish building, with the manager's little office – a small room with space for his assistant, Roger Ballinger, to work in – at one end. Harton was in the habit of working at a high desk, sitting on a stool, immediately next to the window at the very end of his quarters. He was sitting there last night when he was shot from a little grove of beech trees at the edge of the property, exactly a hundred yards away. He was shot with a rifle carefully supported by the trees and bushes of the copse, which was in line with the window."

"You recovered the weapon?"

"Yes, Mr. Pons."

"Is that not somewhat unusual in cases of murder, Sergeant?"

"Indeed it is, Mr. Pons."

Pons smiled. "I detect a note of uncertainty in your voice, Sergeant. What struck you?"

"Mr. Pons, it was his own rifle with which he was killed," answered Hetherman. "Furthermore, there was a cord attached to the trigger, and this cord was looped around the broken end of a stout twig, and carried back to the open window through which he was shot."

"Only to it?"

"No, over the sill and into the room."

"Within reach of Harton?"

"Yes, Mr. Pons. He could have pulled the cord."

Pons' eyes danced. "I believe my illustrious predecessor demonstrated his remarkable abilities in a matter of like nature on a country estate near Winchester, if I am not mistaken. Shall we find it similar, I wonder? A hundred yards of cord! I fancy we have to deal with a remarkably cool intelligence. You have removed the rifle, Sergeant?"

"We examined it, of course, but we replaced it this morning specifically for your scrutiny. We have removed the body, however."

"Naturally, naturally. Now then, if we accept your conclusion that there was no motive – at least not a patent one – for suicide, did Harton have enemies who might wish to see him out of the way? Or who might wish him grievous harm?"

"I doubt it, sir."

Pons chuckled. "Dear me, Sergeant. Again that note of uncertainty. Why?"

"Mr. Pons, it's like this. Harton was quite a man with the ladies. He was engaged for a good while to the daughter of his landlord, Miss Ethel Coster, but their engagement never seemed to get anywhere. A fortnight ago it came out that Harton had taken up with Miss Alice Fisher, and meant to marry her. She'd been engaged to Ronald Farrow, and had broken their engagement. Perhaps she was tired of waiting for him. Sometimes engagements run a long time in the country."

"Had this one?"

"Yes, Mr. Pons. Three years. And naturally, Farrow was furious. He put the blame on Harton, though it's my opinion that if there's any blame to be fixed it should be fixed on the lady, since she's the one to make up her mind and the man usually hasn't much to say about it. Now there's talk about that Farrow made some threatening remarks concerning Harton. But Farrow is known to be a blustering sort, unlikely to take any kind of action. All promise and no fulfilment, if you know what I mean, Mr. Pons."

"Ah, but sometimes the worm may turn, Sergeant."

"I know, Mr. Pons. I'm afraid that people hereabouts really think it has turned. That's why they're all so close-mouthed and so eager to believe in Harton's suicide. Because, for all his bluster, Farrow is more popular than Harton was. Harton wasn't a good mixer, if it came down to it – didn't drink much, even though he went down to one of the pubs now and then for a game of darts."

"Everyone is capable of murder, Sergeant," reflected Pons. "Even if you are convinced Farrow is innocent."

"I am, it's true, sir. But then, you may be right, and I wrong. You come to know people one-sided like, and you set them in your mind in a sort of groove. They might not be that way at all. But here we are at the scene, Mr. Pons. Now you may have a look around for yourself."

As he spoke, the car drew up into the driveway of a building some sixty feet in length, before which two constables stood on guard. From it rose the voices of several dogs, which carried sharply to the ear in the damp morning air. The mists were now rising a little, but still held to the countryside, filling the vales, so that trees seemed to rise out of them without trunks, making a spectral appearance in the landscape.

Sergeant Hetherman led the way into that end of the building which was clearly not used for kennels. The door opened upon a large room, obviously that of the manager and trainer. From this room another door on the right opened to an inner room, adjacent to the kennels, and a second door opened into a small room with a desk and some shelving, from which in turn two rather wide windows opened on the lawn outside the building. It was obvious that it was in this small room that Harton had died, for the high stool on which he had been sitting to work at the old-fashioned desk still lay on its side, and chalk marks, together with a splash of congealed blood on the floor indicated the position of the body when found. Sergeant Hetherman led us directly into this room.

"As you see, Mr. Pons, this is where the body lay. And there," he said, pointing to the sill of one of the open windows, "is the cord. The bullet entered Harton's head just above and behind the left eye, passed through, and lodged over there in the wall. You can see where we dug it out."

Pons walked over to the window and examined the cord. "Sixteen-ply," he murmured. "And seven feet of it in over the sill." He looked out the window. "It lies slack down the wall and across the grass. I take it that is the copse over there – just coming through the mist, Sergeant?"

"Yes, Mr. Pons."

"Dear me. He would have had to reel in the cord to get a tight enough hold on it to set off the rifle."

"Yes, sir."

Pons gazed at the end of the cord. "Cut with a scissors, I see."

"I hadn't noticed."

"I fancy you can't miss the obvious pressure marks from both sides," said Pons. "A knife tears from one side. The cut is very clean. I submit it was made by a small pocket scissors, not a large shears."

He dropped the cord and scrutinized the window sill, running his fingertips lightly over it along the course of the cord. He leaned out the window once more, peering intently at the grass-covered ground beneath, and made clucking sounds with his tongue.

"Prints, too," he murmured. "Did any of your men walk up to this window, Sergeant?"

"No, Mr. Pons."

"Well, well, let us just see."

Pons turned and went out of the building. Presently he came into view outside the window, where he immediately went to his knees to peer intently at scarcely visible footprints in the still wet grass. A heavy dew made a faint outline of footprints leading up to the window and back toward the copse – or, quite possibly, the other way round. They were the prints of a man's heavy shoes, but were not, I judged, exact enough to enable the shoes themselves to be identified from them, for the dew outlined only the general indentation, and some of the grass forming its outline had already sprung back into place from the previous evening, when the footprints had presumably been made, for dew lay in the depression of the prints as well as outside.

Pons, meanwhile, paced off several of the steps. His stride was manifestly longer than the stride of the man who had made the footprints, even at an area where the steps indicated that whoever had made them had been running. He looked back at us, watching him from the window.

"Are these not short steps for a man with such large feet, Sergeant?" he asked.

"I would say so, Mr. Pons."

"Hm! Singular, singular indeed." He got down on his knees once more, peering intently at one footprint after another. "Uneven, too," he said. "In one area, he has been running. This suggests nothing Sergeant?"

"I fail to see it, sir."

"Would someone about to commit suicide act in such haste? Surely deliberation is the key to suicide."

"In most cases. An exception certainly isn't impossible."

"But unlikely."

Pons picked up a strand or two of what I took to be cobweb; in another place he took from the footprint he was examining what appeared to be the torn fragment of a long leaf.

He got up finally, brushing at wet patches on his knees. "I commend these prints to your earnest attention, Sergeant," said Pons. "They are highly significant. Come along."

We hastened outside to join Pons, who was following alongside the line of footprints toward the copse. From time to time he bent down, picked up some minuscule object, and flicked it away or returned it to the place from which he had taken it. He was careful not to tread upon the white cord which lay beside the prints and ran up through the bushes to vanish behind the leaves of the copse. His eyes were aglow with suppressed excitement, as if the footprints told him far more than was visible to any other eye. In this manner we reached the copse.

Pons walked carefully around to where he could see the rifle propped in the crotch of a tree and supported by a limb under the stock. It was aimed from among leaves and pendant branches directly at the window. The white cord was still tied to the trigger. For the moment, however, he gave this but a cursory examination; he was still intent upon the prints, and he studied their leaving and entering the copse. Not satisfied with his scrutiny from his knees, he lay prone, regardless of the wet grass, and gazed at the prints with singular care. On the far side of the copse the prints were lost in deep grass which divided the copse from a gravel path.

Having seen so much, Pons returned to the rifle. His face wore the look of a dog on the scent. Without a word, he examined the loop of the cord around the broken branch.

"Freshly broken, I see," said Pons.

"Yes, sir."

"I submit it was for this purpose. Would not the sound of a breaking branch have disturbed Harton?"

"It might have."

"He could have heard it, in any event. But there is nothing to show that it was not broken after Harton's death."

"No, sir."

"Just come over here, Sergeant. Let me call your attention to the bark of the twig at the point of contact with the cord, and to the cord itself where it passes over the twig."

Sergeant Hetherman turned puzzled eyes upon the twig and the cord. His honest young face reflected his perplexity, but he forebore to put it into words.

"Most instructive," murmured Pons in his most irritating manner, without any intention of enlightening us.

Pons now turned his back upon the rifle and again resumed his scrutiny of the ground, now and then again dropping to his knees, as he progressed through the copse. When he came to the little open stretch of deeper grass beyond, he paused.

"Your men have walked through here, Sergeant?" he asked.

"Only along the near edge, Mr. Pons. We were looking for the footprints."

"You did not find them."

"No, Mr. Pons. Someone had passed through during the previous twenty-four hours – a child, perhaps, or a large animal – but certainly not the owner of the shoes or boots which made the prints leading to the kennels."

"So that it may have been that the tracks we followed came out from the kennels and returned there."

"We haven't discarded that possibility, Mr. Pons."

"It is always wise to keep an open mind. Sergeant. The obvious is sometimes most to be distrusted."

Pons pushed on through the deep grass to the gravel path, at which he looked with some annoyance.

"Where does this path lead, Sergeant?" he asked.

"To the road on the one side, and on the other to a lane which doubles back into Haslemere."

"A pity it is here. And the road?"

"The road is a continuation of the one we followed to the kennels, sir. It goes on to Bordon and turns north again for Godalming."

Pons stood for a moment deep in thought. Then he turned abruptly back toward the copse, passed through it, and went on to the Cloverdale Kennels once more, returning to the room where Harton had met his death. We were at his heels.

"If Harton sat at this desk, he must have been working," Pons said as Sergeant Hetherman came up behind him. "At what?"

"Mr. Pons, he was writing a personal letter."

"To whom?"

"I have it here." The Sergeant took a single sheet of notepaper from a leather folder in his breast pocket and handed it to Pons.

I read it over Pons' shoulder.

"The Kennels.
"Fifth.

"Look – aren't you making rather a fool of yourself with all this threatening and so on? It sounds like the devil, and it makes you look a good deal worse than if you just kept still. I've destroyed your notes – because you'd really look a fool if they fell into anybody else's hands, wouldn't you? By the way, I'd be obliged if you'd send back my..."

Thus far Harton had got in his letter when he was interrupted. There was, however, nothing to show that he was at work on this letter when he was shot – no blot of ink, or scrawl of the pen, which might have been expected if the writer had been shot at this point.

Pons' thoughts had taken the same direction. "There would seem to be no way of demonstrating that this letter had not been begun earlier in the day, Sergeant."

"No, Mr. Pons."

"So that, if he were engaged on a report which someone might find expedient should never see the light of day, for example, such a report could have been abstracted from the desk before the body was discovered."

"It's quite possible, sir. But I wouldn't know what kind of a report, Mr. Pons."

"Suppose he were preparing a report on his assistant, Sergeant. There are any number of possibilities."

"I see, sir," said the Sergeant dubiously.

"At what time, approximately, did the event take place?"

"That seems to have been determined quite exactly, Mr. Pons," said Sergeant Hetherman with some animation. "The shot was heard by several people. Roger Ballinger was walking dogs, as was his custom at that hour. Coster was in one of his fields, just finishing trimming the edge. Mrs. Coster was in the house. Miss Ethel was out beside one of the buildings on the farm teaching a new dog to retrieve. While none of them looked at a clock, all are agreed that the shot sounded just at dusk – a few minutes past nine o'clock I make it."

"Did anyone investigate it?"

"No. Coster thought someone was shooting at jackdaws. Mrs. Coster heard it but didn't register it clearly as a shot. Miss Ethel thought it was the backfiring of someone's motor. And Ballinger took it for boys at target practise. He had heard shots earlier in the evening, and seen some boys from Haslemere cycling out to a target range; he thought one of them might have fired a parting shot for the evening before returning to the village."

"Then Ballinger discovered the body?"

"Yes, Mr. Pons. When he came back, he put the dogs into their kennels; then he went around to the office and found Harton."

Pons looked at his watch. "It is now eight. Presumably Costers will be up and about. I should like to talk to them."

"You'll find them very straightforward people, sir," said Sergeant Hetherman. "We follow that lane beyond the copse; that will take us directly to their farm."

The three Costers were at breakfast when we arrived at their pleasant little country house. Learning that Pons and I had not yet broken our fast, Mrs. Coster, a buxom, capable woman with flashing brown eyes, insisted upon preparing bacon and eggs for us, while Sergeant Hetherman explained our presence.

"It was a great shock to all of us, Mr. Pons," said Mrs. Coster. "Edward was like one of the family, you might say. Of course, he was planning to leave us, now that it was likely he'd be married.

"Did he at any time show signs of nervousness or irritability, of being afraid for his life?" asked Pons.

"Never," said Mrs. Coster firmly.

"'E wasn't afraid of nought nor anybody," said Coster in rough tones. His voice rumbled up from deep within his stout, hard-muscled body.

"But he told me just last week he'd had some threatening notes," said Miss Ethel in a gentle voice.

"Could we see them?" asked Pons.

"I believe he destroyed them," she answered. "He didn't take them seriously."

Mrs. Coster gave her daughter a hard look.

"How did Harton react to these threats, Miss Coster?" pressed Pons.

"He was annoyed."

"He didn't mention their author?"

"No, Mr. Pons. I suppose they weren't signed – though he didn't say so."

"Did he acknowledge any enemies?"

Here Coster put in an answer. "Them as didn't like Pelham didn't like Harton. You know how 'tis with people."

"Mr. Coster," said his wife warningly.

"And there are people who don't like Mr. Pelham, I take it," said Pons reflectively.

"'Tain't so much him, as what 'e does with his dogs."

"Mr. Coster," said his wife again.

"And what is that, Mr. Coster?" insisted Pons.

"They do say – crooked racing."

"I see. And people would quite understandably believe Harton had a hand in it."

"People who didn't know him might," said Mrs. Coster quickly. "None of us would."

Pons gazed at her thoughtfully. "Where were you, Mrs. Coster, when you heard the shot?"

"Right in this room, Mr. Pons."

"And you, Mr. Coster?"

"Up field."

Pons turned to Miss Ethel.

"I was outside," she said.

"Can you show me, Miss Coster?"

"Certainly."

She rose at once and led the way outside. She was not so much attractive as appealing, a woman close to thirty years of age, I judged, and there was a confident ease about her movements. She was plainly what most men would call "all woman." As soon as she stepped outside, her dog fell in at her heels.

She paused beside a long crib for grain. "I stood about here, Mr. Pons."

Pons bent, picked up one of a pair of heavy brogans lying there beside the crib. He threw it, turning to the dog as he did so to cry, "Fetch, sir!"

The dog gave Pons a curious look, but did not move.

Miss Coster began to laugh. "You don't seem to have any power over dogs, Mr. Pons. Perhaps the ladies resist you, too?"

Pons smiled. "I remain dogless and a bachelor by choice, Miss Coster. But of course your dog is not really a retriever, is he?"

"No, Mr. Pons. I tried with little success for an hour or more last evening to teach him to retrieve. You see how little he has learned."

Pons turned and looked back in the direction of the Cloverdale Kennels. "The shot must have been quite clear from here," he said thoughtfully.

"It was, Mr. Pons. But you know, with all the calling to the dog, and the dog's barking, I couldn't be sure it was a shot. It was only afterwards – when..." Here she paused and bit her lip, the only sign of emotion she had so far shown at the death of the man who had until so recently been her fiancé.

"Well, we must not keep Mrs. Coster's breakfast waiting," said Pons briskly.

After a delicious repast, we started back for the Kennels once more, Pons having expressed the wish to talk to Roger Ballinger. The morning mists had now risen; sunlight shone from every drop of dew, and the countryside glowed with green, touched by heather now beginning to bloom. The great mound of Hindhead rose in the northwest, and the slopes of the generally high country where Haslemere lay – the highest land in Surrey – aglow in the morning sun, set Pons to musing of that distinguished citizen of Haslemere named Oglethorpe who had founded Georgia in the United States, and of the Dolmetsch family of musicians who made the town their home – all this somewhat to Sergeant Hetherman's perplexity, for, being unacquainted with Pons' annoying manner of speaking about anything but the matter in hand, he was woefully bewildered.

Ballinger was not alone at the Kennels when we arrived. The owner was with him. Ballinger was a lithe young man of twenty-five, while Pelham was a thick-set man of fifty or more; the one was as polished as the other was rough.

"I'm glad Hetherman had the good sense to call you in, Mr. Pons," said Pelham at being introduced to us. "Though it seems perfectly clear to me. I understand they've detained Farrow for questioning. They'll have it out of him."

"If I have a vice, it is distrust of the obvious, Mr. Pelham," said Pons.

"Stuff and nonsense, sir," said Pelham gruffly. "It's a simple matter. Either Harton committed suicide or he didn't. He had no reason to commit suicide..."

"None at least so far known to us," said Pons.

Pelham brushed this aside. "So if he didn't take his own life, then he was murdered – cord or no cord. If you ask me, the cord's a red herring. I'll say it straight, Mr. Pons – young Farrow had a reason to get even with Edward Harton. Even if Harton didn't send him those notes."

Pons turned to the Sergeant. "Notes, Sergeant Hetherman?"

The Sergeant looked apologetic. "Farrow claimed to have received notes in the mail taunting him with not being a man – to let Harton take his girl from him."

"You neglected to mention it."

"I'm sorry, Mr. Pons. We have no evidence that this is so. Farrow says he destroyed them. He may never have received them."

"How many?"

"Three, he said."

Pelham snorted impatiently. He turned and flung his arm toward the copse. "And there are prints of a man's shoes there. What more do you need?"

"I submit there are one or two points that would seem to need elucidation," said Pons. "For instance, the prints were made by someone who walked awkwardly, as if in some way physically defective. He was also unusually light for the size of the prints, for, if you will observe the prints in the bare soil around the copse near the path, you will notice that no very great indentation has been made. And such as is there is most uneven, indeed. I've not seen Mr. Farrow; I am not sure at this point that it will be necessary to avail myself of the privilege of speaking to him. I rather think there is nothing I can learn from him. Is he, Mr. Pelham, either physically defective or unusually light?"

Pelham glared at Pons in astonishment not unmixed with a little scorn. "Farrow's a big man – almost as big as I am. He's no lightweight."

"So then, let us eliminate him," continued Pons. "Could it be possible that your employee, discovering that he had become unwittingly involved in a scandal, took his own life?"

Again Pelham snorted. "What kind of talk is this, Mr. Pons? What scandal?"

"Let us just speculate for the moment, Mr. Pelham, and suggest that it might be fixed races."

A cloud of rage darkened Pelham's face; his nostrils began to twitch with fury. He half raised a clenched fist as if to strike Pons, but controlled himself with manifest effort.

"I bid you good-day, Mr. Solar Pons," he said, turning on his heel to stalk away.

"Mr. Pelham is a man of strong temper," said Pons after Pelham had driven away.

"Perhaps your example was ill-advised, sir," said Ballinger loyally.

"If so, it was by design," said Pons crisply. He gazed for a moment intensely at Ballinger. "I daresay you will inherit Harton's position, Mr. Ballinger?"

"Mr. Pelham has suggested as much," answered Ballinger stiffly.

Pons nodded. "Now, sir, you were out walking the dogs, I understand, when the fatal shot was fired."

"I was, Mr. Pons. It's my custom to take the two Dobermans out at that time of the evening."

"Invariably?"

"Yes, Mr. Pons."

"Were you seen by anyone?"

Ballinger flushed a little, as if startled by Pons' question.

He cleared his throat nervously and said, "No, Mr. Pons."

"I fancy this custom of yours was known to all persons interested in the Kennels?"

"I believe it was. People who come here at all are generally aware of our routine."

"So that anyone intending harm to Harton could be certain that you would not be in the immediate vicinity of his office?"

"I believe that is correct, Mr. Pons. I take the dogs over along the road to Bordon, and we walk for somewhat over a mile to a culvert where the dogs run loose for a bit. Then we return. I'm usually gone about forty minutes. I leave here at sundown or a bit before."

Pons stood for a moment tugging at the lobe of his left ear. Then he said, "I daresay you knew Harton as well as anyone. Did he seem in any way troubled recently?"

Ballinger grinned grimly. "Troubled? Well, Mr. Pons, he was always having woman trouble, if you know what I mean. Otherwise, no."

"Did he ever make any adverse reference to Donald Farrow?"

Ballinger shrugged. "Only to the extent of calling him an oaf in conversations with me. But perhaps he did so elsewhere; when he was irritated, he wasn't very tactful. I think anyone could tell you that. Try the pub – the Walk Inn on the near edge of Haslemere; he was there often enough, and I suspect they'd tell you the same thing."

"Did you yourself ever have any disagreements with him, Mr. Ballinger?"

"Only such as might arise between a professional and a man coming almost new into the game. And I'd have to admit I had coming what I got."

"In short, Harton lived pretty much for himself, without regard for the reactions of others?"

"Don't we all, Mr. Pons? I mean, we all think first of ourselves. That's only human. Some of us do it smoothly, and some don't care. Like Mr. Harton."

Pons nodded. "Tell me, Mr. Ballinger, was Harton in the habit of bringing his rifle to the Kennels?"

"I never knew him to bring his rifle here, sir."

"He hunted?"

"Yes, sir. Apart from women, it was his only recreation, Mr. Pons."

"Thank you. That's all, Mr. Ballinger."

Ballinger walked back toward the Kennels, leaving us to stand where we were. For a few moments Pons said nothing, but his eyes were fixed on a point in space far ahead of him, and wore that expression of intense concentration which gave evidence of the ratiocinative process. It was Sergeant Hetherman who broke in upon him.

"Mr. Pons, if I might ask – you called my attention to the cord and the twig around which it was looped. I've examined it and found nothing."

"Precisely, Sergeant. That was the point. There was no evidence that the cord had ever been tightened on the twig – no rubbing of the bark, no fragments of bark adhering to the cord, which indicated that the cord had been put up only to distract us from evidence of murder. That should dispose effectively of the inclination to believe that Harton took his own life."

Sergeant Hetherman nodded, as if to confirm his own convictions.

"A singularly well thought out murder, too, Sergeant," continued Pons. "By the way, you ought to lose no time setting Farrow free. He had nothing whatever to do with Harton's death."

"Very well, Mr. Pons."

"As for the murderer," continued Pons, "I rather think that if you pick up that pair of brogans standing beside Coster's grain crib, you'll find that they will fit the prints you've marked off leading into and out of the copse on the side toward the lane. Moreover, a close scrutiny of the grass should reveal to you – as it did to me – tiny fragments of fertilizer, maize-husk, and maize-silk, which indicate that the wearer came from a farm in the vicinity – not far enough away to have worn off this evidence – though I fancy the brogans were carried to the scene and back. Coster would seem to be one of the few farmers who is experimenting in the raising of maize, and the evidence therefore, is conclusive."

"Coster!" cried Sergeant Hetherman. "But why?"

Pons gave him a sympathetic glance. "Alas, no, Sergeant. Harton was slain by Miss Ethel Coster, wearing her father's brogans. Coster in his own shoes would have left a far more definite print, and there would have been no uncertainty about any prints left by him – as there were by Miss Ethel's small feet in her father's shoes. You'll probably find the ball from which she cut the cord on the Coster farm; it's a cord common to farm use in England. Of those people who obviously had reason to hate Harton, she was the only one who had access to his rifle. Hell hath no fury like a woman scorned! I fancy she tried at first to provoke Farrow into violence against Harton – if we can believe him about the notes he had received, and there is no reason why we should not. And, Sergeant, I should not be surprised if you found that Miss Ethel is a devotee of the adventures of my illustrious master."

While Sergeant Hetherman stood in amazement slowly giving way to belief, Pons looked at his watch. "I daresay we have just time to catch the 11:19 for London, Sergeant, if you will be so good as to run us back into Haslemere."

"It is really elementary, when you consider the problem," I said, once we were comfortably seated in our compartment on the short run back to Waterloo Station. "Circumstantial evidence was certainly deceptive in this case."

Pons sighed. "My dear fellow, circumstantial evidence is deceptive only to those who have no ability to interpret it properly. Facts are facts, and any unbiased, ordinarily intelligent approach to them cannot fail to read them without error.

"Consider, for example. The cord was cut with a scissors – moreover, a small scissors, of a type commonly used by women rather than men. A man customarily cuts with a knife, looping the cord and slashing it. While this in itself is hardly conclusive, it struck me at once as most suggestive. Next, the tracks left by the murderer. These were clearly made by a man's shoes, worn by someone with unusually small feet – such as Miss Coster obviously has. But again, this too is highly speculative. Add to it however, anonymous notes sent to goad Farrow to violence, and you begin to perceive a feminine intelligence in the matter. Let us go on to Harton's unfinished letter. Did nothing about it strike you, Parker?"

"Certainly. It supported the known fact that Farrow had made threats against Harton."

"Dear me," said Pons testily. "I thought it quite the contrary. How did he phrase it? 'Look – aren't you making rather a fool of yourself with all this threatening,' he began. And he went on, 'I've destroyed your notes – because you'd really look a fool if they fell into anybody else's hands...' And then he asks that something of his be sent back to him. Now, my dear Parker, I submit that this is patently not the kind of letter a man sends to another man; no, this letter was clearly being written to a woman. Moreover, it was to a woman who had threatened him – not publicly, but privately, in 'notes', a woman who has something of Harton's – very likely letters. Who else could this be but his former fiancée, Ethel Coster? Certainly it could not be intended for Farrow.

"Further, when at last I saw the girl, I was more than ever convinced that she was our quarry. She was calm, collected, cool. But she made two little slips, quite apart from the fact that she had manifestly *not* been training her dog very much at retrieving – retriever or no, every dog can be taught to retrieve after a fashion, and had the dog been so taught, he would have made after the brogan when I threw it."

"If she made slips, as you say, they were beyond me," I put in.

"Ah, Parker, you've always had an eye for the ladies – exterior first – and I am considerably more interested in what goes on inside their pretty heads. Miss Ethel said that Harton had had 'some threatening notes'; who would know this better, since she sent them? Unfortunately for her, when she dropped the cord inside the Kennels after killing him, she did not take time to look at the letter Harton had been writing, or she might have seen her notes mentioned.

"Secondly, she made a curious and tantalizing slip in our conversation at the maize-crib. She said, if you remember, 'You don't seem to have any power over dogs, Mr. Pons. *Perhaps the ladies resist you, too?*' Now, I submit this is *not* the kind of remark one makes casually to someone one has only just met. No, indeed. It came up from deep in Miss Coster's subconscious, for she was very much bound up in the problem of lovers and engagements – particularly broken engagements – and fading hopes of marriage, and in the concealment of that fury of hatred at being thrust aside for another woman which drove her to take the life of the man she had hoped to marry.

"Miss Ethel had the strongest motive of all – revenge. When young Ballinger told us that Harton never brought his rifle to the Kennels, the matter was plain as a pikestaff. Where was it, then, but in the Coster home, where Ethel need only walk into his room and take it? She had the opportunity to use it, and she knew just when to do so, for the crime was patently committed by someone who knew the routine of the Kennels. She walked over to the copse, coolly shot Harton, then boldly attempted to make his death look like suicide – borrowing a gambit from Doyle. Thin, true – but it might have taken in someone less observant than Sergeant Hetherman."

"Yes, it is all perfectly clear now," I conceded.

"I daresay this little problem established a sort of record, Parker – though I cannot be certain; you are more fond of these inconsequential details than I – but I cannot recall a puzzle which has consumed less time. Three hours, I make it."

VI

THE ADVENTURE OF THE BLACK CARDINAL

"That unbelievable conspiracy," Solar Pons was accustomed to call the affair of the Black Cardinal, which began for me early in January of a year which must remain nameless. I had spent Christmas in the Austrian capital, attending a medical conference there. As I was preparing to entrain for Calais a week later, I received an enigmatic wire from Pons, instructing me to present myself at a certain address in Vienna and accept papers which would be ready for me. As usual, there was no word of explanation, and the hour set was so near that I had no alternative but to leave my hotel at once and hail a carriage.

I gave the driver the Ringstrasse address Pons had given me.

He looked at me with curious hesitation. "*Haben sie es recht*?" he asked.

"*Gehen sie nur*," I replied, nettled.

He bowed elaborately and closed the door. Then he mounted his box, and in a few moments we were rattling away down the avenue toward the mysterious address Pons had wired me. Our destination was not too far from my hotel, through broad avenues and shadowy by-ways, but it had begun to rain when at last we pulled up before a wrought-iron gate, which was the only opening in a formidable ten-foot wall of stone that ran the length of the entire street on both sides of the gate where two young men stood at stiff attention in national uniform.

Something of my driver's uncertainty communicated itself to me; I turned apprehensively toward him, as if to assure myself that this was indeed the correct address. He sensed my unspoken question and nodded, not without a certain self-satisfaction at what must obviously, to him, have been my error. Summoning my courage, I approached the gate beneath my driver's dubious eyes. At once the guards stepped forward and crossed their guns to bar my way.

"*Nicht vorbei*!" exclaimed one of them. Fortunately, I had brought Pons' wire with me; I now proffered it. One of the guards stepped back and struck the gate three times sharply with the butt of his gun. Then he came forward once more, and together the two of them scrutinized the paper, carefully shielding it from rain. A few minutes passed in silence; then a muffled sound fell to ear from the other side of the gate. A white face peered out between the bars. A hand was stretched forth and received my wire from Pons. It was withdrawn, and the face vanished into the darkness.

More minutes passed, during which the guards maintained a stolid immobility. My wonderment was mingled with some irritation at Pons for having thrust me into what must surely be a matter of some importance without any explanation to guide me. At last the gate creaked open, and I was ushered through.

I found myself now in a large rambling garden, in the background of which rose an antiquated but impressive building, toward which my guide led his silent way. I followed as silently, casting a hurried glance around. To my left I could see tall white streams of water playing from a group of fountains dimly illuminated by a trio of post lights.

My observations were cut short when we ascended a short flight of stone steps, walked a distance along a balcony-like colonnade, and drew up before a heavy, double-panelled door, which my guide opened for me to enter. I stepped inside; the door closed behind me; I could hear my guide's retreating footsteps.

From the far end of the long hall in which I now found myself came a man clad in a long robe, which, as he approached, I recognized as the habit of the Augustinian friars. He came up to me, bowed slightly, and addressed me in English.

"Please follow me, Dr. Parker. His Eminence and His Excellency are expecting you."

I followed him as he returned the way he had come, but I was now more bewildered than before. The presence of this friar, coupled with the tone of respect with which he had uttered "His Eminence", suggested a Cardinal of the Roman Catholic Church. And "His Excellency" could refer to no one but a high official in the Austrian government. Then I recognized my imperfect mental picture of this old house with its group of illuminated fountains and enclosed gardens – I was in the residence of the Archbishop of Vons, chief minister of the Austrian state.

My guide paused before a green baize door, on which he rapped sharply. An answer I did not hear must have come to his ears, for he opened the door and stepped aside, motioning me to enter. I stepped into a darkened room. As I walked forward, two white faces looked toward me from the far side of a huge table.

I had no difficulty recognizing the piercing eyes of the stern man in black who sat on the left, gazing steadily at me through his pince-nez. The other was dressed in a Cardinal's habit, and though I had never seen him, I assumed that he was none other than Cardinal Hoffman, Archbishop of Vienna; his ascetic face seemed more kindly than his companion's, and his eyes twinkled with amusement at what must have been obvious embarrassment on my part.

"Please sit there, Dr. Parker," said the Prime Minister, indicating a chair on my side of the table. Turning, he addressed his clerical superior, "Will you speak, Eminence?"

The Cardinal nodded, bent forward, and singled out a sealed envelope from among the mass of papers arranged on the broad table. He laid it before me. In the dim light at the table, I saw that it was sealed with the arms of Austria and addressed in a cramped hand to Solar Pons.

"I do not know," said the Cardinal in a soft, well modulated voice, "whether you are aware of the importance of your mission to us. If so, it is well; if not, I can tell you very little, and your natural curiosity must rest until Mr. Pons sees fit to explain the matter. It should not be necessary to impress you with the vital importance of this packet in furthering Mr. Pons' investigation."

"I understand," I answered, a little nettled at what I thought unnecessary mystery. "But I should prefer not to travel in total ignorance."

Cardinal Hoffman smiled. "Mr. Pons," he said gently, "has been engaged by His Holiness to find an individual known as the Black Cardinal, a man posing as one of us, who has been stirring up dangerous anti-religious feeling throughout the Continent. He seems to be centering his attention on England at the moment, and the apt suggestion to retain Mr. Pons made by Cardinal Latmer was immediately adopted by His Holiness and the Sacred College."

The Prime Minister now touched a bell-button on the table to signify that our all too brief interview was at an end. I rose and bowed. Behind me, the green baize door swung silently open, diffusing through the room the pale yellow light from the hall.

In a few moments I found myself once more in the dark street, with the two impassive guards staring at me in some curiosity. I saw that my cab had been detained, and lost no time making my way back to my hotel, and from there, taking time only to send a short wire to Pons setting down the hour of my arrival in London, to the airport, for I had already packed in my previous anticipation of entraining for Calais.

Pons met me at Croydon. His brisk manner gave no indication of the nature of his current problem.

"You've brought the envelope, Parker?"

"Your wire caught me just in time to permit a change of plan," I said. I handed the packet over to him.

He slipped it into an inner pocket without so much as glancing at it, only nodding in satisfaction. Then his keen eyes swept the beacon-lit grounds as if in search of someone, after which he rushed me through the struggling crowds to a waiting cab, and in a few moments we were speeding toward London.

I was relieved and relaxed to be in our familiar quarters at 7B Praed Street once more, with the ever forebearing Mrs. Johnson serving us a late breakfast in those pleasantly warm surroundings. I could hardly wait, however, to ask Pons about the problem which had prompted his wire to me in Vienna, and I did so as soon as Mrs. Johnson left us alone.

"Ah, it's a tantalizing little matter," he said offhandedly, "but with decidedly serious possibilities. I do not as yet view it as gravely as the Vatican does, but then, there is a difference in perspective. I may say that ever since Cardinal Latmer called upon me and laid before me the problem as His Holiness viewed it, I have been working constantly. I've never before worked so much and accomplished so little."

Pons pushed back from the table, went over to his files, and drew out a thick packet of newspaper clippings which he threw down before me. I saw at a glance that the packet was composed of numerous lesser packets of clippings, each held in a rubber band.

"Just glance over the headlines of any group of these clippings, Parker," said Pons.

The clippings had been cut from many Continental papers, as well as from American and British periodicals. It needed but a cursory examination to reveal that the headlines were of a most foreboding tone – *Vatican Attacked by Spanish Government in Sharp Note, Anti-Catholic Feeling Rising on Continent, Russian Foreign Office Flays Papacy, Catholic Cardinal Predicts Religious War, Fascist Ties to Vatican,* and the like.

"What does it all mean?" I asked.

"It would seem to be the work of one man, operating through puppets and petty criminals not worth the trouble to find," said Pons. "As nearly as I can ascertain, he operates a rumor factory and he plants rumors carefully designed to inflame suspicion and prejudices, which always exist in regard to the Catholic Church, as you know. He has called himself variously 'Cardinal Niger' and 'Cardinal de Noir' – hence the 'Black Cardinal'. Now and then he has been audacious enough to send supposedly official announcements to the press on his own stationery, and it is no tribute to the newspapers that these announcements have been taken as *bona fide*, and printed – for the members of the College of Cardinals are all well known, their names can be ascertained with only a little trouble, and the absence of a Cardinal Niger or a Cardinal de Noir from that College could be proved with only a minimum of effort. But in the main he tends to rely upon rumor mills and those inevitable 'reliable sources' on which the wildest rumors are blamed."

"But surely no responsible person takes such stories seriously," I said.

Pons shrugged. "One cannot count on the affairs of our world being conducted only by responsible persons. The danger is not in these wild rumors *per se*, but in the possibility that they may be seized upon as a pretext for violence against the Roman Church. You know how uneasy the German situation is, what with the post-war privations and economic difficulties which the Allies have never properly resolved, due largely to the intransigence of France – and, I must admit – in part our own country. Moreover, there is still fresh in many minds the unhappy role of the Vatican, which unwittingly harbored a spy for the Central Powers in the person of Msgr. Rudolph Gerlach."

"I recall the incident," I said.

"Even more recently," Pons continued, "there has been the struggle within the church between the Modernists and the Integralists. The Modernism movement began under Leo XIII, as a determination to recognize and adapt the church to contemporary realities – within the framework of traditional Catholicism, of course. The movement had developed under Pius IX but Pius X took a stand against it and specifically condemned it in 1907 in his *Pascendi* encyclical. This resulted in driving the movement underground. The Integralists, who opposed the Modernists, organized a secret society, the *Sodalitium Pianum*, designed to bring to light the activities of the Modernists. The center in Rome was led by Msgr. Umberto Benigni, who used his paper, *Correspondenza Romana* – later *La Correspondance de Rome* – as well as other lesser papers to reprint confidential reports on the Modernists and the activities of the Integralists, all of whom were disguised by pseudonyms. Benigni and his paper carried on a campaign of vilification against the Modernists, whose most potent voice was that of Cardinal Rampolla. The Integralists flourished until Cardinal del Val, then Secretary of State, became aware of the Rome center, and carried his opposition to Benedict XV, who in his first encyclical, *Ad Beatissimi*, late in 1914, condemned Integralism, hard upon Cardinal del Val's suppression of *La Correspondance de Rome*. Only so recently as 1921, Benedict XV declared the *Sodalitium Pianum* defunct. It is understandable that the Church might wonder whether the present activities of the individual known as the Black Cardinal are not a further outcropping of this internal struggle in the hierarchy."

"Do you think so?" I asked.

Pons shook his head. "It seems wholly unlikely. I took the trouble to look up some of the figures of the struggle. Cardinal Rampolla is dead. Benigni turned his by no means inconsiderable talents to writing the social history of the Catholic Church, and now lives in retirement in Rome, his health failing. No, I think we have in the Black Cardinal an individual obsessed with hatred for the Roman Church, one by no means untalented in his ability to stir prejudices and inflame street rioting. He must also have means at his disposal. I should guess him to be an unfrocked cleric."

"If I may interrupt your train of thought," I put in, "what is in that envelope I brought from Vienna?"

"Detailed reports on the Black Cardinal's activities in Austria, compiled by the *Polizei* of that country. He evidently began his work there, but the Austrian Prime Minister, as a Bishop of the Church, was not slow to understand the direction taken by the spurious Cardinal, and the work of the police soon made Austria too uncomfortable for him. Of his activities in France and Germany, less is known – but newspaper headlines tell us all we need to know. What is important is that we have every assurance that the Black Cardinal is now in London. The unpleasant part of his activities – as the Black Cardinal knows – is that to the inexperienced layman, it is made to look as if a Catholic plot were burgeoning."

"Have the police any clue to his description?"

"From Austria we have only the slightest notes. He is described as tall – well, tall men are common in England, perhaps more so than on the Continent. He is referred to by some people as benign in appearance, by others as sinister in aspect, which only suggests that our man is a consummate actor, which I have no doubt he is."

"What has been done to turn him up in London?" I asked then.

"All the customary avenues of information have been explored. I dispatched Frick and some of his friends to make the rounds of the underworld. I had some hope of discovering something of use in Limehouse or Whitechapel, though the hope was dim, for our man did not seem likely to have accomplices there. Frick found nothing, of course. Scotland Yard sent Dunstan and his sophisticated crew to move about in higher circles. Nothing came of this either. And my brother has not been idle at the Foreign Office." He shrugged. "All to no end, save the usual farcial events which always attend such matters – like the Park Lane servant who had had the bad grace to suggest that cardinal red as a color for the cardinalate smacked too strongly of royalty and to propose that cardinals in the future wear black. The poor fellow was frightened out of his wits by the Yard and had to be freed at once." The sound of the outer bell attended Pons' words.

Pons glanced at the clock on the crowded mantel. "That will be Inspector Jamison, right on time."

In a moment the portly Inspector crossed our threshold, looking as self-important as always. "Glad to see you back, Doctor," he said to me, after he had greeted Pons.

"I observe by your manner that you have nothing to report," said Pons crisply.

"I don't know how you do it, Pons," said Jamison. "But you're right – nothing's the answer, nothing at all. To tell the truth, I'm beginning to think there's no such person at all."

"You've been at it for three days," said Pons. "And turned up nothing in all London?"

"Done no better than you, Pons," said Jamison, not without some satisfaction. "Unless you count those little mistakes – like the cab-driver."

"Cab-driver? Tell me about him."

"A slow-witted fellow. Said he'd driven a man who wore nothing but black robes to the home of Cardinal Latmer." Jamison chuckled. "Well, we took him out there over my protests, and of course he identified one of His Eminence's priests as the arch-criminal."

Pons smiled thinly.

"He thought as he had picked him up at the docks..." began Jamison.

"Has a general alarm gone out?" Pons interrupted.

"No, nothing of that kind, Pons. We've sent word only to public carriers. After all, the fellow has to move about somehow."

Pons grimaced. "With so little description, too! A futile move. It only results in giving us less time than I thought we had. Once he is aware, he can slip out of the country with ease."

Jamison shrugged this off. "What troubles me, Pons – how does this man work? How can one man set the stage for – well, call it a religious war?"

"By preying upon the prejudices and biases which afflict us all," answered Pons. "You know his methods – how he approaches gullible Catholics, sometimes in priestly garb and proposes sending out notices, cleverly associated in exaggerated form with some incident of little importance – how he directs notices to the press under a false letterhead and the like. Some of his agents have been caught, only to turn out to be dupes – innocent people who had been persuaded to believe that they were working for Rome. He has used gullible Catholics in lesser positions in governmental offices, and there is some reason to believe that minority parties, like the Communists, have been playing a hand here and there.

"I think we are justified in assuming the Black Cardinal to be a man of great wealth – since otherwise he would have to have some organization to supply money for his activities. There is thus far no evidence to support the belief that any organization is connected with his plans. His capture therefore will end the 'conspiracy'."

"If only we knew who he might be!" said Jamison.

"Knowing who he is is not nearly as important as knowing where he is," said Pons. "He could be one-time Fr. Jannichon, unfrocked four years ago; ex-Bishop Vradlica, whose whereabouts are unknown since he left the Danube Valley three years ago; he could be Msgr. Schleicher, once of Berlin, and known to have been active in intrigue during World War I. There are half a dozen others." He spread his hands in futility. "But now, if you will excuse me, Jamison, I must be on my way to Ambrosden Avenue."

"Let us hear from you, Pons," said Jamison, preparing to take his leave.

Within moments Pons, clad in his deerstalker and Inverness cape, and I were on our way by cab down Edgware Road toward Victoria Street and Westminster.

At the home of Cardinal Latmer, we were shown into a small, darkened room manifestly deep in the house, for we had walked a lengthy corridor to reach it. There was no window, and the panel through which we had entered seemed to be the room's only entrance, though it might well have been that one or more of the other panels bordering the wall were also disguised doors.

The prelate we had come to see sat at a combination desk and table near the wall opposite the door, backed by heavy portieres; he was an old man, tall and gaunt; he wore horn-rimmed glasses, and, in the glow of the small lamp which illuminated that part of the room in which he sat, he wore an air of great and benign composure, so often to be noticed in the hierarchy. He did not wait for us to speak.

"I am glad to see you again, Mr. Pons," he said. "I am at your service in this matter at the express order of His Holiness. How can I help you?"

Pons introduced me. He acknowledged the introduction graciously, but with the patent understanding that his business was with Pons. Curiously, the first instinct aroused by the prelate at this proximity was a professional one; I was forcibly struck by the old man's extreme nervousness, which stood out in my sight. His fingers were so unsteady as to appear palsied, and his lips twitched often, while his eyes blinked fast.

"I have had time to study the papers sent from Rome," said Pons, "and it seems to me as it did to Cardinal del Val that the man who best fits the description and qualities of the Black Cardinal is ex-Bishop Vradlica. What can you tell me of him up to the time of his excommunication?"

"His activities prior to 1914 can hardly be of interest to you, Mr. Pons," said the Cardinal. "At that time he had been a bishop for seven years. With war imminent, he began to appeal to Rome to come actively into the Balkan situation. You know, surely, how abhorrent the very thought of war was to the late Pope, and it must be evident to you, then, how much he was distressed by this appeal from Bishop Vradlica – as he was later by disclosure of the activities of Msgr. Gerlach."

"No one aware of events could question the sincerity of that saintly Pope in his efforts toward peace," said Pons.

"I was at that time working in the Vatican library," continued Cardinal Latmer, "and had frequent opportunities to read and discuss his letters with other clergymen. I had not at that time been elevated to the cardinalate, of course. Bishop Vradlica's letters were very powerful in their appeal, and in some ways cogent in the argument that the Church could gain by allying itself actively with the Continental coalition then in formation. I need hardly tell you that Bishop Vradlica found no sympathy in His Holiness, who instructed the Papal Secretary to warn the bishop that such entreaties must cease, and that his thoughts must turn from terrestrial matters to a higher plane.

"For some time, then, nothing more was heard from Vradlica. Then the man opened a new correspondence directly with the Secretary of State. At the same time, other influential members of the cardinalate began to receive urgent communications from Vradlica. His letters clearly proved that Bishop Vradlica had gone ahead on his own authority to begin negotiations with Austrian and Hungarian secret agents, and Cardinals Colonna and Valdini appealed to Benedict to take some drastic action, particularly since war had now actually broken out, and the activities of the bishop were putting the Church in a most awkward position, at a time when His Holiness had publicly appealed to the nations to submit their problems to arbitration.

"His Holiness took no action for two weeks, pending the arrival of further reports. When these came, only confirming the Vatican's worst fears in regard to the bishop's activities, Benedict sent the bishop a formal order to abandon his activities under threat of excommunication. This is the customary procedure in such matters, Mr. Pons. Rome is extremely reluctant to invoke the action of excommunication, and gives the offender every opportunity to repent.

"Bishop Vradlica defied His Holiness. He was excommunicated, and soon after dropped from sight, though we assumed that he had retired to his ancestral estates."

"He was, then, independently wealthy?"

"Mr. Pons, he was a member of an old Hungarian family. He was the only heir to a substantial fortune."

Pons meditated for a few moments. Then he spoke again.

"You say you had opportunities to read some of Bishop Vradlica's letters. What would you say of them as letters."

"Oh, sound, Mr. Pons, very sound – so much in his favor," said the prelate. "But I think they expressed clearly what is called a power complex. There was great yearning after power in his letters. It was the declaration of that ego which recognizes no barrier and no power greater than its own. And with time they grew increasingly arrogant."

"And distraught?"

"Perhaps. This could be said, of course. The letters gave evidence of a shrewd, calculating, ruthless mind. Cardinal Colonna believed Vradlica to be mad."

"And you?"

Cardinal Latmer shrugged. "I am no judge."

"Did his proposals to His Holiness seem feasible to you?"

"Feasible, but stupendous, Mr. Pons."

Answer followed question, and question answer. My attention wandered to the prelate's nervous fingers. He seemed to be insistently tapping the flat arms of the chair in which he sat, and his right index finger was engaged in tracing over and over again some kind of design. Pons' eyes fell to the restless fingers; whenever he looked away from the Cardinal, the prelate's fingers tapped sharply as if to command his attention again.

I studied his face. The prelate seemed pale even in the diminished light of the room. And perhaps a little drawn, as if he were overly tired. I thought him physically run down, perhaps even ill, and glanced at Pons to determine how long this interview might yet take.

But at this moment the Cardinal began to cough, and, as if at signal, the portieres behind him parted. I caught a glimpse of an open panel behind them as a tall, stoop-shouldered priest stepped into the room and came forward with tender solicitude to stand behind the prelate's chair.

"Forgive me, gentlemen," he said softly, "it is not good for Eminence to talk so much. He is not as well as he should be. If you will excuse him, he should rest."

"There is nothing further," said Pons, rising at once to go. The priest was evidently the Cardinal's personal physician. He was a man no longer young, with dark, lustrous eyes. He favored us with but a fleeting smile and turned anxiously to his charge.

His Eminence bowed in farewell, and we left the room.

The priest who had conducted us to the prelate's room still waited outside his door.

"How did you find His Eminence?" he asked anxiously.

"Well," said Pons shortly.

"He has been virtually in isolation for a month," said the priest, "at work on a monograph. He gave orders that he was not to be disturbed, and, save for his physician, no one has seen him except on his obligations. Even you would not have been received, had it not been for the orders from the Vatican."

"Are not princes of the Church always at the service of bishops, archbishops, and priests responsible to them?" asked Pons.

"In ordinary cases, yes, sir."

We were shown out to Ambrosden Avenue. I was about to hail a cab when Pons stopped me.

"As long as we are in the vicinity, let us just stop in at Bancroft's office."

We made our way to Whitehall, and there, after some difficulty – far more than we had encountered at Ambrosden Avenue – we found ourselves in the little cubicle in the cryptography department which served Pons' seldom seen brother as an office.

Bancroft Pons looked out from behind a desk piled high with papers of all kinds, and surrounded by other papers. Even this tall, formidable man was dwarfed by the evidence of work surrounding him. He was not pleased to see us, and showed it.

"Solar, you impose on me," he said. "You have permitted this trifling matter of the Black Cardinal to persuade you to disregard my rules. I come to see you, not the other way round."

Pons only smiled. "I'm happy to see you your usual cantankerous self."

"Spare me your wit, Solar. I can give you one minute, which hardly allows for your conversation. You have Dr. Parker to run your errands. I am as aware, you see, of what goes on in Vienna as I am of what takes place in Rome. As for this little matter of the Black Cardinal – he can be in one of only two places – either down very deep or up very high. Let me call your attention to Mr. Edgar Allan Poe's story, *The Purloined Letter*."

"I know it well."

"Good, I need say no more. It only depends then on which letter-rack."

We were dismissed with the wave of a hand.

Bancroft Pons called after us, "There will be a cab waiting for you out in front."

And so there was.

Back in our quarters at 7B Praed Street, with Pons clad in his mouse-colored dressing-gown and ensconced in his favorite chair, we sat considering the problem in hand.

"You noticed Cardinal Latmer's tension, Parker?" asked Pons.

"I certainly did. Nothing would please me more, professionally, then to have him under observation for a while. Such striking features! I couldn't help noticing that his physician..."

Pons looked up quickly. "You took the priest for his physician?"

"So he struck me. He was extremely solicitous of the Cardinal."

"Hm. His Eminence seemed ill to you?"

"Let me say rather that he seemed under exhausting strain."

"In seclusion writing a monograph," mused Pons. "I saw no evidence of it."

"Nor I. But there were drawers in his desk in which the manuscript could have been kept."

"And the Cardinal's general pallor suggests that he has not been out of the house for some time. He seemed actually a little underfed."

"What, specifically, caught your eye?" pressed Pons.

"His right index finger."

"You saw it then?"

"I could hardly help noticing its insistence. You regard it as important?"

"I submit that His Eminence was trying to tell us something he could not put into words," said Pons.

"Absurd! We were in his private study, adjoining his bedroom. It must be soundproof. Why should he not be able to speak?"

"I shall know that when I learn what it was he was trying to tell us. You undoubtedly noticed how he drew attention again and again to his finger by tapping on the arm of the chair?"

"A subconscious nervous reaction," I said.

"Come, come, Parker. It was to draw attention to the design he was indicating."

"I saw no design."

"I am not surprised. Yet he constructed it over and over – a simple circle with a right angle drawn in its center. It reminded me of that childish puzzle of the man in the fenced-up lot." As he spoke, he reached over to the table for an envelope and a pencil. "Like this," he said, drawing rapidly.

I gazed at the drawing he had made – a circle with a sort of check mark in it.

"Meaningless," I said.

Pons shook his head. "On the contrary. He drew it almost without variation."

"Almost?"

"I observed that at intervals the Cardinal appeared to go through the construction of making cuts in his circling line, then closing them again. No more."

"You've read more into this than you were meant to read."

"I've not read enough," said Pons.

I watched him continue to draw designs on the envelope, then turned to take up a medical tome I had begun to read well before my Continental sojourn. I had hardly read more than a half dozen pages, when I was aroused from my engrossment by a hoarse shout from Pons. I looked up, startled.

Pons stood with one hand clapped to his head, while in the other he held the envelope, which was, I now saw, covered with replicas of the design Cardinal Latmer had outlined with his finger.

"Now what?" I asked.

"I have it!" he cried. "How blind I have been! Bancroft was right." He thrust the envelope before my eyes. "Look at it – it's not a right angle in the circle; it's the letter *L*, the capital *L*."

I looked at him in astonishment. "That conveys little to me," I said.

He paid no attention. He strode rapidly to the telephone and called Scotland Yard to ask for Inspector Jamison.

"Are you there, Jamison? Come over to 7B, will you? I have my finger on our man and need your men to take him in."

Pons' casual announcement sent me scrambling after the envelope he had dropped, curious to learn how he had made anything of this simple design. I stared at it, bewildered.

"Supposing this isn't a right angle, but a capital L," I said. "Where is the hidden message?"

"Elementary, my dear Parker. You're looking too hard – as I was initially. The thing is too simple. *L* stands for the Cardinal's name; the circle stands for his prison."

I looked open-mouthed at Pons. "Then it follows that his physician is his keeper," I said.

"And the Black Cardinal."

"Incredible!"

"Not so," retorted Pons. "Consider – for the past month Cardinal Latmer has been largely incommunicado, presumably engaged on a monograph. According to information transmitted to us, the Black Cardinal has been in England approximately a month. What more natural than that he should take the citadel of the enemy by seizing the Primate of all England? To hide himself in the bosom of the Church he would destroy is the acme of cunning. This is the gambit Bancroft had reference to – the purloined letter in Poe's story was in plain sight in the letter-rack, only under cover of another envelope. So it is with the Black Cardinal."

"Still incredible," I cried.

"Not at all," replied Pons. "Let us reconstruct the circumstances as they very probably occurred. Vradlica comes in the guise of a priest or bishop on a visit to the Primate. He gains admittance to the prelate's study, which, as you observed, leads off into his private chambers. Once alone with Cardinal Latimer, Vradlica forces him to submit to him. This is much more simple than you imagine; the Black Cardinal must only capture the Primate and hold him prisoner in his own quarters, and once he has seen to it that the order goes out that the Primate is not to be disturbed, he is safely in charge."

"But we had no difficulty gaining admittance," I protested.

"Such a contingency was prepared for, as you saw, by the attending presence of the Black Cardinal, concealed behind the Cardinal. You could hardly help noticing that the Primate had just time to fulfil his obligation to any Vatican directive in regard to my interview, when the Black Cardinal, acting as physician, appeared and made it clear that we should go."

"These things are always far clearer to you than they are to me," I said.

Pons smiled. "Well put, Parker. That is why I am the private enquiry agent, and you are the doctor."

"And the business with the index finger?" I asked.

"You will remember that I said his little design reminded me of the childish game of the man in the fenced-up lot; the problem is, find a way out without having the man climb the fence. The principle of the maze. The circle suggested an enclosure; the cuts he indicated, open doors which were nevertheless closed; the *L* at the center – all spoke as clearly as need be: 'I am imprisoned in my own house!'" Pons shook his head disgustedly. "How unfortunate that I failed to read him correctly at the time. I could have bagged the Black Cardinal when he came to take the Primate again into his charge!"

From outside came the sound of hastily applied brakes and the slam of a car door. Hard after came footsteps pelting up the stairs.

"That will be Jamison," said Pons.

Inspector Jamison threw open the door to our quarters and entered the room. "Where is he, Pons?" he asked.

"In Cardinal Latmer's house on Ambrosden Avenue," answered Pons.

Jamison fell back, his face flushing. "Alone?" he cried, incredulous.

"Alone," answered Pons. "He is holding the Primate prisoner."

Pons gave Jamison no time to protest, but launched into a detailed explanation.

"We'll take him at once," said Jamison, when Pons finished.

"Gently, gently, Jamison," cautioned Pons. "We must not fail in this. At the very least, this fellow is an international nuisance – at the worst, he is capable of provoking a bloody religious war. I propose that you set up a cordon around the Cardinal's residence and also the cathedral – there is doubtless a passage connecting them. Parker and I will go to the house once more and ask to see His Eminence – we must do all we can to prevent his being harmed, even though our reappearance there may put Vradlica on guard and cause him to flee, for your men to take him, for he must emerge either from the house or the cathedral.

Jamison's dubiety showed plainly on his rotund face. "How much time will you need?" he asked.

"Give us twenty minutes. If we're not out in that time, you and your men come in."

"I don't like it, Pons, but I'll agree to it. We'll need time to place our men."

Pons glanced at the clock on the mantel. "Shall we say seven o'clock?"

"Seven o'clock it is."

Promptly at that hour, we presented ourselves at the house on Ambrosden Avenue. We were admitted without question, though the young cleric showed some surprise at the untimeliness of our visit. He listened impassively to Pons' request to see the Primate on a matter of some urgence, making no secret of his doubt that we would be received.

"I will see, gentlemen. Please be seated."

He hurried away.

Three minutes passed before he returned. "His Eminence will see you now," he said.

Pons flashed me a quixotic glance. Evidently our quarry had not become suspicious.

We were shown to the same room where we had visited with the Primate that morning. The lights, however, were very low, so that it was difficult to adjust our eyes to the darkness. But once the door had shut behind us, the lights were turned up only to disclose before us, with his back to the prelate's desk, not His Eminence, but the man we had come to take, looking at us coldly and not without amusement from above the gleaming barrel of a revolver.

"Ah, Mr. Solar Pons, we meet without dissembling," he said. "Not really our first meeting – but very probably our last."

I saw now that our quarry had affected his robes; he stood in princely splendor, with the gleam of madness clear in his eyes.

"You realize, of course – you are surrounded," said Pons.

The Black Cardinal bowed. "The house, Mr. Pons – *I* am not. I do not intend to be taken. At this point, it would hardly be convenient for any government to allow me life. In less than five minutes, I will be on the river. The United States – Boston, perhaps – will offer me haven. I can begin my private war anew."

He stepped backward around the desk.

I gathered myself for a leap. Even the capture of the Black Cardinal was not sufficient price for Pons' life.

"You cannot shoot us both," I said.

The Black Cardinal laughed harshly. Then, instead of pulling the trigger, he threw the weapon at Pons, and vanished behind the portieres. Pons caught the weapon, aimed it, and pulled the trigger. There was no explosion. The weapon was empty!

Pons flung himself through the portieres upon the panel. His deft fingers traveled swiftly over the woodwork in an endeavor to find the spring which would release the panel.

"The Primate, Parker – see to him," he cried.

I ran into the adjoining chamber. The Primate of all England sat bound and gagged in a chair. His alert eyes welcomed me.

I cut him loose.

"So, it is over," he said quietly. "I heard. I submitted to his indignities for I believed him less harmful here at my side than loose upon the world."

He staggered to his feet and hastened to Pons' side to touch the spring that opened the panel.

He waved us into the opening. "To the cathedral," he said. "Go! I am unharmed."

Pons sprang into the opening, I at his heels. We raced for some distance along level floor; then we came to a sharp descent which Pons made in three great steps. We found ourselves then in a long stone passage, at the end of which an ascent of eleven steps brought us to a blank wall. Pons sought and found the spring which opened the wall to us in the same fashion that the Primate had opened the first panel. We found ourselves now behind the high altar of the cathedral. Without ceremony, Pons rushed around the altar and down the steps to the lower level of the side altars. A few startled worshippers stared at us in amazement. We ran down the long center aisle and came out through the vestibule to the outer steps of the cathedral.

Pons' wild appearance immediately attracted the attention of a constable who recognized him. "Mr. Pons!" he cried.

"Who are you, Constable?"

"Wilson, sir."

"Has anyone come out within the past few minutes, Wilson?"

"An elderly gentleman, sir. One of the worshippers."

"Tall, thin?"

"Yes, Mr. Pons."

"Wilson, were you not instructed to stop anyone who emerged?" demanded Pons.

"Sir, only clergyman."

"Ah, the glory of Scotland Yard! A pox on Jamison's literal mind! That was our man. Round up your men and notify the river detail. He is making his escape on the Thames." Pons stabbed the dusk with his index finger. "Is that a police car down there, Wilson?"

"Yes, sir."

"We will take it. Notify Jamison."

Pons leaped down the steps and out into the street, where he commandeered the police car. In moments we were careening up the Avenue and out upon Victoria Street, only to stop at the first telephone booth to catch Pons' eye. There he spent fully ten minutes, while I fidgetted in the car.

When he came back, we drove furiously southward.

"Where are we going?" I asked finally.

"To Croydon. I managed to find Bancroft. There will be an armed plane waiting for us. The river detail may be too slow."

"An armed plane!" I cried. "Pons – you don't mean to shoot him?"

Pons smiled grimly. "He cannot be allowed loose on the world, Parker."

I need not dwell on that wild ride to Croydon, nor on the gaping wonder with which we were greeted on our arrival. The armed aeroplane was there, right enough; Bancroft had moved with his customary dispatch. Our pilot was impressed with the importance of his mission, and we were soon zooming away over London along the line of the Thames at a speed that more than made up for the time we had lost in London.

Out of Woolwich, our spotlight found the police boats going at a good rate toward Erith. We swept the line of the river, seeking our quarry on either shore as we went along.

We were almost at Erith before we caught up with the Black Cardinal. We had begun to think he had vanished into the recesses of the docks when suddenly the spotlight passed over a speeding boat on the water below.

"Lower!" cried Pons.

The pilot banked and turned. The spotlight swung in a great arc and again flashed over our quarry as we approached the countryside and the river. Pons leaped to the machine gun.

But as the light caught and held the speeding figure, and the pilot regulated the aeroplane's speed to that of the fleeing figure in the boat below, the Black Cardinal leaped up and away from the boat and was lost in the swirling water.

Boat and aeroplane shot forward; we were out of range of our quarry.

The pilot banked again and turned.

"Worse than futile!" cried Pons. "See there! The green lights of the police boats. Back to Croydon."

We had failed in our desperate gambit.

It was not until noon of the following day that we learned the outcome of the police search. The Black Cardinal had not, after all, made good his escape. His drowned body had been found just prior to Jamison's telephone call; the Thames had quenched his flaming hatred and drowned his grandiose dreams forever.

VII

THE ADVENTURE OF THE TROUBLED MAGISTRATE

"Justice," said Solar Pons, as we sat on either side of the fire in our lodgings one misty November evening, "is a comparatively rare commodity, perhaps because it is so difficult of definition. I daresay, therefore, it is altogether fitting that one of His Majesty's magistrates should be uneasy in mind. Tell me, Parker, does the name Fielding Anstruther mean anything to you?"

"I can't say that it does," I answered after reflection.

"It was but one chance in a thousand that you might have seen the name in the lists appended to some of those ridiculous petitions for the abolition of capital punishment which come up from time to time. He is a magistrate in the West country, and it would appear, unless his daughter is in error, that he is very much disturbed. This came for me half an hour before your arrival."

So saying, he reached into the pocket of his dressing-gown and tossed an envelope to me.

I opened the letter inside and read it.

"Dear Mr. Pons.

"As I am visiting in London for a few days I am taking the liberty of addressing you to learn whether I may call to discuss my father's trouble. He is Mr. Fielding Anstruther, magistrate at Ross, and I fear the curious events following the assizes have upset him most grievously. If the messenger fails to bring me an adverse response, I will expect to call at No. 7B at eight o'cock this evening.

"I am, sir, yours respectfully,
Violet Anstruther."

I looked up. "This is surely an intriguing little note."

"Is it not?" agreed Pons, his eyes dancing. "And one would have expected that the curious events to which Miss Anstruther refers might have achieved some public notice. But search as I may, I find little in the columns of the newspapers to suggest what it is that troubles the honorable magistrate. Save, perhaps, this little item from the *News of the World* a week ago."

He picked up the newspaper from beside his chair and read, "Death of Percy Dixon. Percy Dixon was found dead this morning at Ross, Hereford. Mr. Dixon had recently been charged in the matter of Henry Archer, who was the victim of foul play six months ago in his place of business in Ross. Dixon was discharged because of insufficient evidence. He appeared before Mr. Justice Anstruther.'"

"There is surely nothing curious about that," I said.

"No, since coincidence is far more usual than people like to believe," observed Pons. "Nevertheless, I find it interesting in the circumstances."

"Our client's letter mentions 'events' – so these must have been plural."

Pons glanced at the clock on the mantel. "It lacks but a few minutes of eight, and I fancy we shall have to abate our curiosity until that hour."

He filled his clay pipe with the abominable shag he smoked and settled back to wait. But he had hardly done so, when there was a ring at the outer bell, and within a few moments Mrs. Johnson showed in a young lady in her late twenties, a fine figure of a woman, with challenging black eyes and a provocative mouth, who, with the unerring intuition of her sex, instantly addressed herself to Pons.

"Mr. Pons, I am Violet Anstruther."

"Come in, Miss Anstruther. Dr. Parker and I have been awaiting you."

I had got up to draw forward a chair for our client, who thanked me and sat down as she loosened the fur piece about her neck. She betrayed a certain agitation only in the nervous way in which she clenched and unclenched her hands.

"I'm at my wits' end, Mr. Pons," she began, "or I would never have come to you."

I flashed a glance at Pons, but this little "compliment" appeared to have escaped him.

"And I'm sure that if my father knew I had come, he would be furious. He is a very reserved and proud man – very sure of himself within his world, which is that of law and justice – and certain matters would seem to have conspired to unsettle him."

"You mentioned 'certain events' in your note, Miss Anstruther, and now speak of them again. Do you do so with direct knowledge from your father?"

"No, Mr. Pons. That is the problem. For some months now father has paced the floor long hours in the night. His appetite has fallen off. He cannot seem to sleep, yet he looks dreadfully tired. He is often so preoccupied that he is sometimes not aware that we've spoken to him."

"'We'?"

"My Aunt Susan, father's younger sister, lives with us." She went on. "He has lost weight, and makes some little joke or other when I call his preoccupation to his attention. Of what is on his mind, he has not said a word, I've not asked him directly, but I know if he had any intention of speaking, he would do so.

"Mr. Pons, I thought at first that perhaps money matters were at the root of his trouble. But this is not so. I have assured myself of that. His investments are sound, and our income hasn't fallen off in the least. We're comfortably situated; at mother's death she left a considerable sum, which was an adequate amount even after death duties. Nor could I find any variation in his daily habits, other than those I've just mentioned, that would suggest some important alteration in his personal life. He has received no unusual mail; no one, other than the customary companions of his lifetime, has called upon him; indeed, Mr. Pons, I can think of nothing but that he is concerned over the way in which some of his cases have been disposed of, post-trial, so to speak."

"Ah, then Mr. Dixon is not the only gentleman who has appeared before your father to have subsequently died?" put in Pons.

"No, sir. He is only the most recent. This day week, in fact. He is the third, altogether. The first was Hester Spring. It seems probable that she smothered her baby. My father is a very just, upright man, and he felt there was a possibility of accident. She died about a month after her discharge. The coroner's jury decided that her death was an accident; she had been drinking and smothered in her bed."

"And the next?"

"The second was Algy Burke. He ran down old Mr. Carter one night months ago. He served four months and paid a fine, too. He died in an accident – run over one night when he stepped out of his yard to walk up the street toward the pub. The driver of the car was never found."

"And Mr. Dixon?"

"That was apparently something to do with his heart, Mr. Pons."

"What of the matter in which he was charged?"

"Mr. Archer was held up and robbed in his shop. He seems to have put up some resistance and was brutally struck on the head. He died in the hospital a day later, as a result of this blow. The general feeling in Ross is that Dixon did it, but my father felt that the case was not proven, and again directed a verdict of acquittal. I know it sounds typically like a woman's reasoning, Mr. Pons, but I've looked everywhere else for something to fix upon, and I can come up with nothing other than these – well, they are simply coincidences."

"Are they?" asked Pons thoughtfully. "I wonder. I am always suspicious of coincidences, no matter how frequently they take place. They may not be the work of the Prime Mover."

He cogitated for a moment, then asked, "These events were consecutive as you narrated them."

Our client hesitated briefly. "Yes, Mr. Pons."

"I detect some hesitation in your voice, Miss Anstruther."

"That is to say, Hester Spring, Algy Burke, and Percy Dixon died in that order. Actually, though, Dixon's case was first in order before my father – then Burke, then Spring."

Pons sat for a moment in deep thought, while our client preserved a respectful silence, intently watching Pons' lean face as he sat with eyes closed, contemplating what she had told him. Presently he opened his eyes and gazed soberly at Miss Anstruther.

"These little coincidences have all taken place in Ross?" he asked.

"Yes, Mr. Pons."

"Yet Mr. Justice Anstruther sits elsewhere in the assizes?"

"Yes, of course, Mr. Pons."

"And have these coincidences dogged his decisions elsewhere?"

"Not to my knowledge."

"Curious," murmured Pons. "Most curious."

"Mr. Pons, will you look into the matter for me?"

"I confess my interest in what you have told me, Miss Anstruther," said Pons, "but if your father is determined to lock his trouble inside him, it may be difficult to approach him."

"Father sits tomorrow at Ross. It is the case of a wife beater, and father will have little sympathy for him. I propose to invite you and Dr. Parker – if he will come – " (here she smiled very prettily in my direction) – "to be my guests at dinner in our home so that you may see father for yourself. If you have no objection, since father may know your name, I propose to introduce you as – let us say Professor Moriarty of Kings' College."

Pons smiled. He got to his feet and said, "Done."

"Paddington in the morning, Mr. Pons. The train will bring you to Ross by late afternoon. I myself leave by the last train tonight."

After she had taken her leave, Pons returned to the fireside and sat for a long time in thoughtful silence, his eyes closed, his fine, lean fingers tented before him. Presently he glanced over at me and spoke.

"What do you make of it, Parker?"

"I'm afraid I can say only it is all an emotional woman's imagination," I replied.

"What!" cried Pons. "Three people have died. I should hardly call that imagination."

"God disposes in His mysterious way," I retorted. "It may sound trite, Pons, but that seems to be the long and short of it.

"Ah, but even He may have a little help now and then," said Pons, smiling enigmatically.

"Pons, you aren't serious!" I protested. "This is surely nothing more than a series of coincidences."

"I have not said it is other than that," said Pons amiably.

"I fancy that far more than three people escaped justice at Mr. Anstruther's hands, in deference to his horror of wrongly punishing anyone, and that they are all in good health."

"Well, that is a very sensible conclusion."

"I hope I may always be, as you put it, 'sensible,'" responded Pons, with a wry smile and a twinkle in his keen eyes. "But perhaps Mr. Justice Anstruther does not think the author of these events Providence."

"I have often found that judges tend, after a long term, to equate themselves with Providence."

Pons smiled. "I daresay it is idle to speculate in the matter. We have too few facts to assimilate. If your wife can spare you, pray give me the pleasure of your company tomorrow."

Late the following afternoon we crossed the lovely Severn and were soon entering Ross, a country town above the left bank of the Wye, and one little spoiled by industrialization. Our client herself waited at the station in a pony cart.

She seemed completely recovered from her agitation of the previous evening, as she announced that she had taken rooms for us at the Swan and added, "Nothing has changed at home, Mr. Pons. But you'll see for yourself when you meet father at dinner tonight."

"I look forward to it, Miss Anstruther."

Our client drove us to the Swan, where we left our valises. Then we went around to her home on the far edge of the village. It was a gracious Victorian house, surrounded by a hedge. A two-car garage was attached and, beyond it, a small shed and stall combined, which doubtless housed our conveyance when it was not in use.

"For the time being," explained Miss Anstruther as she led us into the house, "we are quite alone except for the cook, who is preparing dinner. Aunt Susan spends a few hours every afternoon assisting at the local hospital – she has had some nurse's training – and the two of us take turns at the type-scripts of my father's notes and papers."

"These no doubt include the records of his cases," said Pons.

"Yes – and of course, lectures he often gives, and letters to the press – he feels very strongly opposed to capital punishment, Mr. Pons."

"I was aware that he is," said Pons. "I hope you will not take it amiss if I seek to draw him out on the subject at dinner."

"By no means. It is perhaps the only subject that will stir him from his preoccupation."

Pons' glance now lingered on what was obviously a man's easy-chair, with a little rack of books beside it and one open on its arm, turned face down. I looked at its title – *Somnambulism and Its Causes* – and observed three other books on similar subjects mingled with obviously legal tomes on the rack.

Noticing our interest, our client said, "That is where father spends much of the night, when he is not pacing the floor. Oh, Mr. Pons, do you think you can help him?"

"We shall see."

We had not long to wait for the arrival of the other members of the household. As it happened, they came together in the car driven by our client's aunt, who had driven around to court to give her brother a lift. He appeared to be a man not much over fifty, and she perhaps not quite ten years younger. They were rather dour-faced people, clearly brother and sister, and their features had a curiously equine appearance, being long and rather more broad than the average, with firm, almost prognathous jaws, wide mouths, and clear, direct eyes.

They did not seem very much surprised to meet guests at their table, which suggested that our client was left perfectly free to lead her own life – as, plainly, each of them led his.

"Professor Moriarty?" repeated the magistrate. "Sir, that is a familiar name. What is your field?"

"Sociology," replied Pons without a trace of guile. "I am in a very real sense a student of my fellowmen."

"The proper study of man," agreed Anstruther.

Our client called us to the table for dinner as Pons and Anstruther were talking. As we sat down, Pons continued. "And you, sir, have you not made a name for yourself in your efforts to make capital punishment obsolete?"

The magistrate seemed mildly pleased. "If I may say so," he said.

"It does not occur to you that the entire direction of the movement for abolition and all the concurrent goals may be a trifle unnatural?"

Anstruther frowned. His eyes fired. "In what way, Professor?"

"Why, sir," said Pons, waxing to his little game, "surely it must have struck you that the whole matter is against nature. Here we are engaged in preserving the unfit at the expense of the fit, decades after Mr. Darwin pointed out that in nature only the fit survive to best perpetuate the species."

"That is certainly a novel idea," said Miss Susan Anstruther, not without lively interest. "I had never thought of it that way."

"Hardly novel, dear lady," said Pons. "It's only the broad view. I've always found that opponents of capital punishment, devotees of correctional treatment over punitive action, and the like, are incapable of seeing the forest for the tree – for the sake of one human being, they are quite willing to ruin society." He turned again toward our host. "Does this strike you as heresy, Mr. Anstruther?"

"I suppose," said the magistrate with a fine edge of sarcasm, "it is what you might call evolutionary."

"*Touché*!" cried Pons, smiling. "And what do you call your view?"

"I am a simple humanitarian, Professor."

"Ah, yes," said Pons, resuming the attack with spirit, "I have never known it to fail but that every one of these theorists – call them welfare workers or psychoanalysts or even sociologists – would have us believe theirs is the humanitarian view and any other is brutalization of the finer instincts of mankind. They are all perfectly willing to consign half a dozen worthy human beings to the grave, if they can 'rehabilitate' – I believe they call it – one lost sheep who would have left society somewhat richer if he had been quietly executed without delay in the first place."

Our host was plainly astounded, if not outraged. "Sir, that is a medieval view!"

"Another catchword. Another label," said Pons. "Mr. Justice Anstruther, I put it to you that the essential fabric of society would be vastly improved if we could liquidate a basic ten percent of mankind without quibbling about these purely false moral issues."

"Professor, that is monstrous," cried the magistrate in tones of horror. "I cannot believe you are serious."

"I was never more so," said Pons.

"There's something in what Professor Moriarty says," said Miss Susan Anstruther, her eyes glinting with excited interest.

"It is all there," said Pons.

Our host was by now almost speechless. "You hardly talk like a sociologist," he said with a touch of asperity in his voice. "Unless you've taken your training in one of the Continental countries where they hold that certain types of humans are superior to others – or in the Orient, where they consider human life of no consequence whatever."

"My education, sir, is much humbler. Public school and Oxford. *Summa cum laude*, I should add."

If Pons had set out to outrage our host, he could have taken no other course with equal success. Justice Anstruther was by now almost purple with suppressed anger; he had not lifted a morsel of food to his lips since Pons' position had come clear to him, but he was too much the gentleman to forget his place as our host and could not give himself to venting the anger he manifestly felt. Pons, however, had achieved his goal, and he now spoke in more mollifying tones.

"But at least you, sir, practice what you believe. Your court has a reputation for lenience."

Mr. Justice Anstruther swallowed. "I try to be fair, sir."

"My brother bends over backwards," put in Miss Susan Anstruther, not without indignation. "He gives every consideration to the criminal."

"And none to the victim," said Pons, chuckling. "An all too human trait. One does not see before one what is safely in the grave."

I thought Mr. Justice Anstruther would burst with fury. I put in quickly, "In my profession, too, we prefer to save lives – not destroy them."

Our client was beginning to show signs of puzzled distress. She looked from Pons to me, from me to her father and back to Pons. She no more than I knew what Pons was about, but she shared my hope that Pons would soon drop the subject. Quite as if he read our minds, Pons abruptly did so.

"But our positions are patently not reconcilable, sir," he said quietly, "and perhaps I have not given this matter as much thought as it needs. Of late, too, I have been much engaged in the study of somnambulism. Tell me, sir, do you ever walk in your sleep?"

The effect of this simple question upon our host was positively astounding. The angry red and purple washed out of his face as if a drain had been opened to draw these mottled colors away. Mr. Justice Anstruther went deadly pale; his fork clattered to the table, though he had been holding it in his clenched fist like a weapon during Pons' outrageous discourse; his fingers fell to the table's edge and gripped there; and his eyes fixed on Pons as if he looked upon a ghost.

I leaped up. "Sir, you are unwell!"

He shook his head, not trusting himself to speak. Slowly he pushed his chair back from the table. Our client flashed Pons a glance of mingled dismay and perplexity as she went around to her father's elbow.

Mr. Justice Anstruther came slowly to his feet, regaining his dignity. He bowed formally. "Pray excuse me, gentlemen."

Then he walked steadily from the room, our client at his heels.

Miss Susan Anstruther got to her feet, too, somewhat agitated and reproachful in her manner. She meant to escape the scene, but Pons was not yet ready to let her go.

"I could not help observing that your views are directly opposed to your brother's, Miss Anstruther," said Pons.

"Oh, yes," she said, her expression altering at once, and the same kind of fire coming into her eyes as had burned in her brother's during his anger at Pons. "There are so many who get away. Week after week. Rapists, wife-killers, drunken drivers – all kinds of murderers – turned loose on technicalities which are a mockery of justice. To rape and stab and shoot and butcher again and again!" She bit her lip suddenly. "I try to tell my brother."

"You feel strongly about this, Miss Anstruther."

"I do, I do indeed. But it is Fielding who is the justice – not I. Besides, Henry was my friend – a very dear friend." Here her eyes grew misty with tears and her agitation increased. "*He*... just lets them go!" She seemed to shudder, controlled herself, and said quietly, "If you will excuse me – it's time for me to go to church."

Pons and I both rose and bowed as she went out.

Now that we were alone, I could no longer hold back my sentiments. "In all the years I've known you, Pons," I cried, "I have seldom witnessed anything more disgraceful than your conduct this evening."

"Was it not!" he agreed enthusiastically.

"How can you sit there so calmly and admit it?"

"Because it is perfectly true," he said with equanimity.

Miss Violet Anstruther came back into the room, her eyes flashing, her hands clenched.

Pons was equal to the occasion. "Pray forgive me, Miss Anstruther. I must apologize for what must have seemed to you an inexcusable display of bad manners. But I trust you have seen that it had its *raison d'etre*. Your poor father, for all his convictions, has all along had some doubts about certain of the cases up before him, and, since the hand of Providence seems to have made other disposition of his discharges, he has become obsessed with the conviction that he himself has been the instrument of Providence as he walks in his sleep.

"I observed as I came in this afternoon that your father was reading books about somnambulism and ventured a shot in the dark; it struck the bull's eye."

Our client sank down into her chair, bewildered. "Mr. Pons, I am dreadfully upset. I fail to see that you have resolved my father's doubts – rather the contrary," she said haltingly.

"My dear young lady, I have only begun to look into the matter. And now, if you will excuse us, I wish to pursue my inquiry elsewhere."

Miss Anstruther hurried to the vestibule where she had hung our outer clothing.

Pons paused at the threshold. "By the way, has your father ever left the house at night, to your knowledge?"

Miss Anstruther's face paled a little. "I believe he did go outside once or twice."

Pons nodded, satisfied. "Your aunt left us for church," he said then. "I take it there are evening services?"

"Not always, Mr. Pons. My aunt is a retiring sort of woman. She spends much of her time in charities, hospital work, and in church."

Still Pons lingered. "I daresay the inquest on Mr. Dixon will have been held by this time."

"Yes, Mr. Pons."

"Can you give me the coroner's name?"

"Dr. Allan Kirton, King's Head Road. I could drive you there, Mr. Pons, if you wish."

"We'll walk or take a cab, thank you, Miss Anstruther. I believe you should be at your father's call. Do not hesitate to reveal our little deception to him if he should question you."

We bade her good-evening and were off into the village.

"Pons," I said, once we were out of earshot of the house, "this is incredible. It is hardly likely that a man with Anstruther's convictions should have such deep-seated doubts as to give rise to such a delusion as you suggest."

"Is it not? I submit, Parker, that the fantasies of the human mind are virtually unlimited. Mr. Justice Anstruther is an honorable, self-righteous man, satisfied with his way of life, confirmed in his convictions. But there are chinks in his armor, and that he could even for a moment entertain such a fantasy is proof of it."

"Do you intimate there is more to it than that?"

"That, in fact, Anstruther did take some kind of somnambulic action? It may be so. You're a medical man, Parker. Can you deny that the possibility exists?"

"Such things have happened," I was forced to admit. "But it is a well-known truth that no man asleep would perform any act which it is against his nature to do when he is awake."

"I am not adequately acquainted with Mr. Justice Anstruther's nature," said Pons dryly, and thereafter said no more until we presented ourselves to Dr. Allan Kirton.

The coroner was a cheerful little man, pink-cheeked, white-haired, and voluble. He could hardly have been more than sixty years of age, and welcomed us with a lively manner.

"I certainly never expected to see Mr. Solar Pons in Ross," he said, bustling us into his house.

"A little challenge has been put to me here, Doctor," explained Pons. "I should dislike to fail it. You may recall that my illustrious predecessor once undertook to solve a crime in the vicinity – in Boscombe Valley."

"I recall it, indeed I do, sir. But we have nothing of that sort to invite your talents."'

"I am interested in Percy Dixon."

"A scoundrel."

"Dead."

"And good riddance."

"He died a natural death?"

"He did. We found heart failure."

"No suggestion of violence?"

"Not a mark on him, other than what you'd expect."

"And what would one expect, Dr. Kirton?"

"Well, Mr. Pons, he'd been in the hospital for a day or two, and naturally there was the mark of a hypodermic injection."

"Only one?"

"Only one."

"I take it you required the hospital chart for the inquest?"

Dr. Kirton smiled. "I still have it here, Mr. Pons. Would you like to see it?"

"If I may."

"You shall."

He bounced out of his chair, retired into an inner room, and returned with the chart in question. He handed it to Pons, who gazed at it with narrowed eyes which did not conceal his keen interest.

"Hm! Blood pressure, 178/101. A trifle high."

"A bit. Consistent with his situation. He had been found unconscious in the street. They thought, of course, he'd been taken suddenly ill." The coroner chuckled.

"Pulse, 48. Low. Respiration difficult. Oxygen and ice-pack."

"He was only drunk, Mr. Pons. The fellow was a lout. No wonder his heart gave out."

Pons handed the chart to me. It represented nothing but the standard treatment for anyone brought into a hospital unconscious, with irregular respiration, pulse and blood pressure. "You held the inquest on Hester Spring?" asked Pons then.

"Of course, Mr. Pons. A clear case of suffocation. Ironic, too. That was the way her baby died. She was cleared of that, but chiefly because of Anstruther's softness."

"I take it there was no suspicion of foul play?"

Kirton shook his head vigorously. "Absolutely none. There was a complete absence of motive."

"I see."

"I'm afraid you're on a wild goose chase, Mr. Pons," said Kirton cheerfully. "Open and shut cases, both of them. Open and shut. Both inquests were purely routine matters. Oh, carefully done, sir – I saw to that. But routine, just routine." After a few pleasantries, we bade Dr. Kirton good night and withdrew.

At the Swan half an hour later, Pons made himself comfortable, while I sat to wait upon his inevitable question. It came presently.

"You noticed nothing unusual about the hospital chart on Dixon, Parker?"

"Nothing. The treatment was standard. I looked in vain for evidence that he might have fallen – contusion, bruise, something of that sort; but since there was none, he plainly did not hurt himself when he fell."

"Otherwise, nothing?"

"Oh, come, Pons – I've read thousands of hospital charts."

"All the more reason for studying each with care," said Pons, with that infuriating air of having observed something that had escaped me, which was ridiculous, because I had looked over the Dixon chart with such care that I could have recited it from beginning to end if called upon to do so.

He subsided into thoughtful silence, and sat tugging the lobe of his left ear, his eyes half-closed. He sat thus for a quarter of an hour before he spoke again.

"An interesting problem. I shall regret leaving it."

"Ah-ha! Then it was as I said," I could not help pointing out. "I think, Pons, before you go, you ought to apologize to Mr. Justice Anstruther."

"I intend to do so," replied Pons. "No later than tomorrow breakfast. In the meantime, I have a few little enquiries yet to make. While you sleep, I shall go out into Ross and look about a bit more."

He put on his long grey travelling-cloak once again, bade me good night, and slipped out of our quarters.

Early next morning we presented ourselves at the home of our client, who herself opened the door to us. At sight of us, her left hand flew to her lips, as if to prevent an outcry.

"Good morning, Miss Anstruther," said Pons. "I trust your father is still at home?"

"He is, Mr. Pons. He's at breakfast with Aunt Susan."

"Good, good! I should like to speak to him at once. Have you disclosed our little deception?"

"No, sir. I lacked the courage."

"No matter."

She stood aside reluctantly. Pons, however, pushed into the house and made directly for the dining-room.

Our host of the previous evening looked his astonishment at sight of us. He would have come to his feet, had not Pons spoken.

"Pray keep your seat, Mr. Anstruther. I have come primarily to offer my apologies for my conduct at dinner last night."

"I am sure, Professor..." began the magistrate stiffly.

"Sir, my name is not Moriarty," interrupted my companion. "It is Solar Pons. I am not even a professor."

But my companion's name was evidently familiar to Mr. Justice Antruther, for, though his face paled at Pons' disclosure, his apprehension now gave way to a strange air of resignation.

"So it has come, Mr. Pons," he said quietly.

"Yes, sir. But hardly, I daresay, as you expected."

"A police enquiry?"

"A private investigation."

"They *were* murdered!"

"I have reason to believe so. But not by a man who might have walked in his sleep! You should discipline your conscience, sir. There might have been more murders – for they are technically that, even though they were conceived as executions – save that other potential victims were simply not available to the murderer. And there is, too, the suggestion that the compulsion toward murder had been satisfied with the death of the one person the murderer desired to see punished.

"The murderer had to be someone thoroughly familiar with the cases before you, with access to data perhaps not wholly available through the press or even in the course of the trials. It had to be someone who could slip into Hester Spring's house beside the church – or who could follow or accompany her in when Spring was intoxicated and smother her when she was too addled to save herself – someone who could bide his time and run down Algy Burke, or who could do it on impulse after long design when the opportunity presented itself – someone who could pump a bubble of air into a man's vein without suspicion."

"A nurse," said our client.

"And last night, after learning that she was on duty at the hospital just before Percy Dixon was discharged, I took the liberty of making a close scrutiny of your sister's car..."

"Not Susan!" cried Anstruther.

Our client stifled an outcry.

Miss Susan Anstruther, however, only smiled. "They deserved to die," she said with an air of triumph. "My brother always was soft-hearted. It's monstrous to realize how many criminals are being turned back upon society."

Mr. Justice Anstruther gazed at her with an expression of absolute horror on his face, and our client, too, listened as if she could not believe what she heard.

"Those indentations on my car could have come from any source, Mr. Pons," said Susan Anstruther contemptuously. "And an embolism is hardly traceable. I'm afraid you would be chided if you came before my brother with such evidence, and he would direct a verdict of acquittal. Isn't that true, Fielding?"

Mr. Justice Anstruther was speechless.

"You needn't answer," she went on. "And you couldn't sit on the case. But I don't think Mr. Pons has any intention of going into court with such a mass of theory unsupported by sufficient fact, or he would never have come here with his story. Do you, Mr. Pons?"

"There would appear to be another way to dispose of the matter."

"Commitment," said Justice Anstruther. "It can be arranged."

"Oh, no!" cried our client.

"Dear Violet would rather have a sensational trial," said the older woman. "But there won't be any trial. There are more madmen outside than in the institutions set aside for them. I'm tired – and now Henry's gone..."

"Henry?" repeated Anstruther.

"Henry Archer – Dixon's victim," said Pons. "Miss Susan's 'very dear friend' – it was his death that fired your sister's zeal to become the public executioner."

Miss Susan Anstruther smiled bitterly, closed her eyes, and bowed her head.

"Sister! Sister! What have you done?" murmured Justice Anstruther.

Pons took out his watch. "If you will excuse us, we have just time to catch the train."

In our compartment, while the train sped toward London through the lovely land that is Herefordshire, Pons could not help pointing up my failure.

"It was not, you see, what *was* on the hospital chart that was important – but what *was not*. The coroner distinctly mentioned having observed the mark of a hypodermic injection. Yet no record of such an injection appeared on the chart. One could hardly have expected Miss Susan to set down: 'One bubble of air, intravenously injected,' could one?

"Anyone might have had the opportunity to kill these three, but why then were other cases left untroubled if not because whoever did in these three had more ready access to them than to others? Furthermore, Mr. Justice Anstruther sat elsewhere but in Ross; yet it was only in Ross that Providence seemed inclined to intefere with his disposition of his cases. Access was thus of prime importance.

"Miss Spring's house stood beside the church Miss Susan frequented. Miss Susan worked in the hospital to which Percy Dixon was admitted – and to which he had been admitted many times previously as a victim of *delirium tremens*, as she well knew. Algy Burke's death might have been the result of sudden impulse – or it might have been planned; I submit, however, that it was impulse, because premeditation would have meant that Miss Susan would have had to watch his place, and that might have made her conspicuous and thus directed suspicion to her. Perhaps Mr. Justice Anstruther's fear of his own sleepwalking was only a blind to prevent himself from seeing what his sister did – for he certainly knew that she disagreed vehemently with his concept of justice.

"The whole matter, however, was elementary, if different. The only possible motive for altering the court's decision to a fatal disposal of the cases seemed to be a compulsion to exact justice as the murderer conceived it. Such a compulsion rises easily in many of us when justice seems to go awry, but those who feel it seldom act upon it. Miss Susan Anstruther must have known it for many years, but it took the murder of Henry Archer to drive her to action. What we shall never know is this – did she kill out of pure compulsion? – or were the executions of Spring and Burke planned to conceal the death of Dixon, for which there existed a possible motive in her friendship – or romance – with Archer?"

He shrugged. "However, when it comes to people playing God, I'm not sure I don't prefer the Susan Anstruthers to the mass of do-gooders – the self-appointed humanitarians, the psychoanalysts, the sociologists. The Susan Anstruthers of this world at least eliminate people who are in all likelihood guilty of crimes against society, while the do-gooders all too often, if indirectly, by their freeing of dangerous individuals in the delusion that they have been 'rehabilitated,' eliminate the innocent."

VIII

THE ADVENTURE OF THE BLIND CLAIRAUDIENT

"Ah," murmured Solar Pons from where he stood at the window of No. 7B, looking down into Praed Street, "I fancy we are about to have the offer of a case. What a pity I shall not be able to take it!"

I interrupted our packing for a holiday on the Continent and came over to his side to follow the direction of his gaze. A cab stood at the kerb, and, getting out of it were an elderly lady and her companion, a man of thirty-odd years.

"She must be quite infirm," I ventured. "See how she depends on her companion."

Pons chuckled. "No, Parker, she is blind. Observe the way she holds her head – she doesn't look down for the kerb, and her companion walks slightly in advance of her, guiding her steps."

"You didn't mention an appointment."

"I have none, so I am free to listen to the problem the lady is bringing to me."

"Why not the young man?"

"Oh, come, Parker! Why would a blind woman put herself to such trouble if only for a companion perfectly able to tell us his own story? No, the problem is hers.... Ah, they have roused Mrs. Johnson."

In a few moments our estimable landlady knocked gently on our door, then opened it and stuck her honest, scrubbed face, surmounted by coils of heavy hair, into the room.

"A lady to see you, Mr. Pons."'

"Send her in, by all means, Mrs. Johnson," said Pons.

Mrs. Johnson withdrew, swinging the door wide as she did so, revealing our prospective client and her companion. She did not now seem either so aged or infirm as I had taken her to be at first sight. She was a stout woman of about sixty-five. Her hair was greying, but the skin of her face was curiously little lined and had a kind of translucence, heightened by the black glasses which concealed her eyes. Led by her companion, a young red-haired man with a mottled skin and bushy brows over pale blue eyes, she stepped into the room.

"Mr. Pons," she said uncertainly. "Mr. Solar Pons?"

"Pray be seated," said Pons, motioning her companion to a chair.

"I am Lily MacLain, Mr. Pons. You may have seen my card in the papers."

"I've seen your card, Miss MacLain. 'Clairaudient Readings.' On Oakley Street, just around the corner from Cheyne Walk."

"I've been in Chelsea ever since I did a turn on the stage," said our client. "It's a good place for anyone with what they're beginning to call extra-sensory powers. This good young man is my nephew, Theodore Holt. He has served as my eyes since he came to live with me three years ago – after the most faithful of companions died."

"I daresay your problem hardly pertains to the future, if you can read it," said Pons

"Well, Mr. Pons, I do read the future. I do, indeed." She spoke slowly, as if she were choosing her words with care. "But there are limitations under which we all fall – all of us who have the gift. And the principal one is that few of us – very few of us – are ever able to penetrate the veil when it comes to ourselves. That picture seldom comes clear – it remains murky. But for others, no. For instance, Mr. Pons, I can tell you that you will soon solve an extraordinary series of crimes in which a bird serves as an accomplice to a murderer; you will be asked to investigate another series of murders involving a suspected werewolf; you will be instrumental in exposing a rather well-known doctor who has successfully done away with one wife and is only thwarted by your good offices in doing away with his second. But if I were to step out into the street within the hour only to be run down by a cab, I could not in all probability foresee it."

Pons' eyes twinkled; the ghost of a smile touched his lips. "But you haven't come here to expound upon my future, Miss MacLain."

"No, Mr. Pons. On mine. I want to pose an unusual problem for those talents which are especially yours. I'm not without funds. People pay well for my services. So few are content to let the veil be; they want it lifted. I am as well prepared to pay for your services as most of them are for mine. In short, Mr. Pons, I want you to avenge me."

"In what connection?"

"I want you to see to it that my murderer is punished."

Pons' eyes danced. "You anticipate being murdered?"

"'Anticipate' is not quite the word, Mr. Pons. Let us say rather that I will be murdered. It is not my future I've read. I've heard the voices. And they speak of murder."

"Let us start at the beginning, Miss MacLain," suggested Pons.

Our client pursed her lips thoughtfully. "I suppose you might say it began when I did a reading for a man who called himself Alistair Green. I say 'called himself' because many people fail to give their real names. He had marital difficulties, and I saw no future for him with his wife. In fact, I saw danger for him if he remained with her. Evidently he went home and began an argument which resulted in her leaving him. As a consequence, he developed a strong hatred for me; like most weak men, he tried to put blame for his own shortcomings elsewhere. He came to see me again and again – usually he had been drinking – and once he created such a disturbance, in the course of which he threatened me, that Theodore had to take care of him. Isn't that true, Theodore?"

"Yes, Aunt Lily," said her companion. "Mr. Pons, he threatened to kill my aunt."

"After which, of course, Theodore threw him out."

Her nephew nodded in confirmation. "He came five times in all – so far. He'll come again."

"Perhaps it is needless to say," said our client, "that we looked up Alistair Green at the address he had given us, but his address was as false as his name."

"Did you lodge information with the police?" asked Pons.

Our client shook her head with a faint smile. "Could they do any more than we did?"

"But you could have described him, Mr. Holt," pressed Pons.

"Mr. Pons, he came by night. My aunt keeps her place dimly lit for atmospheric reasons. I saw him, yes. He was short, blonde, with hair closely trimmed; he wore a moustache and he looked to be a sporty type – not the kind who usually consult my aunt."

Pons looked quizzically at Lily MacLain. "Would it not be simpler to apprehend this man and turn him in for having threatened you?"

"No, Mr. Pons. The police have never been kind to those of us who have the gift. They would dismiss such a charge brought by one in my calling, since in their eyes no very great crime was committed. I would only end up by angering him so much more."

"So you feel he is earnest enough in his threats to eventually carry it through?"

"Mr. Pons, I will die."

She said this as calmly as if she had long been resigned to it.

"Why need this be so?" pressed Pons. "In the face of warnings?"

"Mr. Pons, it will happen. A knife will be used. I invite your particular attention to the weapon. This man will come to my house in the night. As a result of his coming, I will die. You ask about 'need'. I can do nothing to prevent it. I'm not asking your pity; I ask only simple justice."

I could not help interrupting, not, I fear, without a trace of skepticism in my voice. "How can you know this, Miss MacLain?"

"Dr. Parker, I can understand the profound doubt of a medical man," our client answered. "Sir, in my calling, as I have said, we are unable to read our fate. But in projecting ourselves into the future through our gift, there is a point at which we lose awareness of ourselves; after that point we cease to exist. I am not aware of myself very far in the future."

"A police guard might be obtained for your home," I suggested.

"The police are needed on far more tangible difficulties than mine," said the clairaudient. "Mr. Pons, can I count on you?"

"At the moment, Dr. Parker and I are off to the Continent. Perhaps I can call on you on our return?"

"Thank you."

She extended one arm for her nephew and, supported by him, came to her feet. Then she bade us good-afternoon.

Once our client had gone, I could not prevent my protest from bursting forth. "I have a particular dislike for charlatanry of this kind, Pons – all this sort of clairvoyance, fortune-telling, palm-reading, and the like. It is all nonsense, designed to prey upon the hopes and fears of the ignorant."

"Who demand to be preyed upon," added Pons. "A healthy skepticism is a good attribute. I like to keep an open mind. One can never be positive in matters of this kind, however rational it seems to deny out of hand the manifestations of the so-called supernatural or extra-sensory."

"Pons, this woman's story was a rigmarole of the ridiculous," I cried. "Fancy retaining someone to avenge a murder not yet committed!"

"I am not nearly so positive as you, Parker. You have a happy faculty for seeing only the evidence which supports your prejudices. I can hardly afford such a luxury."

"Pons, you cannot believe this woman has foreseen her death!"

"*She* is certainly convinced that she will be murdered," replied Pons. "As to whether she has foreseen it in the reprehensible manner you infer – that is another matter. She has some reason quite beyond the clairaudience in which she professes to be adept. She has been actively threatened in the presence of at least one witness besides herself. On that score, her fears are not entirely groundless."

"A thousand persons are threatened for every one who is done to death," I said.

"Perfectly true, my dear fellow. It did not strike you, then, that there was something cogently convincing about Miss MacLain's appeal?"

"Not in the slightest."

"Did it occur to you that she may have had some ulterior motive in coming to me?"

"Perhaps."

"What, then, could it be?"

I shrugged. "You are the expert on ratiocination, Pons. Not I."

"Which makes it all the more a puzzle that you, who are not, should think her guilty of some ulterior motive. It suggests nothing to you that she avoids the police?"

"She explained that herself. The police, like myself – very wisely, too, if I may say so – have a natural distrust of charlatans."

"Let me put it this way – it does not seem to you that she may distrust the police as much as they may distrust her and that therefore she has come to me convinced that if she is slain the police are entirely likely to bungle the solution of her murder?"

I laughed. "Forgive my laughter," I said.

"My dear Parker, it reassures me." He smiled himself. "Nevertheless, there are certain aspects of this little problem which delight and challenge me. I believe it is the first time in all my years of making private enquiries that the victim of a murder..."

"A projected murder," I put in.

"Very well, a projected murder," agreed Pons imperturbably. "It is the first time that the victim has retained me to solve her murder before it has taken place."

"Pons, do you honestly expect her to be murdered?"

"I should not be inordinately surprised if her death by violence came about."

"As she has predicted?"

"Let us say, more or less as she has predicted."

"Pons, this is fantastic!" I cried. "That you, of all people, who rationalize everything, should be taken in by a type of predatory charlatan who is quite common the length and breadth of England!"

"Our client has been faced with certain premises and has drawn certain conclusions from them. Her clairaudience has played only a minor part in the matter. She has now laid before us these same premises, and it is plain to see that each of us has drawn diametrically different conclusions from them. But let us examine this little matter of clairaudience. What do you conceive it to be, Parker?"

"Simply stated, it is said to be the ability to hear sounds which are ordinarily beyond hearing. It is the aural equivalent of clairvoyance, which is presumed to be the ability to see events beyond the perception of others."

"By that definition a man whose ears are attuned to certain high-pitched sounds – like cries of birds and frogs – not commonly heard by other men, would be clairaudient?"

"Well, not exactly."

"Or a dog, that hears whistles which make no sound to our ears when we blow them, is then a clairaudient?"

I protested in exasperation. "No, no, it isn't like that at all. It's hearing something which could not possibly be heard! Like voices from next week or a conversation in another city, like those conversations from the future of which Miss MacLain spoke but a short time ago. You know very well what clairaudience is."

"Indeed, I do. But do you? I submit that it is perfectly possible for one person to be far more developed in one sense than most of the people who surround him. And this is particularly true of those who have to rely on the senses that remain to them after the loss of one – especially one so important as sight."

"I don't deny it. But I draw the line at someone who pretends to hear voices from the future. Lily MacLain professes to do so. She has said as much in so many words in our presence. You've heard her – so have I. This is charlatanry."

"Why? Because you do not have this gift?"

"Not at all. Because it refutes science!"

"Strong words, Parker! Strong words! Let us just say it goes against what we know of science at this point in the development of man."

"That's strong enough for me."

"And if science next week or next year or a half century hence uncovers a perfectly logical explanation for clairaudience in its currently most reprehensible form – I use the terminology your attitude suggests – then you, too, will subscribe to it?"

"Certainly."

Pons chuckled. "I must admit your attitude is scarcely different from that of those of our ancestors who proclaimed, 'This golden calf is All!' or 'This stone image is All!' or 'God is All!' In your case it is Science that is to be worshipped. Scientist though I take pride in being, I would be the last to suggest that our scientific discoveries to date have reached such a stage of perfection that we have achieved ultimate knowledge and no further advances are open to us."

"I've said no such thing!" I protested vehemently.

"You inferred it. But our problem here does not depend solely upon the issue of clairaudience," he went on. "We have a tangible potential murderer in the fellow who calls himself 'Alistair Green', and we have certain keys to his identity, despite Miss MacLain's pessimism. His wife has recently left him, and we know that he is a man who is slight of stature, light of weight, and much given to anger and bluster."

"How do you arrive at stature and weight, if I may ask?"

"You had a good look at our client's companion. Would you say he could be described as husky?"

"Hardly."

"Yet he 'threw Green' out of the house on Oakley Street. 'Green' must therefore be of even less weight and slighter of stature than Mr. Holt."

"Of course! I should have seen something so elementary."

"The most astonishing feats of ratiocination in the history of mankind seem elementary upon elucidation of the steps between premise and conclusion," observed Pons.

"But all that is hardly enough to put you on Green's trail."

"True. But did it not strike you that our client was not anxious that we *should* be set upon his trail?"

"Now that you mention it, she didn't seem particularly enthusiastic."

"So that, in effect, our client may have what the psychoanalytical gentlemen in your department would call 'the death-wish'. If she does not actively wish to die, she is resigned to the idea of death. Her wish is not for me to prevent the event she foresees, – take note – but to avenge it. Does this not strike you as singular?"

"Far-fetched, but not singular."

"Indeed! I submit it is one of the most provocative little puzzles I have ever had put before me. Time will tell us its meaning. I confess to some concern for Miss MacLain. Perhaps we could shorten our holiday by a week."

As we were stepping out of our cab in the early morning hours of a day just a week later, our landlady, who had been expecting us and had evidently been waiting upon our arrival, came hurrying down the steps of 7B, and called out, "You'll want that cab, Mr. Pons."

"Indeed!" said Pons.

"Inspector Jamison just left word you were to step around to Miss MacLain's house on Oakley Street," explained Mrs. Johnson.

Pons flashed me a cryptic glance. "We are too late," he said. "Take our bags into the vestibule, Parker, and we'll be off."

Inspector Jamison waited for us in the house on Oakley Street, enthroned in self-importance in the ornate parlor, which was furnished in quasi-Victorian fashion. Theodore Holt, manifestly dejected, sat silent nearby in the room to which the constable at the door admitted us.

"Well, Pons," said Jamison, "your late client has been murdered in the manner she told you she would be. We have the murderer, but in view of her application to you, Mr. Holt here insisted that we should send for you."

Pons turned to our late client's nephew. "Perhaps we may hear from Mr. Holt just what took place."

Holt looked up haggardly. "Certainly, Mr. Pons. I was awakened at just about midnight by an unusual sound. It was probably the breaking in of the window in my aunt's bedroom, but for a while then as I lay awake I heard nothing. Then my aunt stirred in her bed. I heard her call out, 'Is that you, Ted?' So I slipped out of bed at once, knowing she'd heard something I hadn't. I was on the stairs when I heard a kind of muffled blow. Aunt Lily groaned. I ran into her room to find this fellow bending over her bed. I had armed myself with a poker. I struck him – hard."

"Green?"

"Yes, Mr. Pons. That's what he called himself."

"Oh, he coshed him, all right, Mr. Pons," said Jamison appreciatively. "He was still out when we got there. We've only just sent him away."

"I'm sorry to say I was too late to save my poor aunt," concluded Holt. "Her visit to you was prophetic, Mr. Pons – more prophetic than I dreamed."

Pons listened attentively to this recital, and for a few moments stood in that attitude of deep thought so characteristic of him – head sunk on chest, eyes closed, the fingers of his right hand stroking his ear lobe. Then he stirred, his eyes opened, he looked at Jamison.

"Let us just have a look at the bedroom."

"Look all you like, Pons. It can't do any harm."

Holt came to his feet. "This way, Mr. Pons."

The adjoining bedroom was in disarray. The bed particularly was much disturbed. The body of Lily MacLain had been removed, but bloodstains lay in mute testimony to the crime which had taken place there only a few hours before. A window across the room from the bed in which the blind woman had lain had been opened by means of a pane broken in so that a hand could reach through and get at the lock; glass still lay on the sill and the carpet. It was the sound of this breakage which had undoubtedly awakened both Lily MacLain and her nephew.

"Where did you find her murderer?" Pons asked Jamison.

"Right there beside the bed, Pons. Just where he fell when Mr. Holt struck him."

"Who is the fellow?"

"His name's Jasper Howells. Employed by Instow & Son as a book-keeper. Wife recently left him. He's been around here several times. Had too much to drink each time. He admits that."

"Ah, you've had a statement from him?"

"Oh, yes. He came around before we took him in."

"He denied he had killed Miss MacLain, of course."

"Not in so many words, though most of them do. Said he couldn't remember all he'd done. He said he had called on his victim at half after nine – not half past eleven, the time he killed her. You could still smell liquor on him, and he talked like it, though it was a pretty sharp blow Mr. Holt gave him. He's got a skull fracture. If he hadn't been so hardheaded, he'd have been killed. He claims he fell into a stupor here and can't remember what happened. A very common defense, if I may say so – he's setting it up for his line at the trial. But Mr. Holt tells me Miss MacLain told you about his threatening her, Pons."

"True. If this is the same man who gave her the name 'Alistair Green'."

"It is, Mr. Pons," put in Holt.

Pons turned to him. "Tell me, Mr. Holt, is there anyone else who might have had enough animosity against your aunt to wish her dead?"

"I cannot say, sir, but I doubt it very much," Holt said somewhat reluctantly.

"I observe that you hesitate, Mr. Holt. Who is it?"

Holt attempted a weak smile. "There was a middle-aged man who had paid some attention to Aunt Lily. I believe he'd proposed to her. She spurned him. It upset him badly, and he talked a little wildly. But I'm sure he entertained no real animosity."

"When was this?"

"Oh, six weeks ago. He used to come here for readings at first. He'd been coming for all of seven years, Aunt Lily told me. She foretold his wife's death three years ago, and other little things."

Pons crossed to the window and looked out.

"Of course," continued Holt, "there were people who were dissatisfied with Aunt Lily's readings. There are always those. They go away disgruntled, sometimes angry, and sometimes they come back to tell her so. I could set down a list, if you like. But once they've got it off their minds, so to speak, they've done it and they forget all about it."

"A low window," murmured Pons. "The room is easy of access. The walk below would effectively eliminate footprints."

Jamison smiled indulgently. "We've been all about the place, Pons. Fine tooth comb, you might say. Now, in regard to what Miss MacLain told you a week ago – you'll be available for the trial, Pons?"

"Certainly, if the prosecution is generous enough to accept the testimony of amateurs."

"Oh, you amateurs sometimes do us a little service or two, Pons," said Jamison with unwonted generosity.

"Your flattery touches me, Inspector," said Pons, and turned again to Holt. "What is the name of that middle-aged fellow who was attentive to your aunt?"

"Gerald King, sir."

"Where can he be found?"

"He lives nearby. Over on Flood Street. Number 71."

"We've already had a go at him, Pons," said Jamison. "He denies he was turned down. Just the opposite. It would trouble his vanity to admit being turned down, wouldn't it? Some of these middle-aged fellows are touchy."

"Quite, quite," murmured Pons. "Now, if you don't mind, I'll just have a look around. The kitchen, I take it, lies at the back of the house?"

"This way, Mr. Pons," said Holt, starting from the room.

In the kitchen Jamison pointed to a carving knife on the table. "It was that kind of knife with which he killed her, Pons. Set of two."

"He used Miss MacLain's knife?"

"Oh, it was no risk coming out here to get it. She was blind, you'll remember."

"True, true. You have the weapon, of course?"

"Certainly, Pons."

"You've examined it for fingerprints?"

"That's being done. But I can tell you Howells' prints are on it as clear as they need be – to the naked eye – written in her blood."

Pons stood again in deep thought, his eyes partly closed. His fine nostrils trembled, and the entire expression on his feral face was that of a keen-scented animal hard on the track of prey. When he opened his eyes again, he gave the kitchen only a cursory glance. He gazed at Jamison.

"They'll be putting Howells through it at the Yard," he said. "Let me suggest you lose no time advising them to pay close attention to his fingertips – all sides."

Jamison favored him with a blank stare. "Oh, come, Pons," he said at last, "we've got him. Very full prints."

"I suggest you lose no time, Jamison," said Pons icily. "Evidence may be destroyed. At any time they may permit Howells to wash his hands. Get on the telephone and have a report sent back here without delay. Dust his nails, Jamison – his nails."

"The telephone's in here, Inspector," said Holt.

When Inspector Jamison returned, Pons asked, "What of the weapon? It was not found in the victim's body, I take it?"

"No. It was on the floor, next to Howells. By the look of it, he'd struck her once; not knowing whether it was fatal, he was about to strike her again, when Holt's blow dropped him. He let go of the knife."

"I assumed as much," said Pons.

"If I could have been only a few moments sooner," lamented Holt miserably.

"Never mind, sir," said Jamison. "You couldn't know."

"But she had been threatened! I should have been down without delay. He wouldn't have had time to find the knife then."

Pons now busied himself with a close examination of the kitchen, and then again the bedroom. He was still at this half an hour later when the call Jamison expected came through from Scotland Yard. Pons stood listening, the ghost of a smile on his face.

Jamison put down the telephone and turned a perplexed face to Pons. "Prints on the nails, Pons," he said.

"Identifiable?"

"Yes. But not identified. No record."

Pons turned to Holt. "Will you bring me a glass, Mr. Holt – an ordinary water glass?"

"Certainly sir."

Holt slipped into the kitchen and back, carrying a water tumbler.

"Just hand it to Inspector Jamison, Mr. Holt.... Carefully now, Jamison. Just compare those prints with the prints found on Howells' nails."

For an instant Jamison froze. The tableau held – Jamison stared at Pons, the expression on Holt's face melted. Then the scene exploded – Holt struck the glass from Jamison's hand, shattering it, and in the next instant dove for the window. But Pons was upon him with the litheness and speed of a cat and brought him to the floor.

"I give you the murderer of Lily MacLain, Jamison," said Pons, panting.

"But how did you come to this, Pons?" asked Jamison, still shaken, after Holt had been removed by two constables.

"If Lily MacLain was stabbed only once, and Howells was felled in the act of attempting to stab her again, how could it be that his prints can be found *in her blood* on the handle of the knife?" Pons shook his head. "No, Jamison, it won't wash. Howells helped to set himself up for the charge, but he isn't guilty. Holt killed her after he struck Howells down, then rolled Howells' prints on to the handle of the knife. And isn't it a little far-fetched to believe that a man bent on murder would come without a weapon?"

"But what reason had Holt for killing his aunt?"

"He had the strongest of motives. As his aunt's only heir, he would lose her not inconsiderable estate if she married, as evidently she contemplated doing. If you'll proceed on the assumption that Holt did not tell the truth, and that Howells and Gerald King are telling the truth, all the pieces of this little puzzle will fall into place. Spilsbury will supply all the scientific evidence you need."

"Extraordinary," I said, as we left the house on Oakley Street. "Yet the affair offers clear proof of the fallibility of Lily MacLain's clairaudience."

"Miss Lily MacLain's clairaudience may have been considerably more brilliant than either of us is prepared to admit," answered Pons.

"Prescience there was, certainly," I went on, "which is the mark of ordinary intelligence; there's nothing extra-sensory about it. But why did she come to us? And why, if she were not fallible, did she accuse Howells – or, by the name he used, 'Green'?"

"I fail to recall that she did," answered Pons as he hailed a cab coming past in the dawn light. "I submit, Parker, that she told us, as well as she could, that her nephew planned to murder her and put it on someone else."

"Oh, come, Pons!" I cried in protest.

We got into the cab and Pons did not speak for a few moments. Then he answered. "Part of the faculty of observation is a keen ear. You failed to listen. She said 'Green' had threatened her. He had begun to make fairly regular visits and created scenes. He usually did this when he was under the influence, which made him all the easier for Holt to handle. Now, I put it to you, Parker, that a man who means to kill very seldom goes out of his way to warn his victim; no, with each visit to annoy Lily MacLain, Howells was increasingly less likely to kill. Do you fancy our late client was unaware of this? I daresay not."

"Pons, I distinctly recall her saying she would die by his hand."

"No, no, Parker. You didn't listen carefully. She said she would be murdered. She said, 'A knife will be used. This man will come to my house in the night.' She did *not* say he would kill her. Her exact words were, 'As a result of his coming, I will die.' So she did.

"That she could have done more to prevent her death, I have no doubt. Why she did not must remain a puzzle. Her nephew served as her eyes. She did nothing without him. As she had depended upon that companion who died, she now depended upon him. Soon it became subtly altered – she could do nothing without his permission, she could not escape him even when she sensed that his greed for her possessions was overpowering, and her clairaudient powers – or intuition, if you like – told her he would attempt her life. Howells' loud threats gave her the chance to come here, and her nephew fell in with her plan because he knew how well it would serve him. Having thus set the stage, as he thought, Holt had only to wait until Howells came again, then keep him there until he was ready to do his shameful deed."

"Intuition, then – not clairaudience," I said.

"Was it intuition or extra-sensory power which caused her to invite my particular attention to the means of her death: the knife? It is folly to believe that anyone bent on killing another would put himself in the position of searching an unfamiliar house for a weapon instead of bringing his own. It will not be given to either of us to decide whether or not she was genuinely clairaudient," finished Pons enigmatically. "I fancy Lily MacLain will have the final word, Parker."

This, in the succession of cases which came to Pons' attention in the following months – among them those foreseen by Lily MacLain – she did.

A CHRONOLOGY OF SOLAR PONS
BY ROBERT PATTRICK

(From the 1961 Mycroft & Moran Edition)

(The late Robert Pattrick had virtually completed this chronology, save for certain disputed points, when he died early last year. The titles listed include only adventures chronicled in books, and not separately published magazine stories not yet collected.)

CANONS OF THE CHRONOLOGY – 1) All discoverable time-clues are used – such as dates given by Parker or any other person; references to events, dates of which are known; Parker's progress (or lack of) in learning Pons' methods; references to other stories, dates of which are known... 2) Dates given by Parker are accepted as final so long as they do not contradict one another. Where this has occurred, dating has been made on the basis of any other evidence contained in that or any other story.... 3) Should any problem prove undatable in spite of the above, the Chronologist has used his own judgment.... 4) Should any problem be published in the future which specifically contradicts any date given in this Chronology, rule 2 will be employed with *both* stories and adjustment made accordingly. In the event the new problem is one of those which Parker has mentioned (see "Untold Problems" following this Chronology) preference will be given to the new date, assuming, of course, it conforms in all other particulars.

THE CHRONOLOGY

MEETING OF PONS AND PARKER / JUNE 1921

The Adventure of the Sotheby Salesman / August, 1921 / Aldershot

The Adventure of Ricoletti of the Club Foot / September, 1921 / London

The Adventure of the Circular Room / April, 1922 / Richmond

The Adventure of the Purloined Periapt / May, 1922 / London

The Adventure of the Lost Locomotive / June, 1922 / Girton

The Adventure of the Five Royal Coachmen / June, 1922 / The Test River

The Adventure of the Frightened Baronet / August, 1922 / Chiltern Hills

The Adventure of the Limping Man / October, 1923 / Northumberland

The Adventure of the Perfect Husband / 1924 / London

The Adventure of the Dog in the Manger / 1924 / Stoke Poges

The Adventure of the Swedenborg Signatures / 1925 / Canterbury

The Adventure of the Rydberg Numbers / November, 1925 / London

The Adventure of the Praed Street Irregulars / April, 1926 / London

The Adventure of the Penny Magenta / June, 1926 / London

The Adventure of the Remarkable Worm / August, 1926 / London

The Adventure of the Retired Novelist / October, 1926 / London

The Adventure of the Devil's Footprints / January, 1927 / Aylesbury

The Adventure of the Cloverdale Kennels / Summer, 1927 / Haslemere

The Adventure of the Lost Dutchman / Summer, 1927 / London

The Adventure of the Grice-Paterson Curse / August, 1927 / Uffa

The Adventure of the Dorrington Inheritance / January, 1928 / London

The Adventure of the Norcross Riddle / March, 1928 / Norcross Towers

The Adventure of the Late Mr. Faversham / April, 1928 / London

The Adventure of the Black Narcissus / May, 1928 / London

The Adventure of the Three Red Dwarfs / May, 1928 / London

The Adventure of the Broken Chessman / June, 1928 / London

The Adventure of the Hats of M. Dulac / 1929 / London

(Dr. Parker's first Solar Pons story, The Adventure of the Black Narcissus, written in collaboration with August Derleth, published January, 1929.)

The Adventure of the Little Hangman / Summer, 1929 / Combe Martin

The Adventure of the Blind Clairaudient / Summer, 1929 / London

The Adventure of the Man with the Broken Face / September, 1929 / North Coast

The Adventure of the Seven Passengers / January, 1930 / London
The Adventure of the Black Cardinal / 1930 / London
The Adventure of the Six Silver Spiders / 1930 / London
The Adventure of the Lost Holiday / Fall, 1931 / London
The Adventure of the Troubled Magistrate / 1931 / Ross
The Adventure of the Mazarine Blue / 1931 / Stroud
The Adventure of the Proper Comma / March, 1932 / London

(Sometime during the winter of 1931-2, Dr. Parker opened separate medical offices, but continued to reside at 7B Praed Street.)

The Adventure of the "Triple Kent" / Summer, 1932 / Tunbridge Wells
The Adventure of the Paralytic Mendicant / August, 1932 / Bury St. Edmunds
The Adventure of the Trained Cormorant / Fall, 1932 / New Romney

(Early in 1933, probably January, Dr. Parker married Constance Dorrington, and moved to South Norwood from Praed Street.)

The Adventure of the Camberwell Beauty / May, 1933 / London
The Adventure of the Tottenham Werewolf / Summer, 1934 / Tottenham
The Adventure of the Mosaic Cylinders / 1935 / Birdlip
The Advenutre of the Stone of Scone / December, 1935 / London-Scotland

Untold Tales

The Adventure of the Haunted Library / probably 1921
The Adventure of the Missing Tenants / 1921
The Adventure of the Octagon House / probably 1922
The Adventure of the Viennese Musician
The Adventure of the Burlstone Horror / 1925
The Adventure of the Mumbles / Green Stars / probably 1929
The Adventure of the Nineteen Maidens
The Adventure of the Sussex Archers / Summer, 1927
The Adventure of the Italian Letters
The Adventure of the Catalytic Agent
The Adventure of the Reluctant Scholar / Summer, 1927
The Adventure of the Shaplow Millions / Summer, 1927
The Adventure of the Ascot Scandal
The Adventure of the Purple Stain
The Adventure of the Orient Express
The Adventure of the Clubs (a short novel)
The Adventure of the Lost Metternich / 1929
The Adventure of Gresham Old Place
The Adventure of Cagliostro Second
The Adventure of the Pope's Guardsmen
The Adventure of the Gold Lorgnette
The Adventure of the Muttering Man

NOTES ON THE CHRONOLOGY

Meeting of Solar Pons and Dr. Parker – It must not be assumed that this is a "definitive" Chronology. Rather, it is the best which can be constructed from evidence within the stories. Dr. Parker, like his great predecessor, often conceals or confuses vital dates and facts. Indeed, it is the opinion of August Derleth, who is probably the one person who knows Parker best, that the good doctor has actually telescoped time in at least one instance. Internal evidence seems to place the meeting of Pons and Parker in mid-1921. This is on the basis of the stories *The Adventure of the Lost Locomotive* and *The Adventure of the Five Royal Coachmen*. Yet his introductory remarks at the beginning of "*In Re: Sherlock Holmes*" point to mid-1919. August Derleth believes, and I am inclined to agree, that the latter date is correct. This would mean that several other cases, said to have taken place "a year or so" later, may have been actually as much as three years later. If this should be true, Parker has done his work well. And, lacking any proof to the contrary, I have chosen to accept his word at face value save where there is an obvious contradiction.

The crux of the matter lies with the two stories mentioned above. In his opening *Word*, Parker writes, "Within a few months I had begun to take notes on Pons' cases..." *The Adventure of the Lost Locomotive* took place "during the first year of my residence at 7B Praed Street," while *The Adventure of the Five Royal Coachmen* has Pons saying, "Now that I have concluded that little matter of the lost locomotive..." Now, according to history, the Great Naval Conference of the 1920's mentioned in the latter story took place in 1922. If Pons' cases are historically fixed to the history in the books (rather than wandering in a space-time of their own), then this is a fixed and unchanging date. Therefore, either the reference to Pons' having just concluded the affair of the lost locomotive is in error, or the reference in *The Adventure of the Lost Locomotive* to its being in the "first year of my residence" is wrong. And that, in turn, depends upon how many months elapsed before Parker started taking notes. If the references are in error, then *The Adventure of the Sotheby Salesman* took place in August, 1919, and all the other early cases must be moved back accordingly, except *The Adventure of Ricoletti of the Club Foot*, which is fixed by internal evidence.

There is yet one other possible solution – that, although they began occupying the same quarters in mid-1919, Parker took much longer to begin recording the cases, that, in fact, he has given us nothing earlier than *The Adventure of the Sotheby Salesman* in August, 1921. This permits of believing that when either Parker or Pons speaks of "the first year" or elapsed years, he is thinking strictly in terms of when Parker began to play Boswell – and *not* of when he actually took up residence at 7B. He was thus "with" Pons in the sense that they shared quarters, but *not* "with" him in the sense of actually participating in the cases.

Derleth's comments on the problem are worthy of note: "It seems to me only natural that Parker might have telescoped time a little, and referred to many of the early adventures as 'a year or so' after he first met Pons, when in fact they may have taken place as much as three years after that historic meeting. That is the only explanation I can offer. Parker can be as garrulous on occasion as Pons is not.... Nor is it impossible for Parker to set down errors in his accounts. As I recall it, this seems to have been typical of Watson, too."

For more details and a full list of titles:

visit https://www.hachetteindia.com/home/yellowbacks

WELCOME BACK TO THE GOLDEN AGE